Fluffy, Flip Flops, and Foul Play

A Cozy Magic Midlife Mystery

Silver Circle Cat Rescue Mysteries
Book 7

Leanne Leeds

Fluffy, Flip Flops, and Foul Play
Silver Circle Cat Rescue Mysteries #7
ISBN: 979-8-9900434-1-1

Published by Badchen Publishing
2709 N Hayden Island Dr.
STE 103131
Portland, Oregon, 97217

For permissions contact: info@badchenpublishing.com

The Naming of cats is a difficult matter; It isn't just one of your holiday games.
     — T.S. Eliot

Contents

Contents

PARTNER WITH DEAN MILECDS

Chapter One

I watched as Mystico batted a catnip mouse across the floor, Belladonna and Ginger pouncing after it. The three of them were an odd trio—Mystico with her hairless sphinx body, Belladonna sleek and black like a mini panther, and Ginger, the rugged ginger tabby. But they seemed to get along now that Mystico had moved in with Diego Gomez.

Diego sat at the counter of the Silver Circle café sipping an iced latte, the ice cubes clinking against the glass as he stirred his drink. I studied his face, noting the dark circles under his eyes that told of many sleepless nights since Luna's passing. "She seems to be adjusting well, all things considered," he said, nodding toward Mystico. "I'm having a bit more trouble, but that's to be expected, yes?"

It had been a month since the Cinco de Mayo festival, when Diego had taken over caring for his ex-girlfriend Luna's cat after...well, after Luna's murder. That was something we talked little about, the tragedy still too near, but I could see the sadness still clung to him like a morning fog.

"I'm sorry you're struggling, Diego, but I'm glad to hear that Mystico's doing well," I replied. "I saw you come out of the vet wing. Something wrong?"

"Oh, no, no, she's been doing great," Diego said. "I took her for a checkup with Dr. Gray after I saw some things that concerned me and she got a clean bill of health. Eating well, good weight, I'm taking care of her skin. Everything checked out."

"That's wonderful," I said, smiling. After losing her owner, I knew we had all been worried about Mystico's wellbeing.

Diego idly stirred his coffee. "I brought her in because there was this very weird thing, something I never saw when Luna was alive," he said, his brow furrowing. "Dr. Gray couldn't explain why Mystico seems to just meow sometimes. Like she's having a conversation with someone I cannot see."

I raised my eyebrows.

"She'll wander into a room, sit down and look at the wall, then meow a few times, then go quiet like she's listening to someone talk back. Then she'll meow again, over and over. It's just the strangest thing," Diego said, shaking his head. "Dr. Gray assured me it's nothing to worry about health-wise, just some behavioral quirk. But I don't know." He studied her as she jumped on top of Ginger. "It just seems strange."

Ginger ran, and Mystico batted a toy mouse under a table where Belladonna waited in ambush. The hairless cat had always been an enigmatic creature, with her piercing eyes and mystical aura. What on earth, or beyond it, was she meowing at with such conviction?

Josie had insisted her college Ouija board worked, and Mystico claimed through the drink tray whatchamacallit she could talk to Luna...

Could that all have been real?

I thought back to that eerie night; the light flickering over the ominous board as our fingers rested upon the planchette. Maybe I had felt a strange, otherworldly chill in the air as our hands slid across the board...

Or perhaps some curiosities were better left to speculation.

"If Laurie says she's healthy otherwise, I wouldn't be too concerned," I said, hoping to reassure him. "All cats have their little quirks and eccentricities."

Diego nodded, his eyes still full of uncertainty. "Yeah... I guess you're right."

He sounded unconvinced.

"Trust me, I'm the town expert on cat behavior at this point. If anyone can read these furry critters, it's me. She seems happy and healthy, mystery wall chats notwithstanding."

That got a small chuckle out of him, but it wasn't long before his expression turned solemn again. "I just can't stop worrying about her, you know?" he confessed. "She's been through so much trauma losing Luna. I just wish I knew what she was meowing about. Like, is she trying to tell me something? Ask me for something? Call Luna's spirit floating out there?"

I wished I could tell everyone we knew about the cat plate doodad so that people struggling to understand their pets knew there was a way to talk to them—but we couldn't. Oh, my mind often spun with fantasies of going public, imagining the joy and comfort it could bring to so many—but then my practical side kicked in, contemplating all the ways it could go wrong.

People might exploit the cats, or try to steal the platter, or panic at such blatant evidence of magic in the world—and what government wouldn't want to whisk it away for their own purposes?

Diego watched me, a flicker of desperate hope passing over his face before he seemed to catch himself. "Ah, never mind all that," he backtracked with an apologetic laugh. "Forget I said anything. You're right. Mystico's just a regular cat with a quirky habit of meowing at walls and nothing more. I'm reading too much into it."

I could tell by his wistful tone that he didn't quite believe his own words—or if he did, he wished he didn't. I reached over and squeezed his hand, letting him know without words that I was there for him.

He laughed. "You're very good at playing bartender

4

for the daylight coffee crowd, Ellie. Especially when people's problems are cat related."

The bell on the front door jingled as Laurie herself breezed inside.

"Hey, Ellie, sorry I'm late," Laurie said, setting her medical bag on the counter next to Diego. "Emergency appointment after yours, Diego—little Oliver Schwartz decided he aspired to be an outdoor kitty without supervision." She shook her head in amusement. "He met a real outdoor kitty and was quickly disabused of the notion that he was a tough guy."

"No worries," I replied.

"Uh oh, looks like I better rescue Ginger before Mystico gets her claws in him," Diego said with a chuckle, heading over to extricate the hapless ginger tabby from under the table. He turned back and tilted his head in my direction. "Thanks for the talk, Ellie," the handsome artist told me. Diego turned to me, his eyes warm with sincerity. "You always know just what to say —you remind me of a wiser, cooler mom."

"Did Diego just call you... old?" she asked in faux astonishment.

"Oh hush, you," I told her. "I'll take 'wise and cool' as a compliment any day of the week. Thanks very much."

Later that day Zora Hillard strode in, her athletic frame poised with purpose as always. In her arms she cradled a tiny bundle of matted fur—a wee Scottish Fold kitten, its squashed face and folded ears unmistakable.

"Afternoon, Ellie," Zora announced, depositing the kitten on the counter. "Found this little rascal wandering around the hiking trails by the lake. Poor thing's a mess." She gestured to the trail of debris caught in its wiry fur—twigs, leaves, burrs. Between its teeth, it held a filthy black flip-flop, its rubber studded with tiny teeth marks.

I felt a swell of sympathy. "You poor darling."

The kitten let out a squeaky mew and the filthy flip-flop tumbled from its jaws. Eyes suddenly saucer-like, it startled, fur bristling, and scrambled to recapture the shoe, clamping it once again between tiny needle teeth. The flip-flop recaptured, the bedraggled kitten resumed its pitiful gazing up at me, nose twitching.

"It looks to me like one of those fancy purebred folds, like Taylor Swift's cat," Zora went on. "If it does turn out to be pedigreed, I'd love to adopt it from you all. I've always wanted a cat just like a celebrity. If it's a mix, though, I'm sure you can find another home for it."

I fixed Zora with a pointed look.

"What?" she asked.

"We'll have to see about that," I said, scooping up the kitten from her arms and swallowing my indignation. The dirty fluff snuggled against my chest, vibrating with purrs. "I need to get this little one cleaned up and checked out first. And maybe some food, yes?"

"Right, of course. Just remember—I'd take her. Or him."

I thanked Zora and mentally waved away her words like irksome gnats, heading upstairs with the purring fuzzball cradled in my arms. Naturally, Belladonna trotted right on my heels, keeping a curious eye on our new guest.

In the isolation room, I set the kitten down, and it teetered across the tile on wobbly legs. Nose to the floor, it snuffled, exploring every corner and crevice while tugging its filthy flip-flop along like a beloved blanket.

Once they appeared calmer, I wet a washcloth with warm water and gently wiped the kitten's fur and scrubbed its face clean before working a matt splitter through to remove small knots. Finally, I grabbed a soft brush and gently stroked its fur. The kitten leaned into the brush as I smoothed out its coat. Satisfied with my work, I set out a bowl of food.

The poor thing attacked it ravenously and let out squeaky growls whenever Belladonna crept too close to the bowl—or the flip-flop—as if trying to threaten her away from its prize.

"Back it up, Bella—give the little one some breathing room."

Belladonna bounded onto the magic platter, piercing me with her imperious golden stare the moment the eerie glow flared. "Don't just stand there gawking. Let's see what intel we can extract from this vagabond!" she demanded, flicking her tail. "It reeks of suspicion."

"Suspicion of what?"

"Suspicion is a noun."

I scratched Bella's neck. "Easy there, 007. Let the kid eat in peace."

Belladonna scowled. "You could be feeding an enemy agent right under our nose."

"I could be, but I don't think I am. You've listened to one too many mystery novels, Bella."

She bristled, offended. "When we wake up to find our catnip ransacked, don't come crying to me." She cast a withering look at the feasting kitten. "Just look at that conniving little grifter—probably flea-ridden, too."

I turned to the kitten, swallowing down my roiling anticipation. "Okay sweetie, come on over here and hop onto this plate next to Bella." The kitten peered up at me, nose crinkling as it scented the air. "If you sit by her, you can talk to us. We'd love to know your name."

The kitten looked skeptical but walked over, licking its mouth and watching me curiously. It scramble-climbed up one level, then another, and tentatively stepped onto the platter, bumping noses with Belladonna. A pure silvery-white light flowed from the platter, and the cubby shimmered like a diamond.

"There's a good kitten. Now, can you tell us your name, little one?"

"Yes, do tell us where you came from and how you ended up in such a lamentable state," Belladonna's refined voice rang out.

Its ears twisted wildly, trying to pinpoint the source

of Belladonna's voice as its eyes bounced frantically between us, pupils constricted into alarmed slashes. After a few breathless moments, the overwhelmed kitten could only manage a strangled squeak of pure bewilderment.

"It's okay, honey, this is a safe space. Feel free to speak openly with us."

"How safe," Bella said, "depends on your answers."

"Bella!"

It blinked its enormous eyes. "How did you do that?" a young female voice asked.

My heart melted.

I kept my voice soft, hoping to set her fragile mind at ease. "Well, you see, this is a magical plate that lets cats like you speak with humans like me. I know it must be very confusing and strange. But don't be afraid—I promise you're safe here. How did you wind up by the lake?"

"One day I was in a place with soft bedding and warm milk. Then I was wandering outside all alone. I was scared, so I carried my new mom's flip-flop friend, but then I got too hungry and thirsty." She nuzzled against my hand, and then against Belladonna. "The food was good."

"Ugh, child, you smell like dead fish." Belladonna looked affronted at having to share her magic platter with this bedraggled intruder.

"I almost caught a fish once!" the kitten declared, puffing out her floofy chest.

Then her ears drooped.

"But, um... it kinda... flopped back into the water before I could eat it and swam away. Fish aren't as slow on the beach as I thought." The kitten shuffled her paws. "I got a lot soaked," she admitted with a squeaky sigh. "The water was stinky."

"You don't say," Belladonna huffed.

"Do you have a name, honey?" I asked.

The kitten scrunched her smushed face in concentration. "My new mommy called me Fluffy."

"No, no, what she thought you looked like," Belladonna said. "Your proper name and lineage."

"Huh?" Eyes clouded in bewilderment, and she blinked up at Belladonna. "I'm Fluffy."

I lifted the exhausted kitten into my arms. "All right, I think that's enough grilling for the moment," I said, stroking the kitten as she purred. "This little girl needs rest."

Belladonna lashed her tail. "Kittens," she muttered. "I should be the one taking a nap. Kittens are exhausting."

Fluffy drifted off, sprawled on her back with all four legs in the air, still clutching her beloved flip-flop. Once I was sure she was out cold, I pulled out my microchip scanner wand and waved it over her sleeping form. It let out a soft beep and a 10-digit serial number popped up on the display screen. I jotted it down before slipping out the door.

This kitten couldn't be more than a few months old, I thought as I headed downstairs. If she was already microchipped, surely someone must be looking for her. I would have expected to hear from the owner the moment she was missing, since we're the main cat rescue in the area. Anyone within a 50-mile radius who loses a cat lets us know right away in case it turns up here.

I found Darla in the office and gave her the microchip number to look up. She tapped it into the database search bar. "Okay, let's see whose day we're going to make better," she murmured.

After a moment, the results popped up. "Owner is listed as a Lisa Hartman—oh, wait, I know her," Darla said. "She has a boutique called Threads and Trends in Austin. I met her at a wine tasting thing at the lake last year."

"Lisa Hartman," I repeated as Darla handed me the name and phone number. "Doesn't ring a bell. Let me call her real quick."

I dialed, but it just rang and rang before hitting voicemail. "Hi Lisa, this is Ellie from Silver Circle Cat Rescue," I said after the beep. "Someone found a microchipped Scottish Fold kitten out by Lake Wildebridge this afternoon. Call me back as soon as you can and we'll reunite you with..." I hesitated, realizing I hadn't confirmed the cat's name was Fluffy. "Well, with your kitten," I finished.

I hung up and turned to Darla. "What's the kitten's name?"

"Fluffy."

"Fluffy? That's really the kitten's name?"

Darla gave a noncommittal shrug. "Apparently so. Some people just like sticking with the classics."

With no response from Lisa's personal number, I pulled up the Threads and Trends website, scanning for their main phone number. The pages were brightly designed, with photos of happy shoppers browsing racks of stylish clothing. Everything about it gave off an energetic but sophisticated vibe—very on brand for an Austin clothing shop.

I dialed the number listed at the bottom of the "Contact Us" page and listened to it ring. A charming female voice answered on the third ring. "Threads and Trends, this is Evelyn. How may I best be of service to you?"

"Hello, Evelyn, my name is Ellie Rockwell from the Silver Circle Cat Rescue over in Tablerock. I'm calling with an urgent matter regarding your owner, Lisa Hartman—"

"Oh, um, Lisa's not in today," the woman replied, a note of hesitation in her voice. "Can I take a message for her?"

"Do you know when she'll be back? It's rather urgent."

"Well, uh... Uh, I'm not sure..." More odd pausing and stammering.

12

"Do you have a manager? Maybe they can help."

"One moment. Let me transfer you."

After a few clicks and rings, a fresh voice came on the line, crisp and businesslike. "This is Samantha Reeves."

"Are you the manager?"

"I'm the owner. How can I help you?"

"Oh, I'm sorry, I was trying to get a hold of Lisa Hartman." I introduced myself yet again and launched into my explanation about the kitten. As I gave Samantha the quick rundown of finding the abandoned Scottish Fold kitten, I heard papers shuffling on her end of the line.

"Right, I'm going to stop you there. Lisa hasn't been into the shop at all this week. Did you say you found her cat?" Without waiting for me to answer, she added, "I didn't even know she had a cat."

"A very sweet Scottish Fold kitten was found near Lake Wildebridge this afternoon. Lisa's info was on the microchip, so I was hoping to get in contact with her." I felt a twinge of unease. "When did you say you last spoke to her?"

"Let me think... it was maybe Friday?"

I looked at the calendar. It was Wednesday. "Five days ago?"

"Yep, about that. She said she was headed to the lake to decompress for the weekend. I tried to call Monday when she didn't come in, but there was no answer."

"Oh, she normally works there with you?"

Samantha cleared her throat. "Well, not always."

"Do you have her address?" I asked. "Probably best if I just run over to her house and see if I can get her there."

"Sure. Let me give you the address."

After the call, I headed back upstairs to check on the sleeping Scottish Fold. Fluffy was still out cold atop a plush cat bed, flip-flop nestled under her chin. I couldn't help but smile as her squashed face twitched with kitten dreams.

"Don't you worry, sweet pea," I whispered. "We're going to sort this out and get you back home safe and sound."

Fluffy's folded ears gave a tiny flick in her sleep, as if in agreement.

Chapter Two

THE AGED MAROON PICKUP RUMBLED DOWN THE winding country road, its suspension squeaking as we hit the occasional pothole. I glanced out the window at the sprawling countryside zipping past—rolling hills and open pasture blending into thickets of trees as the road curved ever deeper into the wooded hills surrounding Lake Wildebridge.

"So this Lisa lady's place is way out here, huh?" Landon said, one hand draped over the steering wheel as he navigated the truck around a sharp bend.

I nodded, double checking the address scrawled on the notepad in my lap. "Seems so. According to her business partner, she went out to the lake on Friday and hasn't been back to work or answered her phone since. I guess she lives by the lake, too."

Landon's eyebrows pinched together, his mouth twisting with concern beneath his scruffy stubble. "That doesn't sound too promising. You think she just up and abandoned her kitten out here?"

"I don't know. I have no idea who she is, and it is a kitten," I admitted with a sigh. "Maybe she's never had a cat before and didn't know how fast they could scurry away. If Lisa just wanted a weekend away, though, why isn't she back at work now?"

"Good point. Especially one as cute as that little Scottish Fold baby."

I smiled, picturing the bedraggled kitten. "Right? I have a soft heart for all cats, but babies just break my heart extra. Something must have happened to separate them. Fluffy's only three months old at most, and she's already microchipped. That's an on-the-ball pet owner."

Landon nodded. "We'll get to the bottom of it."

I was grateful to have Landon along for the ride. His hulking frame and no-nonsense attitude could be intimidating to some, and thanks to that, he'd proven handy to have around in the past when tricky situations took unpredictable turns and things got... complicated.

Not that things were likely to get complicated.

We were merely trying to contact a seemingly upstanding citizen who had left her kitten unattended by a lake.

What could go wrong?

"Up ahead on the left. That should be it," I said as we approached a driveway flanked by towering pines. Landon slowed and turned, gravel crunching beneath the tires. "Wow."

The house that came into view took me aback.

I'd been expecting some modest lake cottage befitting a small business shopkeeper, but the sleek, modern structure sprawling before us looked like it had leaped straight out of the pages of an architectural magazine, or off the set of one of those house hunting shows about luxury real estate that I definitely never binge watch late at night.

This was the most extravagant home I'd seen in these parts—it seemed about as well-suited to the wooded shores of Lake Wildebridge as I was to runway modeling.

"Wow is right. Swanky," Landon said, echoing my thoughts as we parked.

Clearly, there was more to the stylish owner of an Austin clothing boutique than I had assumed if she also had what had to be a multi-million dollar modernist home tucked away out here.

"Is that where she lives, or is it a vacation home?" Landon asked.

I glanced down at the microchip registry address on my phone, double checking. "Lives here, I think? Though this looks more like a celebrity's vacation villa than a small town shopkeeper's home."

"She's not a small town shopkeeper. Her shop's in Austin, and Austin's not a small city anymore. In fact, I read it's the tenth-most populous city in the United States."

"You hush."

We climbed out of the pickup and studied the house. Its stark white facade was broken up by dramatic windows and accents of rich wood. A sparkling infinity pool jutted out from the back patio, overlooking the lake views beyond.

Everything about it screamed money.

"Let's go see if anyone's home," I said. A quick canvassing of the driveway and garage confirmed no cars were there. Everything was quiet except for the soft lap of water down below and the occasional bird call.

Landon paused, listening. "Maybe nobody's here," he said after a moment.

"Only one way to find out for sure," I said, marching up to ring the sleek modern doorbell.

Chimes echoed through the home's interior.

We waited.

No answer.

I pressed again, listening to the melodic chiming fade once more.

Landon peered through the frosted glass panels flanking the door, trying to glimpse inside. "Looks like nobody's home," he reported.

"Drat," I muttered. "Now what?"

Landon scratched his beard. "Reckon we could look around back real quick, see if anything catches our eye?"

Technically, we had no right to go snooping around someone's private property, but the nagging mystery of Lisa's disappearance and Fluffy's abandonment had my curiosity well and truly piqued. We were here, and...

well, I've never been able to resist the urge to poke my nose where it doesn't belong.

I nodded. "Let's be quick and quiet about it. I'd rather not get buckshot in the backside by some jittery neighbor who mistakes us for burglars."

We skirted the perimeter of the striking modern home, peering through windows as we went. Everything inside looked pristine and untouched. Either Lisa was a fanatically tidy housekeeper, or the place sat empty more often than not.

As we neared the back patio and its picturesque pool overlooking the lake, Landon paused. "You reckon that's her boat down there?" he asked in a low voice.

I followed his gaze down the sloping backyard to a small private boat dock. Bobbing in the water beside it floated a stylish modern boat. And parked in the grass just shy of the dock sat a dusty blue Prius.

The dock creaked as we crept down to examine the sleek white speedboat bobbing in the water. I felt a twinge of guilt, like a kid sneaking a cookie before dinner, as we stepped uninvited onto the private dock.

It faded into burning curiosity as Landon and I began peering around the boat's interior, searching for any clues that might shed light on Lisa Hartman's puzzling weekend lake visit. Running my fingers over the smooth white vinyl seats, I imagined her speeding across the shimmering lake beneath the early summer sun. "Beautiful boat."

"It is, but look here," Landon said, pointing to a canvas tote bag tucked beside one of the seats. Right next to it on the floor sat an insulated cooler.

I popped it open to find several bottles of water and a couple of sandwiches inside, half-submerged in water that had once been ice. "It's not cold anymore at all." I picked one up, peeling back the edge of the wrapping to reveal a soaked French baguette layered with turkey, lettuce, tomato, and an oozy smear of mustard and mayo. "I think these are from Hanzelka's Bakery."

Landon rifled through the tote bag and found sunscreen, a paperback novel, a wide-brimmed sun hat, and a pair of stylish sunglasses—the type of supplies one might pack for a lazy day lounging on the lake.

"Keys are in the boat's ignition, too," Landon noted, glancing at the dashboard. "Gas tank's about half full. Ellie, look—there's a bottle of sunblock tipped over on the floor there."

My eyes followed to where Landon was pointing on the deck. There, a plastic bottle of sunscreen lay on its side, leaking opaque white lotion across the pristine white vinyl flooring.

I stepped closer and crouched down to examine the spilled bottle. The lotion spread in a jagged puddle, edges thinning out as it ran across the gentle sway of the floor. From the positioning, it seemed the bottle had fallen and rolled this way and that as the boat rocked on the water. Trailing tracks cut through the spilled cream where someone's footprints had smeared it.

I touched a finger to the lotion and rubbed it between my fingertips.

Gummy and tacky.

"This was knocked over at least a couple of days ago," I said to Landon. "Whoever did it must have been in a real hurry, too, based on these smudged footprints. They didn't bother to clean the spill up."

Before Landon could answer, a loud crack echoed up from the shore.

I whipped my head toward the tree line and saw the branches shuddering as if something had just pushed through. Visions of an enraged Lisa Hartman bursting from the woods wielding a rake or canoe paddle flashed through my mind—but the figure that emerged with a shotgun gripped in his gnarled hands was not Lisa but an elderly man with a bushy white beard.

My breath caught at the sight of the firearm aimed in our direction.

I shot an anxious glance toward Landon, who looked similarly alarmed. Moving on instinct, he stepped in front of me, gently but firmly grasping my shoulders to position his broad frame as a shield between me and the wavering barrel. I could feel the tension in his muscular hands, a slight tremble betraying his alarm.

"You two!" the armed man barked. "What in tarnation are you doing trespassing out here? Didn't you see the purple paint?"

In Texas, a painted purple post on a property's borders was an unmistakable warning to stay away—a subtle yet potent symbol authorizing lethal force against intruders.

Landon and I threw our hands up in alarm.

"Whoa there, take it easy," Landon called out, his deep voice admirably steady despite the gun aimed our way. "No need for that, friend. We're just looking for the lady who lives in that large house up on the hill. Is this her dock?"

"You know darn well it's her dock." The man's flinty eyes narrowed. "Looking to steal her boat for a joyride, I'll bet." His finger curled around the trigger. "Now tell me who you are before I fill you both with birdshot."

Raising my hands higher to show I meant no harm, I said, "Please, sir, there's been a misunderstanding. I run the cat shelter in town and someone brought in Lisa's Scottish Fold kitten after finding it wandering by the lake. We just want to reunite them."

He squinted at me from beneath his bushy white brows. "You're that cat lady moved into Fiona's old place in Tablerock, ain't ya?"

I nodded. "That's me. Eleanor Rockwell of the Silver Circle Cat Rescue."

Finally, he lowered the barrel with a grunt. "Well, why didn't you just say so?"

Because you had a gun pointed at us, I thought.

"Name's Ethan Henderson. I live just up the hill in the cabin behind this gaudy monstrosity of a house that woman done built." He scowled in the direction of Lisa's large modern home. "I've lived here for fifty years—as opposed to that Hartman woman or that company on the other side of her."

"Nice to meet you, Mr. Henderson. I'm Ellie, and this is Landon."

"You that Tablerock carpenter?"

Landon nodded. "I am."

"Maybe you can tear that damn thing down to the studs and make something useful out of it, then." Henderson eyed Lisa's house with undisguised distaste. "City folk and their fancy architects," he grumbled, spitting over the side of the dock. "All of them came barging in here with their big ideas and cold cash, throwing up houses without a lick of respect for the land or lake or folks already living here."

I bit my lip, mulling over how to respond. "So, I take it you're not friends with Ms. Hartman?"

"Ha! That woman don't have any friends that I ever saw. Just contractors and delivery men traipsing in and out for months getting this eyesore and the one next to it built for her and that city slicker boyfriend of hers."

"What boyfriend?"

"How would I know?"

"When was the last time you saw Lisa?" I asked.

He thought for a moment, scratching his scraggly beard. "Few days back, I reckon. Saw her speeding off in that fancy boat of hers Friday evening. Ain't seen her since."

"Did she often take solo boat trips out on the lake?" Landon asked.

Henderson snorted. "All the time. Disappears on her own for days doing heaven knows what out there." He waved a hand vaguely at the expansive lake.

I frowned. "On this speed boat?"

"She got a fancy yacht, too. One of those ones with a bed down below."

We talked a bit longer, but Mr. Henderson had little else useful to offer. Landon handed the man his business card as we parted ways, asking him to call if anything occurred to him about Lisa's whereabouts.

"Only thing that occurs to me is the lake gave her a comeuppance for coming in here and ruining the shore-line," Mr. Henderson said as he turned and walked back up the hill, chuckling under his breath. "And good riddance, I say."

His words sent a chill through me despite the warm sun on my skin.

⚜

"I think it's time we inform the authorities," I said as we made our way up the hill from the dock. "Something just doesn't feel right about this whole situation."

Landon nodded. "I agree."

"Should we call Mario in Tablerock first and let him know what's going on?"

"Well, the lake itself isn't in Tablerock's jurisdic-

24

tion," Landon reminded me. "It's unincorporated county land. I think we should call the county sheriff's office and get Deputy Markham out here to look around."

"Oh, good thinking. Since this area of Lake Wildebridge falls under county jurisdiction, they might need to get the county sheriff's lake patrol division involved," I said.

The lake patrol was the team tasked with policing the lake. They'd wind up coordinating any water-based search and rescue efforts—and with a missing luxury yacht in the picture, they'd need to search the lake.

Landon pulled out his phone and dialed the sheriff's office, and within seconds, he began explaining the situation to whoever answered.

I stood gazing out at the serene expanse of Lake Wildebridge, its shining emerald green surface rippling in the afternoon breeze. Looking at the calm, picturesque scene, I couldn't imagine anything sinister lurking beneath.

There were only a handful of docks dotting this section of shoreline, and even fewer houses visible set back among the trees. It was an isolated area, quiet and undisturbed. A perfect spot for someone rich who valued their privacy, I supposed.

I looked up to see old Mr. Henderson standing on his back porch, binoculars raised as he peered down at Landon and me. I lifted a hand in an awkward wave, but he just kept staring, watching us like a suspicious sentinel.

Landon finished his call and strode back over. "Don's on his way. He said not to touch anything else and to just wait here for him."

"Got it," I said. "Mr. Henderson up there is monitoring us, it seems."

Landon glanced up at the elderly man still observing us. "I'd guess he doesn't get too many visitors out this way. We're probably the most exciting thing to happen in a while."

"I don't think he finds our presence too exciting. More like a nuisance."

We lingered in an uneasy silence, reluctant to investigate any more. My gaze drifted back to Lisa's sleek powerboat swaying in its slip. What compelled a woman who already owned an impressive luxury house to also have not just one nice boat, but two? It was a decent-sized lake, but not *that* big.

"You think this Lisa lady might have been mixed up in something shady?" Landon asked, voicing my own unspoken thoughts.

"I don't know. I mean, she has a legit clothing boutique, and Threads and Trends seems like a thriving small business based on their website. Would a criminal mastermind also run a ladies' clothing empire on the side?"

Landon shrugged his broad shoulders. "Stranger things have happened."

"And in Tablerock itself." I pictured the stylish, sun-dappled scenes from the Threads and Trends website again. "She could just be a wildly successful entrepreneur who wanted a quiet lake house as a home."

He nodded toward the lake. "Maybe the fish out there know something. We could try chatting with them, see if they noticed anything odd."

I chuckled, picturing us perched on the end of the dock dunking the platter in the water as we attempted to have a pleasant conversation with the fish swimming by. "I can't even imagine how we'd manage that chat."

Lingering on the lawn, we hesitated to delve any deeper into our investigation, acutely aware of Mr. Henderson's unwavering gaze from his perch on the porch. My eyes drifted back to Lisa's boat, questions swirling in my mind. What happened on that boat?

The crunch of tires on gravel drew my attention back up the drive.

A tan cruiser with county sheriff markings came into view and pulled to a stop near us. The driver's door creaked open and Deputy Markham climbed out, boots scuffing on the loose pebbles as he ambled over. One hand rested on his belt while the other tipped the brim of his tan sheriff's hat in greeting. Don had an easygoing manner about him, but a sharp wit lurking behind his polite country charm.

"Afternoon there," he drawled. His crinkled eyes studied us as he approached. "What seems to be the problem here?"

Chapter Three

Once Deputy Markham heard our concerning tale of Lisa Hartman's puzzling disappearance and abandoned kitten, he strode up to her imposing modernist front door and gave it a few sharp knocks. "Ms. Hartman? You home?" he called out. No answer came, and the expansive house remained silent and still.

Next, he tried the doorbell, holding it down so the chimes echoed through the interior. We all waited, but still no signs of life emerged.

Markham turned and walked back down the paved path to where Landon and I stood in the driveway. "So, let me get this straight," he drawled. "Y'all don't even know this Ms. Hartman, and you want me to open up a missing person investigation just like that?" He snapped his fingers for emphasis.

"No, not just like that." I felt a flare of frustration at his flippant tone.

"Okay, like what, then?"

"All signs point to something being off here. I don't have to know the woman to realize that." I summed up everything we knew—Lisa's abandoned kitten, her unexplained multi-day disappearance from work, the stale sandwiches and spilled sunblock on her boat.

"Was the spilled sunblock next to a puddle of blood?" Don asked.

"No, and there was no neon sign pointing to the spot she was murdered, either," I said, unable to keep the sarcasm from creeping into my tone. I crossed my arms and fixed Don with an exasperated look.

He held my gaze steady, the corner of his mouth twitching.

"Don, she planned to spend time out on the lake over the weekend and then just... vanished, leaving everything behind," I said. "Doesn't that strike you as suspicious?"

Markham shook his head. "Well now, Ellie, I know you mean well, but people 'round these parts disappear to the lake all the time without telling a soul. My cousin Dale disappears every few months—turns off his phone and floats around fishing for days, coming back when he pleases. Just because some highfalutin' Austin boutique owner failed to show up doesn't mean she's in mortal peril."

I huffed in exasperation. "But it's been nearly a week! Why wouldn't she be back by now?"

"Well, if you knew her, you could probably answer

that. Maybe she needed some alone time. Wanted to turn her phone off and not be bothered with her fancy boutique's summer sales," he countered, enjoying needling me. "Didn't you say her other boat isn't at the dock? For all we know, she's out there cruising the waters without a care in the world. Or holed up in a lakeside cabin reading one of them romance novels and sipping fancy wine. She looks like she could afford it."

Deputy Don Markham's folksy nonchalance was getting on my last nerve even as a small, irritating part of me had to admit he had a point.

"I know you're frustrated, Ellie," Landon said, placing a gentle hand on my shoulder. "Don's just doing his job. He can't go making this an official investigation based on speculation. I'm glad we called him, but now that he's here, I can see we just don't have much."

"Okay, but what about her pet kitten? Would she leave it behind to fend for itself?" I shot back. "No responsible pet owner would—"

Markham held up a hand. "Ellie Rockwell, you run an animal shelter. You know that the world is filled with irresponsible pet owners, and this gal may well be one of them. You may be right, you may be mistaken. But I can't list someone as missing when there's no evidence a crime took place. She could turn up tomorrow, safe and sound."

I opened my mouth to protest further, but Markham silenced me with a look.

"All I'm saying is, this fancy lakeside mansion

doesn't look like the scene of a grisly crime," he said, gesturing to the pristine modern facade. "No signs of forced entry, no disturbances, not so much as a smear of blood on that polished concrete patio. You didn't find one on the boat, either."

He had me there.

The stylish home and dock showed no hints of violence or struggle.

"However," he continued, "I'll make some calls and put out some feelers, see if any of my lake patrol contacts have seen Ms. Hartman or her other boat out and about. I'll get 'em to cruise past her dock later today and have a poke around. But until we get something more concrete, my hands are tied on assigning departmental resources to look into the matter. All right?"

This was the best I was going to get from Don today. "Thank you."

Markham tipped his hat. "Say now, Ellie," he added, "seems to me a single gal living all the way out here must have someone looking out for her. A sister? Parents? A boyfriend? Gal pals? Might be good to find out who Ms. Hartman spends her time with, see if they know anything that could help you find that poor lost kitten a proper home while we wait for her to turn up. Maybe that Matt Garcia can help you. He's got some tools at his disposal since he's a private investigator."

He gave me a sly wink.

Though his words were casual, that wink spoke volumes. He was giving me permission—and an excuse—

to poke around Lisa Hartman and her relationships. Even if he couldn't investigate much yet, we could.

"That's an excellent idea, Deputy," Landon replied, mirroring his faux-casual tone. "We'll ask around, see if any of Ms. Hartman's nearest and dearest have heard tell of her whereabouts. Discretely, of course."

Markham nodded, the trace of a grin tugging at the edge of his mouth. "Of course."

As we stood in the drive chatting, I noticed old Mr. Henderson still watching us from his porch, binoculars trained on our conversation like a suspicious sentinel standing guard. What a nosy old coot, I thought, bristling at his shameless spying. Did this cranky hermit have nothing better to do than watch Lisa's visitors through his binoculars all day like an overeager bird-watcher tracking a rare species of titmouse?

"Well, I best be heading back to the station," Don said, tipping his hat brim. "But listen—y'all keep those eyes peeled and let me know if you catch wind of anything peculiar. I know you've got a nose for unraveling strange happenings, and I'll admit what you've told me has roused my curiosity." He paused, glancing up at Mr. Henderson as if wary of being overheard. "Especially considering all the drama with that one over there."

"Drama? What drama?" I asked, perking up.

"Call Josie. She can help you out with that."

"But—"

"Will do, Don." Landon cut me off and nodded. "You have a good rest of your day now."

Don cracked a grin. "All right. I'll be around if trouble arises."

With that, the deputy ambled back to his cruiser and headed off, leaving Landon and me standing in the driveway.

"If he told us to call Josie, that likely means these two traded attacks in court," Landon said. "Why don't you call her and see if she has a few minutes? We'll swing by."

"Good idea," I said. "Something just isn't adding up here. I think Don knows that, too—even if he won't admit it yet."

Landon and I stepped through the stately wooden doors into the elegant lobby of Reynolds & Reynolds. The soothing sage green walls and mahogany furnishings exuded an air of refined professionalism, while Marsha's warm smile from behind the ornate reception desk lent a personal touch.

"Hey there! Can I get you folks some coffee while you wait for Josie?" she asked, already moving toward the sleek silver Keurig on the reception desk.

Before we could respond, a sudden eruption of shouting burst from down the hall. Josephine's office door stood gaping open, giving us an unobstructed view of her bookcase-lined walls and massive mahogany desk.

"Now you listen here, Daggett," her voice echoed into the lobby, sharp and commanding as a drill sergeant's. "I've told you a hundred times, there are juniper-oaks on Rosa's property that your bulldozers and backhoes can't touch!"

I exchanged a look with Marsha, our eyes meeting amid Josie's tirade raging on down the hall. The polite, businesslike smile didn't falter, but her eyes twinkled, as if Josie's fiery outbursts were a feature of Reynolds & Reynolds and not a bug.

"But the survey... warblers don't... can't stop progress," a male voice shot back, audibly flustered, even from a distance.

"Don't you dare spout that drivel at me," Josie thundered. "I'll slap you with an injunction quicker than a Golden-cheeked Warbler can sing its morning song if you so much as nick the bark on a single tree before we get this sorted in court."

"Now, see here, Josie—" the man sputtered.

"Are we on a first name basis, Daggett?"

"Did you want some coffee while you waited?" Marsha asked in the same pleasant tone she likely used for every visitor. Her posture was relaxed, her eyes focused on taking our order while her boss's tirade raged on just down the hall.

"I'll take a coffee, thanks," Landon said.

"Me too, please," I added.

"Let me just go get some mugs. I'll be right back."

As Marsha slipped away, I caught more threats to obtain restraining orders and unleash the wrath of unnamed environmental groups.

Another office door creaked open, and Josie's husband Charlie emerged, his salt and pepper hair neatly combed as usual. He greeted us with a friendly smile, his eyes crinkling at the corners—also appearing unconcerned about his wife's ongoing shouting, threatening Daggett with legal damnation.

"Well, hey, there, Landon, always good to see you," Charlie said, shaking Landon's hand. He turned to me. "Ellie, so nice of you to stop in. Can we get you folks anything while you wait?"

I smiled. "Marsha's getting us some coffee, but thank you."

He nodded. "Wonderful, wonderful. Getting warm again, isn't it?"

As he stood chatting about the weather, Josie's voice rang out from the office once more.

"Don't think I won't slap an injunction on that whole lakeside monstrosity, Daggett! I'll tie that thing up in red tape until judgment day if I get one whiff you're disturbing the habitat."

Charlie glanced over his shoulder and said—as if remarking on nothing more than a passing blue jay outside the window—"Exciting stuff at the office today."

A muted string of flustered curses filtered through the phone line, but Josie cut Daggett off. "Don't think this discussion is over just because you're losing your nerve. I expect a revised plan on my desk by Friday, you hear me?"

The speaker phone clicked as the developer hung up.

Josie slammed her palm down on the heavy oak desk with a resounding thwap. "Well, if you hang up on me, I win by default!" she called out victoriously to the dead line and then walked down the hallway. Entering the lobby, she smoothed a hand over her hair. "Sorry about that, folks."

I smiled. "No problem at all."

"What a jerk that guy is. Thinks he can just bulldoze willy-nilly over the environment and people's lives."

"Who do you represent?" Landon asked.

"The golden-cheeked warblers that can make Town Prosperity Investments' stupid gentrifying development too expensive for them to continue in Tablerock. That's who." The hint of a smug smile played at her lips. "They have to pay a lawyer to deal with it. I can write up pleadings while I'm watching reality television."

"They picked the wrong town to develop, I think," Charlie said, eyes twinkling affectionately at his fiery wife. "There's a reason she dresses up as a junkyard dog every year at Halloween."

Josie tilted her head. "I prefer 'tenacious advocate,' but tomato, tomahto."

We enjoyed a chuckle as Marsha returned balancing a silver tray laden with steaming mugs of coffee. "We had the expensive stuff brewing in the back," she told me. "So I just got you some of that."

I glanced at the container of K-cups on her desk and raised an eyebrow. If this coffee was more elite than those expensive pods, it must be quite luxurious indeed. I took a tentative sip, the rich dark roast rolling over my tongue. Mellow with hints of chocolate and cherry.

Josie beckoned us toward the hall. "Well, don't just stand there, come on back and I'll fill you in on whatever it is you want to know," she said, padding down the corridor in bare feet.

I fell in step behind her, Landon beside me.

Behind us, Charlie tagged along,

Josie waved us through the open door and sank into the plush leather chair behind her massive desk while her husband took up a casual lean against the bookshelf, sipping his coffee. Landon and I settled into the cushioned seats across from Josie and I explained why we had come—Lisa Hartman's abandoned kitten, her lake house with no signs of habitation, the untouched picnic on her boat, and Don's reluctance to investigate.

"Deputy Markham suggested you might know something about her disagreement with her disgruntled neighbor, a Mr. Henderson?"

Josie nodded. "Ah, Ethan Henderson," she said, resting her chin on her interlaced fingers. "That old coot's notorious down at the courthouse. It feels like he and Lisa have been battling it out longer than the Hundred Years War."

"That so?" Landon asked. "What's their quarrel about?"

"What isn't it about? Property lines, easements, rights of way, a fence here, a dock extension there," Charlie chimed in. "The legal fees from those two must be paying for at least one junior lawyer's beach house."

Josie chuckled. "He's right. Let's see. How did it start?"

Josie leaned back in her leather chair, steepling her fingers. "From what I understand, the trouble started as soon as Lisa bought that piece of lakeside property from the county after plans for the refuge got nixed. Ethan Henderson had lived in his modest cabin on the adjoining plot for over fifty years, and he took her purchase of it—and her arrival—as a personal affront."

Charlie nodded. "That man views change like a stubborn mule views a new saddle. The moment Lisa's architect walked the land, he came bursting into Slater's office in a righteous fury, ranting about city slickers ruining his lakeside paradise."

"The office that handled Fiona's will?" I asked.

"That's the one. I remember that day too well. I was there on a different case when he burst in to the office with steam shooting from his ears. He slapped every document and photo and news clipping he could find on

Mark Slater's desk, trying to prove he had a legal right to stop her building."

Josie nodded. "From then on, it was one legal skirmish after another—injunctions, lawsuits, appeals. Like ants at a picnic, he pestered and annoyed that woman at every turn." She counted off on her fingers as she listed Henderson's litany of complaints. "The house design was too modern. The construction noise was intolerable. Her fence blocked his view of the lake. She had too many lights on the dock. She played music on her boats too loudly."

"Wow," Landon said.

"Wow is right. And that's just what I remember." Josie rolled her eyes. "That crotchety old geezer viewed Lisa's coming as a slap in the face, and he made it his mission to oppose anything she wanted to do on that property."

I set my coffee mug down on the desk, shaking my head in disbelief. "Goodness. Talk about a neighbor from hell. That's awful."

"You're telling me," Josie said. "Lisa had some hotshot Austin attorney strutting into our courtrooms like he owned the place, Armani suit and all. Even so—with his fancy metropolitan pedigree and everything—every ruling still went in her favor. I was shocked."

Landon frowned. "What do you mean 'even so?'"

"Those old boys on the bench don't take to some upstart big city lawyer waltzing up here to tell them their business," Charlie said. "Around these parts, if you want favorable rulings, your office and your golf club membership better both live in Wildebridge County."

Josie chuckled. "Honey, you're not supposed to say the quiet part out loud. In any case, Lisa had the law on her side, and the old coot didn't have a legal leg to stand on. But he just wouldn't let up."

I sipped my coffee, then asked, "Why didn't they stop him from filing nuisance suits?"

"Have you seen Mark Slater's new boat?"

I shook my head.

"You should. It's stunning," Josie told me. "I think Henderson's legal fees alone bought it and paid for the dock fees at the marina."

Landon looked thoughtful. "You think his hatred of her goes deeper than a normal neighbor dispute, then?"

Josie and Charlie exchanged a knowing look.

"Oh, I have no doubt of that," Josie said. "For Henderson, this feud was personal. Lisa represented everything he hated—young money, fancy architects, disregard for tradition. Austin. Her arrival rattled his entire sense of ownership over that lake inlet."

Charlie nodded in agreement. "To him, she symbolized the beginning of the end for his way of life out there."

If Henderson harbored such bitterness toward Lisa, could it have boiled over into violence when that latest ruling didn't go his way?

As if reading my thoughts, Charlie continued. "The final straw was last month, when the county denied his petition opposing Lisa's plan to extend her dock and add a boathouse to the dock like the house next door to hers. He'd been threatening for weeks to get it blocked, but the approval went through despite his efforts."

Josie nodded. "I was in the courthouse when the decision came down. I've never seen a man so livid. He had steam pouring from his ears. When he lost that battle, I think any last vestige of civility between them vanished." She raised an eyebrow, her expression growing serious. "If anyone around here had reason to wish Lisa harm, it was Ethan Henderson."

Landon cleared his throat. "Now, hold on, let's not hitch the wagon before the horse here."

Josie raised her hands, lips pursed. "You are correct, of course. Just idle speculation. That is, after all, what we do. Is not it? We toss out idle speculation until we hit the bullseye and realize we were correct all along." She turned. "We should gather some evidence, and I need a dress for a banquet—want to go to a certain downtown boutique?"

Chapter Four

THE DOWNTOWN AUSTIN STREETS BUSTLED WITH activity as Josie navigated her sleek black Mercedes through the maze of crowded roads and parked in a pricey garage near Sixth Street. Stepping from the cool, climate-controlled interior into the sweltering afternoon heat felt like diving into a steaming bath.

"Whew, it's a scorcher today," I remarked, squinting against the harsh sunlight reflecting off the rows of glassy high rises surrounding us.

Josie shrugged, unfazed by the blast furnace air as she strode toward the boutique's entrance. "That's Texas spring for you. One day it's sunny and seventy-five, the next day your eyeballs are melting out of your skull."

I chuckled at her frank assessment and quickened my steps to match Josie's brisk pace along the baking concrete sidewalk. All around us, well-dressed socialites ducked in and out of upscale shops shielded from the sun by wide-brimmed hats and oversized sunglasses. I felt woefully underdressed in my casual denim and button-down compared to the elegant patrons swirling around me.

But then again, I'd never been one for high fashion and rarely had occasion to dress up.

We rounded a corner, and I spotted the gleaming storefront for Threads & Trends just up ahead. Sunlight glinted off the sleek metal lettering mounted above the frosted glass doors. Through the windows, headless mannequins posed in chic sundresses beside polished wood displays. I wondered if Lisa had chosen those particular items for the display herself, and felt a pang in my chest thinking of her still unexplained absence.

Inside this posh boutique were clues, I suspected—but to discover them, Josie and I would need to navigate territory where neither of us was on home turf.

As we stepped inside, a rush of cool air greeted us, scented with jasmine and cedar. The lighting was dim compared to the sun's glare outside, and soft acoustic guitar played while my eyes adjusted.

Tidy racks of colorful clothes and neat displays of shoes and handbags taunted me, their price tags as intimidating as a pack of high school mean girls at the mall. Everything gave off an aura of refined sophistication. I scanned the cost of a few insignificant items, and the random tags' numbers made my eyes pop.

This was couture, all right.

Behind a polished wood counter stood a tall, slender

woman with flowing blond hair. She wore an embroidered peasant blouse paired with tight white jeans that showed off her trim figure.

Noting our arrival, the clerk's neutral expression shifted to a practiced smile.

"Welcome to Threads and Trends, ladies. I'm Evelyn. Please let me know if I can assist you in any way as you browse our new summer arrivals." Her tone was polite but detached, as if reciting a script.

Before Josie could respond, the clerk's gaze raked over my jeans and blouse in that split second, judgmental way salespeople sometimes do. Her smile faltered for a blink before returning fixed in place.

"We have some lovely options from local designers that just came in this week," she told Josie, as if I weren't standing right there beside her. Then she added, "All our sizes go up to a US twelve, but there's a plus-sized boutique just two blocks south if your friend needs... extended options."

My eyes narrowed, more annoyed than embarrassed by her assumption. "That's all right, I'm not shopping today." I kept my voice light despite the flare of irritation in my chest.

Josie's chin lifted in aloof confidence. "I'll be needing a dress for myself," she informed the woman, her tone cool and smooth as chilled gin. She arched one manicured brow. "Something classy yet eye-catching for an upcoming lawyers' banquet."

"Of course."

Without breaking eye contact, Josie slipped her sleek designer sunglasses from her face, the movement slow and deliberate. She folded them closed with a soft snap and slid the glasses into her purse. "If you can manage to identify classy. Which—at the moment—I'm not convinced you can."

The clerk stood frozen, her eyes widening almost imperceptibly as they flicked between Josie's aloof expression and her purse, as if struggling to decipher some hidden meaning in Josie's subtle actions and overt words. The moment stretched on a beat too long before she seemed to regain her composure. With a quick, deferential nod, the clerk regained her poise. "Of course, we're showcasing some exquisite cocktail gowns this season that would be perfect. Right this way."

"Not too bright, is she?" my friend whispered to me.

As Josie followed the clerk toward the evening wear section, I lingered near the entrance, wandering between a few racks of breezy sundresses in colors like coral, mint, and lavender. Nearby, a table displayed ironed blouses in intricate lace and eyelet patterns, while shelves along the walls held woven baskets overflowing with embroidered scarves and beaded statement necklaces.

Josie's muffled voice carried over one of the racks. "Do you have this in cobalt blue? Or perhaps an emerald green?"

The saleswoman's muted voice drifted out of the changing stalls as she responded to Josie, the words indistinguishable from where I stood. As their voices faded down the hall, a new sound emerged—a man's tense voice echoing from the back of the quiet store.

I crept closer, keeping low behind a revolving rack of embroidered tunics.

"I just don't understand why everyone is so quick to assume foul play," the man said, sounding defensive. "Has it occurred to you she might have just wanted some time off the grid?"

A woman responded, her low voice sharper.

"I know the two of you haven't been getting along, but we both know Lisa would never leave her business high and dry during the start of summer sales. She didn't even tell me she was taking time off. Her not showing up or calling? It is not like her at all."

Pressed flat against the wall, I peered around and spotted the woman whose voice I recognized from my call earlier—Lisa's business partner, Samantha. She stood with arms crossed, wearing a sleek black dress, her blond hair drawn up in a tight bun. She was facing a man in an expensive-looking suit.

"Oh, please. You're paranoid. I realize you two were close," the man replied. "But she wanted time to herself. You should respect that."

Samantha huffed. "Oh, please? All of a sudden you're the patient, supportive boyfriend? I know you're just hoping she'll resurface so you can patch things up, Derek."

"So what if I am?" He glanced around before

lowering his voice. "I just think everyone is getting ahead of themselves. Lisa is spontaneous. She'll turn up."

"I hope you're right. The deputy that called seemed concerned. He said since she left her car and boat behind, a kitten at a shelter..."

The pair's voices lowered to a murmur, the words lost in the hushed interior of the rear of the boutique. The man—Derek—shifted closer to Samantha, head angled as he spoke rapidly. She gave a quick shake of her head, blond bun bobbing, and replied in a voice too soft to decipher.

After a strained back and forth, the man glanced down to check his watch, the movement sharp and impatient. "I have to run. I've got a meeting. But try not to worry too much yet. You know how she is." His expensive leather shoes squeaked on the glossy floor as he took a step back, increasing the distance between them. "I'll stop by later."

With a dismissive flick of his hand, the man turned on his polished heel and pushed through a plain door at the back marked Employees Only. It closed behind him with a dull thud.

Samantha stared after him, lips pressed tight, eyes stormy. After a long moment, she blew out a sharp breath that stirred the loose wisps of hair around her face and disappeared into the backroom after the departed man, the door swinging shut behind her.

Before I could decide what to do next, I spotted Derek crossing the street in front of the boutique. I ducked behind a rack of dresses, peeking out from between the jangling hangers as he headed straight down the sidewalk with brisk, purposeful steps.

On impulse, I hurried out the door and after him.

As the door swung shut behind me, I glanced back through the window and saw Josie emerging from the dressing room, Evelyn trailing behind holding various gowns draped over her arm. I tapped out a text to her —*Following Lisa's boyfriend, be right back!*—before shoving my phone in my pocket and setting off after Derek once more.

The afternoon sun shimmered waves of heat off the concrete, and I squinted against the glare, keeping my gaze fixed on the back of Derek's pressed suit jacket as he wove through the downtown crowds.

I struggled to match his pace as he turned at a corner and made his way up a tree-lined side street on an incline. My calves burned after just one block of trailing him—apparently my daily exercise regimen of chasing cats wasn't doing much for my cardio fitness, and I was breathing harder than I cared to admit by the time Derek cut down a narrow alley between two mirrored high rises.

I picked up my pace, worried I might lose him in the urban maze, but as I rounded the corner into the alley, I caught sight of him stepping through a set of polished brass doors into one of the buildings...

...that I hoped against hope had air conditioning.

When I got to the doors myself, I slowed my stride, unsure if I should follow him inside. This seemed to be some sort of corporate office building. While they likely allowed random people to just walk in off the street, I had no idea where Derek was going—and following him once inside could be tricky.

Before I could decide, the door swung open again, and I spotted Derek waiting in front of a bank of elevators.

I hurried into the lobby.

Derek jabbed the elevator call button as if trying to poke it into submission. When the doors slid open, he strode inside, eyes fixed straight ahead, not sparing a glance for the plus-sized woman slipping unnoticed into the elevator behind him.

Derek reached out and tapped the button marked fourteen. I hit the button for fifteen without thinking. Out of the corner of my eye, I saw him glance my way, brow slightly furrowed, as though attempting to place me.

I kept my gaze fixed straight ahead as the doors closed.

Once the lift started its smooth ascent, I snuck a sideways glance at Derek. His eyes were fixed straight ahead in a thousand-yard stare, posture ramrod straight beneath his tailored suit.

Everything about him looked expensive and polished, from his expertly styled hair to his mirror-shined leather shoes. His nails were manicured, cufflinks glinting gold at his wrists beneath the crisp lines of his shirt. Even his watch appeared to cost more than my cat transport van.

After a few floors passed in silence, the elevator slowed to a stop and doors slid open with a high-pitched ding. Derek stepped forward, then hesitated, looking back at me curiously.

The doors began to close in front of me, and I breathed a sigh of relief as he turned to walk away. As soon as I was sure he'd gone down the hallway, I punched the "Door Open" button and the polished silver panels abruptly bounced back open.

I walked out into the lobby of Boldman Bracket.

"Hey," Derek's voice called out.

I froze.

"Weren't you just in that shop back on Sixth Street?"

I turned to see Derek regarding me with narrowed eyes.

Fragments of plausible excuses flickered through my mind, but none seemed believable enough to explain why I had followed him here from the boutique. I had to think fast. Why on earth had I been so impulsive?

Now this banker likely thought I was some sort of deranged stalker.

Gripped by anxiety, I resisted the urge to fidget under his scrutiny, not wanting to appear any more suspicious. Come on Ellie, say something clever to throw him off the trail. But my tongue felt leaden, mind blanking on any reasonable justification for tailing this stranger into an office building.

I was well and truly caught.

"Uh, no, don't think so," I faltered, grasping for believable lies. "I'm just checking out a business. On this floor." I gestured around the empty marble lobby.

Derek crossed his arms as he studied my face with searching green eyes. His gaze flicked down, taking in my simple jeans and plain shirt. "You're here to check out our investment bank?"

"Yes?" I answered without confidence.

"That may be true, but you were at my girlfriend's boutique, weren't you?" He tilted his head. "I recognize you. You're that frumpy friend who was with the mouthy lawyer looking for dresses."

My cheeks flushed hot at being called out—and referred to as frumpy.

I grappled for some witty retort that might impress this pompous suit, but the only response my addled mind supplied was, "Excuse me? Is that any way to talk to someone that has access to millions of dollars and might want to invest it?"

Derek took a step toward me. "Millions of dollars?"

I regretted the absurd boast that popped unfiltered from my mouth. The Silver Circle's balance sheet was healthy—but that money was for the cats, not for me. It was earmarked for kitty litter and kibble, not speculative investing. But the technically true claim had tumbled forth in my flustered state before I could fabricate something—anything—better.

Not my finest moment.

"Yes," I told him. "I'm not sure you recognize me, but I'm the woman that was left the Blackwell estate in Tablerock."

Derek's attitude shifted, his eyes lighting up at my claim of access to the Blackwell millions. "Well, now, that changes things," he said, lips curling into an obliging smile. "I do apologize for being short with you. It's been a stressful time since my girlfriend Lisa went missing."

Oh, really?

I thought it was no big deal?

That's what he told Samantha.

He flashed a dazzling white smile. "As it happens, my girlfriend lives out near the Blackwell mansion, too. She has a place right on Wildebridge Lake."

"It's Lake Wildebridge," I corrected.

Derek waved a hand, uncaring of the proper name. "Right, whatever. I never can keep the lake names straight around here, anyway." He glanced at the gleaming watch on his wrist. "Anyway, I have an important client meeting to get to, but I'd love to sit down sometime soon and learn more about your investment needs."

He pulled a sleek business card from his suit jacket pocket and handed it to me. "Call me anytime and we can meet up back at your mansion to discuss potential investment opportunities. I've always wanted to see the inside of that grand old mansion you inherited. It's such an iconic part of local history."

"You could have come by anytime, you know. The lower floor is a public cat café these days." I kept my tone light despite the annoyance at his greedy attitude about face. "It helps support our work with the cat shelter."

Derek looked taken aback for a second before recovering his polished smile. "Of course, of course. Well, regardless, I look forward to a visit soon." He glanced at his watch again and then looked at me once more, as if realizing he was about to let me leave without signing over my millions. "In fact, let's plan to connect this evening. I need to run out to my girlfriend's place—you can meet me there and we'll have complete privacy to discuss your financial needs. How does that sound?"

I couldn't believe my luck.

"Sounds perfect. Call the Rescue later and we can finalize plans."

"Excellent. Until then." Derek flashed me one last dazzling grin before heading down the hallway.

I stood in the marble lobby watching him disappear around a far corner, his Italian leather shoes squeaking on the polished floors.

What a piece of work.

Of all the unpleasant characters connected to this mystery so far, Derek Sutton was shaping up to be the sleaziest by a wide margin.

I headed for the elevator, taking care to hold Derek's

business card by the edges in case there were finger-prints on it we might need later. I had gotten what I came for: confirmation that the shifty Derek was Lisa Hartman's boyfriend (and that he was shifty), as well as an unexpected invitation to visit Lisa's home.

I headed back toward Josie at Threads and Trends—with any luck, she had managed to gather some clues of her own while I was busy tailing the banker.

Chapter Five

I SANK INTO THE PLUSH ARMCHAIR IN MY OFFICE, kicking off my shoes with a relieved sigh. The air inside the Silver Circle headquarters felt like a balm, calming the heat that I could still feel on my skin after following Derek halfway across downtown Austin in the scorching noonday sun.

Landon, perched on the edge of my desk, frowned as soon as he heard how I'd impulsively followed Lisa's alleged boyfriend from the boutique to his downtown office building. His concerned reaction needled my confidence.

"I don't know, Ellie," he said, running a hand through his dark hair. "Seems risky, tailing some stranger through the city like that. What if this Derek fellow had gotten aggressive when he realized you were on his trail?"

"On his trail for what?" I waved a hand. "I had it under control."

"Did you?" Landon leaned back against my desk, the wood creaking under his weight as he crossed burly arms over his broad chest. "What was your plan if he'd confronted you?"

"He did 'confront' me, and I handled it. I was gathering intel, not picking a fight," I said. Why did I bristle so much at his protectiveness? Was it outdated gender roles rankling me, or my own insecurities? "I handled myself just fine, thank you very much. The thing about being a middle-aged fat woman is that almost no one thinks you're a threat to them."

"You're not fat. But you're not Jason Bourne."

Josie leaned in, lowering her voice to an urgent whisper. "Tread lightly, my friend. You're on thin ice." She shot him a pointed look, eyebrows raised in emphasis.

She was right.

I bristled at his insinuation that I couldn't take care of myself. "So I'm just a helpless damsel now, is that it?"

"That's not what I'm saying."

"Sounds like it to me," I shot back. "I've gotten this far in life relying on my wits and instincts. I've done just fine on my own. I don't need you—or any man—to protect me, Landon Rogers."

Charlie cleared his throat, catching Landon's eye with a subtle shake of his head. "Might be wise to reconsider your approach," he murmured.

"For heaven's sake, I'm not implying she's helpless!"

Landon's jaw tensed, the caution in Charlie's tone giving him pause. He drew a long breath, turning back to me as he weighed his next words. "Ellie, I'm not trying to criticize. I'm really not. I just worry about you rushing headlong into risky situations without thinking it through."

"Risky situations? It was the middle of the afternoon on a busy downtown street, not a dark alley at midnight. I knew what I was doing. You're acting like I wandered blithely into a den of ninjas."

He reached for my hand, giving it a conciliatory squeeze. "You know I believe in you. I just want you safe." Sincerity shone in his earnest eyes.

"And I want you to have some faith in my judgment," I told him, but my defensiveness had melted beneath the comforting warmth of his touch.

From her perch on the corner of my desk, Josie watched us, lips pursed in wry amusement as she sipped her coffee. The rising steam wreathed her face, mingling with the hint of smug delight in her eyes as she observed our quarrel. "Oh, don't stop on my account," she said when I glanced at her. "Please, continue this fascinating debate. Though I daresay you've both made your points of view clear."

"You're right, Josie. This is getting us nowhere." I turned back to Landon. "I'm sorry I worried you, but I can handle myself. And I promise to be careful."

Landon's expression softened. "I know you can, Ellie. I only want you safe, is all. No more chasing shifty men down dark alleys, all right?"

I smiled, giving his hand a squeeze—but I felt my hackles rise just a little at his words. I hadn't actually promised not to chase down potentially dangerous strangers again. His assumption that I had agreed and would fall in line stirred a swell of annoyance within me.

For now, peace was restored—but I suspected this wasn't the last time it would come up.

Josie set down her mug. "Excellent. Now that we've resolved this battle of the sexes, let's discuss the actual pertinent information you gathered." She gestured at me. "Ellie, why don't you summarize what you learned about this Derek fellow at the boutique and his office."

I relayed the key details, including Derek's caginess, his invitation to meet at her lake house, and his abrupt change of attitude when money entered the equation. "He seems like a real snake if you ask me, and I couldn't even tell you why—just this energy he has. When he thought I was some rich heiress? His entire attitude changed quicker than a cat spotting a laser pointer dot."

Josie nodded. "Ellie's not wrong. I saw him at Lisa's shop, and he does give off a rather mercenary vibe, doesn't he? That salesgirl Evelyn implied to me that Lisa was single when I asked about him," she continued. "Also said it was irregular for Lisa to disappear from the boutique for so many days without notice. She's the creative force behind their designs, while Samantha handles the business operations."

"So, if this Derek isn't her boyfriend, what's his deal?" Charlie asked.

"Well, from our conversation, he clearly thinks he's her boyfriend," I said. "And Samantha said he was trying to weasel his way back in, so—"

As if on cue, the office door creaked open and Evie poked her head in. "Hey guys, sorry to interrupt," she said. "I just heard you discussing and thought I could help."

This is why we had the isolation room.

"Come on in," I said, waving her over.

Evie slipped inside and perched on the arm of the chair beside Josie. "What's the question?"

"We're trying to figure out if this Derek Sutton is—or was—Lisa's boyfriend or not," Charlie explained.

Evie's eyes lit up. "Oh, I can look into that easy. One quick dive into his SocialBook profile and Lisa's should make it obvious if they were an item or not." She jumped up from her seat. "Let me grab my laptop."

As Evie hurried out, Charlie shook his head with a chuckle. "These kids and their technology skills. Half the time I can barely work my own cell phone camera. Meanwhile, my teenage niece can hack into the Pentagon with a few keystrokes."

"The Pentagon?" Josie asked.

"Might be an exaggeration. But you know what I mean."

Evie returned to my office, her laptop tucked under one arm and balanced against her hip in a manner similar to how waitresses carry loaded trays. She plopped down into the worn leather office chair next to my desk and, with a quick flip of the lid, she powered up her sleek silver laptop.

"Let me just pull up everything I can find on Derek," she said as she logged in. Her fingers moved across the electric blue keys, opening tabs and typing searches. Finally, she angled the screen so we could all see. "Okay, so here's his SocialBook profile. As you can see, he's listed as 'In a Relationship' with Lisa Hartman. From his perspective, at least, they're still SocialBook official."

She navigated to his profile pictures, and I studied the photos of Derek and a stylish brunette who—I assumed—was Lisa Hartman.

In the photos, they laughed and smiled, appearing happy as they clinked cocktails at elegant restaurants or posed on the beach, arms draped across each other's shoulders. I wasn't sure if it was my imagination or if Derek's posed smile really did not reach his eyes, but something seemed off as he beamed at the camera.

"Hmm, interesting," Charlie murmured. "They look happy."

"They do, at least up until a week ago. That picture is the last one." Evie nodded. "Now, check out his Tweeter account." She pulled it up to show a constant stream of posts about closing deals, making money, and living large. "Nothing about Lisa or his romantic personal life at all. His financial life, on the other hand?"

"Guy sure likes to brag about his big deals and lavish lifestyle," Landon remarked, leaning in to scroll through the endless parade of self-congratulatory posts. "Though I can't fault him for being proud of that new yacht. She's a real beaut—probably sleek as a dolphin. Reckon I could cram all my tools and lumber into that baby if I wanted to build lakefront."

"I wonder if that's Lisa's missing boat," I said.

"Are we sure Lisa really has a missing boat?" Josie asked. "Maybe it's Derek's. Those pictures in his apartment look like they're taken from the condos on Red River. Nowhere to keep a boat around there."

I shrugged. "I only know what Mr. Henderson said, and he did call it a fancy yacht. We can call Don Markham at the Sheriff's office. He must know by now what boat they're looking for."

"Does Derek have a lot of followers?" Josie asked.

Evie scrolled down the list of names. "A ton of them, but..." She highlighted a few. "See all these accounts with egg icons and random usernames like MoneyMan300 or DealzQueen84? Those are usually fake accounts people buy on BuyBay to boost their follower numbers."

"So he's a fake," Josie said, shaking her head.

"He cares about what other people think, sure, but that doesn't mean he's a fake." I tilted my head. "I walked in to the Boldman Bracket offices, and they took up an entire floor of that big glass building downtown. That wasn't fake."

"Don't tell me, it was that insufferable blue glass monstrosity that sears your retinas when the sunlight reflects off it, wasn't it?" Charlie asked.

Landon shook his head. "No, it was that green one with the funky angles that looks like a fun house mirror, I think. That also blinds you when the sun hits it."

"It was one of the many identical glass buildings down there," I said, not knowing one from another anymore. "Sometimes I think Austin must've passed an ordinance requiring all downtown architecture to be some variation of blue, black, or green reflective glass. It's a wonder anyone finds anything."

Charlie snorted. "Require? More like subsidize. They must hand out tax credits for each window pane installed."

"Yes, yes, we all know how you feel about Austin politicians, dear. But I agree with you—at this rate, the entire city will disappear behind a massive mirror if they keep throwing up these glass monstrosities," Josie said with an eye roll.

"Huh," Evie said, her voice... odd.

"Huh?"

"Well, Landon was right—Boldman Bracket is in the funhouse mirror-looking building. But get this." Evie turned the laptop again and pointed to an article. "Boldman Bracket is being investigated for shady practices in Herzoslavia."

"What's Hertoslavia?" I asked.

"You mean Herzoslovakia?" Josie asked, furrowing her brow. "That tiny Baltic nation known for its top-quality textiles?"

We all stared at Josephine.

"What? Their artesian springs yield the softest waters in Europe. Or, at least, they used to until that Lake Stempka business. It was ideal for processing fine wools and silks. I imagine the value of those textiles might go up since they're having problems now."

"How on earth did you know that off the top of your head?" I asked.

"I read an article, watched a show. I don't remember. The villagers historically relied on weaving and textiles as their livelihood for local trade, and generation after generation cultivated the craft. They claim Herzoslovakia's master weavers produce the most luxurious tapestries and garments this side of Milan."

Charlie raised his eyebrow. "Which side of Milan?"

"We live on a gigantic ball, Charles Reynolds. We're always east and west of Milan, so what does it matter?" She pointed her finger at him. "Quit teasing me."

"I would never."

She tapped a manicured nail against the desk. "Like I said, that Lake Stempka thing with the pollution has caused a slowdown with it. What on earth could Derek be involved in over there?"

Evie scanned the text. "I don't know. It doesn't mention him."

"That doesn't mean much. BB is a local, independent investment bank, and everyone knows everything." Josie sat up straight, eyes flashing with recollection. "Wait a minute!" She jumped up and hurried over to a garment bag hanging on the coat rack. Unzipping it, she held up the elegant emerald gown.

"Check out the tag on the dress I bought at Lisa's boutique," she said, facing the label outward.

We all leaned in to read the tiny print.

Made in Herzoslovakia.

A cacophony of voices erupted as everyone began talking over each other, their words tangling together into an incomprehensible din over the potential connections between Lisa's disappearance, the boutique's Herzoslovakian fabrics, and the shady dealings of Boldman Bracket in that country. The chaotic cross-talk escalated as they batted contradictory clues and conjectures back and forth like a tennis volley spinning out of control.

I couldn't make out a thing.

"Quiet, everyone!" I called out, holding up my hands. "I appreciate everyone's theories here, but you've lost me. I don't know the first thing about international finance or investment banks. Could someone explain— one at a time—in simple terms what these connections might show?"

Josie and Charlie exchanged a look.

"In basic terms, investment banks have a long history of shady dealings when it comes to securing lucrative contracts," Josie explained. "They've been caught engaging in illegal activities like bribery of foreign officials and bid rigging schemes."

I felt a swell of unease in my chest as she detailed these corrupt practices. My knowledge of high finance was limited at best, and the unscrupulous world she described was foreign to me.

Charlie nodded. "Right. They try to buy favor with politicians and officials in charge of awarding contracts. The more money they contribute as 'campaign donations' or 'gifts,' the more likely they are to win the contract."

"Even if their bid isn't the best or most competitive," Josie added.

"Exactly," Charlie said. "It's institutionalized corruption. And just from what we know, my guess would be that Boldman Bracket may have been playing that game in Herzoslovakia to get business related to the textile industry. If that's true, and word got out, it could be very damaging to their reputation. Lawsuits, fines, even criminal charges could follow."

Could Derek be ruthless enough to kill an innocent woman to protect his crooked empire? Was Samantha involved? The notion turned my stomach.

"You deal with cases like this?" I asked.

"I have in the past." Charlie thought for a moment.

"If Lisa had proof of their activities, or was threatening to expose them..." He trailed off meaningfully.

"So you think they might have gotten rid of Lisa to silence her?"

"He does not. It's all just speculation at this point," Josie told me. "We have no direct evidence linking Lisa's disappearance to Boldman Bracket's activities overseas. We still have no evidence, frankly, that Lisa's disappeared. Her business partner says she heads out to parts unknown by herself all the time."

"And her employee says she never does."

"True." Her expression turned serious. "Look—the connections are concerning enough that we should talk to that kitten. Fluffy was with Lisa at the lake and may know things that could shed more light on all this."

"She's just a child, Josie."

"Children know more than you think. Remember what happened with Fluff during the ice storm? Without that cat's memories as a kitten I doubt we ever would have figured it out."

"I know, but questioning a 3-month-old kitten about a criminal conspiracy seems like a stretch. That was an adult remembering her childhood. This is interrogating a child."

"Desperate times call for desperate measures." Josie's eyes darkened with conviction. "Fluffy may be our best bet to unravel this mystery. We have to at least try talking to her—she may have clues we desperately need."

"Now hold on," Landon said, holding up a hand. "I wouldn't go saying these are desperate times just yet. We're still just working with hunches and hearsay at this point. Seems to me we need more solid clues before we go stirring up a ruckus—especially with folks in powerful places. Can't go making wild accusations without proof."

Josie clicked her tongue, regarding him with an arched brow. "Darling, you take my turns of phrase far too literally." She waved a hand. "I speak in metaphors and hyperbole. I know the circumstances aren't desperate... yet. But why wait until they are to get more information from the only one of us that knows Lisa and has no agenda? The longer we delay, the colder the trail grows."

Landon leaned back in his chair, rubbing his stubbled chin as he mulled over everything we had discussed. "I get why everyone's focusing on this Derek guy, but seems to me there may be more clues buried in those legal disputes between Henderson and Lisa," he said. "Evie, any way you could do some more digging into the court records, see what those quarrels were about?"

Evie perked up, fingers already drifting across the keyboard. "I'm on it. I'll search the county database and see what I can turn up."

"I can give you my county database login if you need more information than what you can see publicly," Josie told her.

Landon nodded. "Might also be worthwhile to loop Matt in on this."

Evie paused her rapid typing and bit her lip. "Matt's away for a bit. He took his abuela down to Galveston to visit family for her birthday." Seeing Landon's eyebrows rise, she added, "I can still poke around online and try to connect the dots in the meantime. I got it. Don't worry."

He stood and stretched. "I never worry," he told her.

Uh huh.

Chapter Six

Fluffy sat on the silver platter, her tiny paws barely covering the etched symbols along the edge. The moment her soft fur made contact, the crystal inlay glowed, casting an otherworldly silvery light over her tan and brown floofy coat.

"Hi everybody!" a young female voice squeaked through the air. "You wanna talk to me again? That's so fun!" Fluffy's eyes grew wide as she took in the sound of her own voice projected around the room. Her folded ears swiveled. "Really, that's so weird, too. Fun. But weird."

"Hello, Fluffy," I said. "How are you doing?"

"How does this thing do that? My paws are warm. Did you know it makes my paws warm?" She turned to Belladonna. "Did you hear me talking? I sound so big!"

Belladonna flicked her sleek black tail in cool response from her regal perch atop the tall carpeted cat tower, her piercing golden eyes narrowing to calculating slits.

"Yes, we can hear you," I said. "Good to talk to you again, Fluffy."

"My name's Fluffy! I'm a fluffy kitty, see?" The eager kitten flopped onto her back, revealing her soft belly fur. She waved her paws in the air as her legs kicked about with joyful energy and added, "Ooh, rub my tummy, please!"

Josie leaned in, scratching the kitten's fuzzy belly while Fluffy purred with happiness, back leg thumping in bliss. "Fluffy, can you tell us about your human mommy? What was her name?"

After a few moments of delighted tummy rubs, Fluffy popped back up, tail curled above her back. "My fur's the fluffiest and softest ever!" she declared, giving her coat a little shake to show its plush texture. "I love my mommy. She lets me sleep on her pillow." Fluffy tilted her head, nose twitching. "One day she put me in my carrier and we went for a ride in her car. Then she brought me to a big house by the water. There were trees and birds and lizards to chase!"

Josie looked at me.

"The equivalent of a four to six years old," I reminded her.

"Do you remember your mommy's name?" Josie asked the kitten.

Fluffy tilted her head and blinked in confusion. "Mommy."

"Do you know what other people called her?" I asked.

The kitten's ears twitched in confusion.

Landon leaned down closer to Fluffy's level. "Hey there, little one," he said in a gentle rumble. "Can you tell us what your mommy looked like?"

Fluffy's tail curled up at the sight of the burly carpenter. "You have fur on your face just like me!" She batted at his chin. "Mommy is big like you and has long fur on her head that's brown and wavy and it smells like flowers," she declared. "And her paws are always moving around, holding things in and out of this enormous machine that makes a scary noise. She makes lots of sounds with her mouth when she's happy. And she gives the best ear scratches!"

I couldn't help but smile even though it was clear piecing together concrete details would be a challenge with our youthful witness.

My eyes drifted down to the flip-flop behind her.

"Fluffy, can you tell me about your flip-flop friend there?" I asked.

"Floppy!" Fluffy exclaimed, seizing the battered flip-flop and chomping on it. "This is my bestest buddy, Floppy. He keeps me safe from monsters."

"Where did you get Floppy from?"

Fluffy's nose scrunched. "Mommy left him on the beach when she ran. I was scared of the big water when I was alone. Because it was Mommy's floppy, I thought Floppy could protect me."

My mind spun with questions as I visualized the craggy landscape surrounding Lisa's modern home. No sandy shores in sight. Only jutting rocks and gnarled tree roots descending into the rippling water. The lake had a few man-made beaches along its shoreline, but none near Lisa's home.

Landon looked at Charlie. "They were on one of the lake beaches."

"The big, noisy water that splashes up on the land," Fluffy clarified as she gnawed on Floppy's mangled strap. "That's where I was. And then I went to find Mommy. Can we stop talking and do belly rubs now?"

"Just a minute, sweetie." I turned to the others. "So Lisa and Fluffy got separated along one of the lake shore beaches—and Lisa was running fast enough to lose her shoe."

"Those are all public beaches, Mom." Ellie scratched the kitten's belly. "Wouldn't someone have found her stuff or the other flip-flop? If they were on a beach, they probably had towels or a cooler—"

"Unless they were just going for a walk." Josie pointed out. "Maybe they had no stuff."

"They had to have a car. There's no beach near Lisa's house. So where is it?" Landon reached for the flip-flop. "Here, let me just take a closer look at that for a minute, okay?"

"Nooo!" Fluffy cried out, her small body tensing as she snatched the tattered flip-flop back from Landon's outstretched hand and scrambled backward, fur bristling. After placing it behind her once more, she let out a tiny hiss of warning. "You can't take my Floppy!" Her wide eyes were filled with distress and mistrust, ears folded back.

Despite her chipper chat with us, I could see how deeply attached she was to this last relic of her missing mother.

He held up his hands in apology. "You're right, I'm sorry."

Fluffy watched him for a moment before relaxing her guarded stance. She stepped forward and allowed Landon to scratch her under the chin in an additional apology. Seemingly satisfied he meant no harm, Fluffy plopped down and resumed chewing her flip-flop with tiny teeth.

The kitten's fragmented story left more questions than answers, but one thing was certain—it was up to us now to find the answers.

And the other flip-flop.

Charlie and Josie lounged on the plush cat beds, laughing as the shelter cats tumbled and played around them in the third floor loft. As I scooped kibble into the row of food bowls Landon had lined up on the counter, my thoughts kept drifting to the meeting with Derek that evening. I hoped he would provide some solid clues, but the idea of chatting up a suspect that may have chased Lisa on a beach made my stomach knot with nerves.

"I talked to Deputy Markham, and he said he's putting some feelers out about Lisa's other boat and her car," Charlie told us between tossing cat toys across the floor. "If it's out on or around Lake Wildebridge somewhere, the lake patrol should spot it."

Josie nodded, stretching out across a plush beanbag shaped like a bass fish as two tabby cats wrestled for the feather toy in her hand. "That will tell us a lot. I have a good feeling about this lead Ellie's following tonight, too. Derek's differing answers seem mighty curious."

"Are you going alone?" Charlie asked.

I shrugged. "Probably."

Evie popped up from where she was sprawled belly-down on the floor, a calico kitten kneading her shoulder. "Oh! Let me run and grab that tiny spy cam from Matt's house so you can wear it tonight, Mom. Darla can drive me."

She took off before I could respond.

Landon straightened, the bag of kibble slipping from his fingers back into the bin with a thud that made me jump. My heart sank as I realized a quarrel was imminent. "You're not seriously going to a disappeared woman's house to meet with her suspect ex-boyfriend alone?"

"Is that an actual question?" I asked.

"I hope not, because that implies there's more than one answer."

I bristled, keeping my voice light despite the irritation flaring inside me. "It's not confirmed by anyone that he's shady."

"I can go if you want, Ellie." Josie sat up on the fish bed, gently interrupting the building tension. "It's only natural I'd accompany you to a meeting like this in my capacity as the shelter's legal counsel. It wouldn't arise any suspicion."

"Except you were at the boutique today."

"Well, so were you."

Landon frowned. "I don't like the thought of you two going there at night to confront a potential suspect."

My hackles rose further at his patronizing tone, but I swallowed the sharp retort on my lips, striving to stay polite. "Landon, we're not confronting anyone, simply gathering information."

"I should come along, too."

I held in a frustrated sigh. Here we went again with the overprotectiveness. Since he'd moved in, it seems like Landon viewed me as less competent, not more—when did he stop seeing me as capable on my own?

I turned away before he could read the insult on my face, busying myself scooping more kibble. "There's no need for that. Josie and I can handle ourselves just fine."

Landon's jaw tensed. "Right, but—"

Sensing the rising tension, Charlie interrupted. "No need to worry yourself, Landon. I'm sure the ladies know what they're doing."

"Another person couldn't hurt," he responded sharply. "For backup."

I looked up. "Josie and I can handle it."

Silence.

He held my gaze, his eyes clouded with concern. His broad shoulders tensed beneath his shirt as if bracing for an argument, the muscles in his arms flexing. One large, callused hand drifted almost unconsciously toward his belt, while the other raked through his tousled waves of salted brown hair—a gesture I knew betrayed his unease. His brown boot tapped out an agitated rhythm on the smooth white tiles of the shelter floor.

"Josie and I will have each other's backs. I appreciate your concern, but we've got this covered."

His shoulders drooped like a balloon losing air, as if the weight of my refusal had pressed all the energy out of him. I could see the dark cloud forming over his head, a tiny storm cloud raining only on him. "If you insist. Just... call me when you get there." He paused. "And when you leave."

"You'll have a live stream of the entire event, Landon," Josie told him before I could respond. She rose from the fish bed, gathering her things. "It's not like we'll really be by ourselves. You, Charlie, and Evie will watch every minute, I'm sure. I'll pick you up at seven, Ellie?"

I nodded, hoping we could move on, but an undercurrent of tension lingered in the air. I suspected Landon's overprotectiveness would keep resurfacing until we addressed it properly.

And by address it properly, I mean cut it off like a gardener pruning back an invasive vine.

The buttery soft black leather enveloped me as I settled into the plush passenger seat of Josie's sleek Mercedes. Through the tinted windows, the setting sun glinted off the polished hood, and I felt a swell of excitement in my chest at the prospect of seeing inside Lisa Hartman's lakeside home.

Josie cruised up the snaking highway leading out of Tablerock, expertly navigating the curves north toward Lake Wildebridge as thick stands of oak and cedar closed in around us. Dappled evening light filtered through the canopy of boughs stretched overhead, and the heady aroma of pine and ripening wildflowers drifted through Josie's cracked window.

"So what was that thing with Landon about earlier?" Josie asked as we cruised up the highway. "He seemed quite perturbed at the notion of us ladies venturing out on our own tonight, but you seemed even more annoyed that he said anything."

I sighed, leaning my head back against the headrest. "Just Landon being overprotective as usual. Since he moved in, it appears that he believes I can't handle myself without a big, strong man around."

"Oh, come on. Can you blame the man for wanting to keep you safe?"

"No, but it's patronizing. I've gotten by just fine on my own all these years. Having him questioning my judgment and trying to insert himself everywhere just rubs me the wrong way." I shifted in my seat to face Josie. "Does Charlie do that with you?"

Josie considered for a moment as she switched lanes to pass a lumbering RV. "Not overtly, no. Though I'm certain a part of him would prefer if I avoided chasing criminals and corruption as a hobby. I think he thought I would have dropped this by now." She chuckled. "Charlie respects my independence. He knows I'd claw his eyes out if he tried to police my activities."

I laughed along with her, though a twinge of envy pinged through me. Why couldn't Landon show me a similar respect?

The highway wound higher into the hills surrounding Lake Wildebridge, the road dipping and rising with the undulating topography. Josie maneuvered the curves as dusk settled over the rugged landscape.

In the distance, glimpses of the massive lake shone between the trees.

"I don't know," I said after a few moments of companionable silence. "Landon means well, but his overprotectiveness just feels infantilizing sometimes. I'm a grown woman. I can assess risks and make my own choices."

"I can understand finding it grating. We women bristle at any perceived attempt to limit our autonomy.

But consider it from his perspective—his protective instinct arises from a place of care, not control."

"Does it though? It feels an awful lot like he doesn't trust me."

"Oh, no way," Josie countered. "A man wants to protect his lady. That's just nature's way, pure and simple. Mother Nature herself gave him that driving need to keep his woman safe from harm—"

"*His* woman?"

"It's instinct, ingrained over eons of evolution, honey. So don't go taking offense when Landon gets all protective. He can't help it. The good Lord above hard-wired that protective streak into his masculinity—let him exercise it! It reassures him you're not gonna get hurt on his watch. And if it comforts him to know you're safe? Let him have that."

"They're going to confiscate your feminist card, Josie."

"Bite your tongue. Your man builds catios, Ellie. Everything has a balance. Give him this."

I wasn't convinced. Josie seemed to accept men's controlling tendencies far too readily in my view. Then again, she'd been married far longer than I.

We crested a ridge, and Lake Wildebridge sprawled before us, a vast rippling sheet of water stretching to the horizon. The fading sunset painted its surface in dazzling hues of orange and pink that shifted and morphed as the gentle waves caught the slanting light. In the fiery glow, the water almost seemed to burn with otherworldly flames.

"It really is beautiful out here."

"I suppose," I conceded. "Look, I hear what you're saying, but I still don't love feeling like I suddenly can't take care of myself now that a man's around."

"You're like a dog with a bone. Don't see it as him believing you cannot take care of yourself, but as him wanting to take care of you because he cares. I'm telling you, Ellie, I do think he bumbled, but you're not cutting him much slack. And, one more point—independence does not prevent you from accepting help at times."

As the Mercedes hugged the curves of the winding hillside road, I mulled over Josie's perspective, watching the dusky waters of Lake Wildebridge slip in and out of view through the trees.

Perhaps I had been too quick to jump to uncharitable conclusions about Landon's motivations. I pictured his concerned eyes and tense shoulders back at the shelter, saw again the way his strong hands had raked through his dark waves of hair as he fretted over my safety. Though his delivery irked me, Josie had a point—his overbearing protectiveness likely arose from affection and an earnest desire to keep me from harm, not from any aim to dominate or control.

I felt a twinge of regret recalling the heat in my own harsh tone, the biting edge in my voice when I had rebutted his concerns.

I resolved to approach the issue again with Landon,

but this time leading with empathy rather than indignation. I would make clear I appreciated his caring intentions, while still asserting my need for independence. With open communication and willingness to listen, I felt hopeful we could find the right balance in this new phase of our relationship.

"Maybe you're right. I'll try to be more understanding," I told her. "After so much time alone, navigating a serious relationship is unfamiliar territory. Compromise takes some adjusting to."

Josie smiled. "It certainly does. But you two care for one another. Have faith you'll find the right balance in time."

"I'll talk to him when I get home."

"Probably no need."

"Why's that?"

"Well, we've been live-streaming this entire heart-to-heart over your spy cam, so Landon likely heard every word." She flashed a cheeky grin. "I believe the awkward work of discussing feelings has already been handled for you."

I blushed, sinking down in my seat as Lake Wildebridge disappeared into the darkness up ahead.

Chapter Seven

Josie's Mercedes glided to a stop at the end of the long driveway leading up to Lisa Hartman's imposing modern lake house. As we climbed out, the faint sound of gentle waves lapping against the shore below mingled with a chorus of crickets and frogs serenading the descending night.

The stark white facade of the stylish home became muted in the deepening dusk, and the last fiery glow of sunset clung to the highest windowpanes, setting the glass ablaze with reflected rose-gold light even as darkness gathered beneath the jutting eaves.

"Well, here we go," Josie murmured, coming to stand beside me. Her keen eyes roved over every detail. "I wonder if our slippery banker friend has already arrived."

Before I could open my mouth to reply, a detail caught my eye—the dusty blue Prius Landon and I had spotted parked near the private dock on our earlier visit now sat in the driveway, looking freshly detailed. The dirt and grime coating its panels had been scrubbed away, leaving the vehicle almost sparkling beneath the exterior lights.

"That's odd. Lisa's car—well, if that's Lisa's car—wasn't here last time. It was down by the dock. But now it's parked right there looking like it just got a wash and wax," I said, pointing it out to Josie.

"Huh. You're sure it's the same car?"

"I don't remember the license plate number, but I think so."

"It could be Derek's."

I raised an eyebrow. "He didn't strike me as a Prius driver."

"If you're correct, that means someone has been here looking after things in Lisa's absence." Josie arched a knowing brow and inclined her head toward the front door. "Shall we?"

The modern chimes echoed through the silent home. After a moment, footsteps approached, distinct even through the solid door. Finally, it swung open.

"Ellie, welcome!"

Derek stood in the doorway, flashing his too-white smile. He had changed from his crisp banker's suit into an open-collared shirt and sport jacket, yet still exuded moneyed elegance.

Well, that's rather forward of him, I thought to myself as I schooled my features to remain neutral. We weren't bosom companions, and I didn't recall extending an invitation for this smug banker to address me by my nickname—though I supposed formalities and social boundaries were of little concern to Derek, seeing as he had no qualms about making himself at home in his missing girlfriend's lakeside mansion.

I allowed his impertinence to slide for the moment, swallowing the tart retort perched on my tongue along with a healthy dollop of irritation at his presumption. "Evening, Mr. Sutton. I hope we're not late."

His eyes flicked to Josie, and for an instant, his polished smile faltered.

I could see the gears turning in his head as he struggled to conceal his displeasure at my bringing a guest— not informing him in advance had been a clever move on Josie's part. If he was this annoyed at Josie, I wonder what he'd think about the hidden camera spying on him from my lapel.

"You remember Josephine Reynolds, don't you?" I asked. "From the boutique earlier today. I asked her to join since she's the legal counsel for our cat shelter."

Derek's smile wavered as he shook Josie's extended hand. "A pleasure to see you again, Ms. Reynolds."

"Likewise, Mr. Sutton." Josie gave Derek's hand a firm, prolonged shake as she held his gaze with an amused challenge in her own. "Looking forward to hearing your proposals."

Derek stepped back, gesturing for us to enter. "Please, come in and make yourselves comfortable."

Again, treating his girlfriend's house like it was his, I thought with a huff of irritation. We crossed the threshold into the elegant home and followed Derek down the hallway toward the back of the house. My eyes darted everywhere, searching for clues as we walked.

Lisa's home appeared cleaned and tidy, with no hints of neglect or disarray. The sleek surfaces gleamed, white walls unmarred, minimalist furnishings meticulously arranged. Whoever had cleaned had been thorough—almost suspiciously so. It reminded me of crime shows where someone scoured a location to eliminate evidence—though on crime shows they usually used bleach, not lavender scented cleaner.

"Have a seat," Derek said, leading us into an airy space flanked on one side by windows stretching from floor to ceiling with views of the lake's dark waters.

An open laptop sat on the table, folders spread out beside it. Derek swept these items into a pile and folded his hands atop the polished wood surface as Josie and I settled into the minimalist chairs. "I must apologize for not having refreshments prepared. I wasn't expecting company beyond Ellie and—"

"No need to apologize on my account," Josie replied, flashing a businesslike smile. "I had dinner before we came, and we'll no doubt stop for drinks on the way back to the house."

I wondered if my mere millions didn't rate a glass of water.

Josie's presence had thrown Derek off-guard, and her

manner was keeping him there; he was already floundering to regain control of the conversation he'd intended to dominate.

"You and Lisa have a lovely home," I remarked, casting my gaze toward the floor-length panes of glass. A strategic silence followed, allowing the delicate lapping of waves down below to emphasize my implied question. "It's beautiful."

"I'm sorry?" he managed after a beat, eyebrows pinching together.

I waved a casual hand toward the windows. "Your home. I was just admiring the beautiful lake views you must wake up to every morning in this tranquil oasis." I flashed a polite smile but kept my eyes trained on him. "I'll bet you got out on the water this weekend for a bit of fun."

"This weekend?" At this, Derek shifted in his seat, the sleek leather squeaking beneath him. "Oh, uh, no." He gave a twitchy shrug, eyes darting toward the darkened lake, then back to me. "I don't live here."

"My mistake," I said, arranging my face into an expression of apology. "I just assumed this was your house as well, since, you know..."

"We're here," Josie deadpanned.

Derek gave an attention-getting cough, collecting himself. "Right, no. As I mentioned at my office, this is my girlfriend Lisa's place. I don't live here with her. I visit a lot, and she lets me use the place, but I live in downtown Austin."

"Really? I'm just impressed with how spotless it is," I continued. "I could never keep white walls so pristine. Especially not with a new kitten. Lisa must have an excellent cleaning service."

I watched Derek to gauge his reaction, but he showed no obvious signs of suspicion. If he was uneasy fielding my probing questions, his poker face didn't show it.

Josie jumped in. "I bet she does. White walls near water require diligent care. I once toured a lovely Mediterranean villa, all cool tile and white stucco, inside and out. They had a team of three just for touch-ups and scrubbing."

As Josie launched into a monologue on European luxury villas, I scrutinized Derek. The man's expression remained polite as he weathered this assault of inane small talk from two middle-aged women, and if the talk of Lisa had rattled him, he didn't show it much.

Finally, Derek cleared his throat.

"Shall we get down to business, then?" He tapped the folder on the table. "I compiled an overview of Boldman Bracket's services and why we're the ideal firm to grow your assets through strategic market investing."

I had no idea what strategic market investment was, but I bobbed my head in feigned comprehension, hoping Derek would attribute any confusion on my face to his own brilliance dazzling my simple mind—rather than my complete ignorance of high finance.

Josie maintained her composure with ease.

Of course, she probably knew what he was saying.

Derek droned on about leveraged portfolios and optimized asset growth, his slick financial jargon washing over me in an incomprehensible stream of buzz-words and percentage return claims. While he talked himself breathless with his slick sales pitch about lever-aging wealth and targeted growth, I subtly craned my neck, eyeing the visible portions of the home for any details.

My inquisitive eyes landed on a framed photo of Lisa and Derek on the credenza. In it, they posed on the deck of a boat, Lisa flashing a radiant smile, her arm draped across Derek's shoulders.

His own smile appeared forced to me, eyes cold and calculating even then.

"But with the current uncertainty around interest rates, wouldn't it be wiser to remain in more stable, fixed-return products until the market stabilizes?" Josie asked Derek.

Before he could answer, a sudden chime rang out from the open laptop. He glanced toward the screen, shoulders tensing as his amiable smile faded. Eyes narrowed, Derek leaned closer to peer at whatever alert or notification had popped up. His eyebrow gave an agitated twitch.

"Excuse me one moment," he muttered, the slick assurance absent from his tone. "I need to take this call."

Without waiting for a response, Derek shoved back his chair and strode from the room, the tapping of his shoes on the hardwood fading until a heavy door clicked shut, muffling the sound.

Josie's eyes narrowed, homing in on the closed door that Derek had disappeared behind. She leaned toward me, lips barely moving as she whispered. "I'm going to see what I can overhear."

Before I could respond, she was up and tiptoeing across the room with catlike stealth, her own heels soundless on the polished wood floors. I watched wide-eyed as Josie pressed close to the door, turning her head to position one ear against the smooth white paneled surface. Her eyes slid shut in concentration, brow furrowing in focus as she strained to make out the conversation on the other side.

What was she doing?

Eavesdropping felt risky, with Derek liable to pull that door open any second.

"Can you hear anything?" I whispered.

"No," she whispered back. "He's too far from the door. I'll tell you if I hear him coming."

With Derek distracted, I took advantage of the opportunity to return my attention to the visible areas of the home. In the hall, a bowl full of keys sat next to a leather-bound book. More framed photos of the stunning couple decorated the living room, featuring them smiling on boats, clinking wine glasses at candlelit dinners, and posing on exotic beaches. The snapshots depicted a happy, glamorous couple, but I wondered how much was a ruse.

One photo gave me pause—the pair on a dock, with a third man whose face seemed familiar. I leaned closer, eyebrows knitting together. Wait a minute, I do know that man. Don't I?

Then I gasped.

That's Ronnie Earle, I realized with a start.

I'd read an in-depth feature article on the elusive figure who lurked at the fringes of high society. He started out small time, just a two-bit hustler, but somehow cultivated relationships with the rich and powerful. Prison bigwigs, corrupt officials, shady businessmen—they were all linked to Earle through his vast network of fronts and shell companies concealing the illicit sources of their money. His name provoked fear in some circles, envy in others.

But no one disputed the man's influence from the shadows.

I straightened up, my gaze sweeping over the cavernous interior of Lisa's lavish lakefront mansion with new eyes. The floor to ceiling windows overlooking the shimmering waters, the original artworks worth more than my annual shelter budget adorning the walls, the luxury furniture...

Could Lisa's quaint downtown clothing boutique really be financing this extravagant lifestyle all on its own? Or were more nefarious funding sources behind her wealth?

My mind spun with questions.

For now, though, I filed away this new puzzle piece for later consideration when I could pick Josie and Landon's brains. But one thing was obvious—there were hidden depths to Lisa Hartman's life.

Josie waved and scurried back to the table just in time, settling into her seat and arranging her features into a look of idle curiosity as the door handle turned.

Derek's polished smile fixed in place but tension was evident in the set of his shoulders and the way his eyes flicked briefly around the room like he was looking for something. "Sorry about that."

"No problem!" I gesture to the framed photo on the mantel. "While you were gone we were looking at your photos and I have to ask—is it you or Lisa that knows the notorious Ronnie Earle? That article I read in Western Monthly portrayed him as quite a character."

My questions made Derek visibly uncomfortable once again for only the briefest of seconds before he recovered, a broad smile snapping back into place. "He's not at all the person the article made him out to be. The media never gets it right." Derek waved a dismissive hand. "Ronnie owns Boldman Bracket. He's a brilliant investor."

"Really?" I raised my eyebrows. "The article certainly painted him in a different light—and I don't remember it mentioning his owning an investment bank."

"See? It's just tabloid nonsense trying to stir up drama, that's all. The man's a saint." Derek went on, perhaps overcompensating now. "Boldman Bracket is one of the top boutique investment banks in the country, you know. We pride ourselves on working with small to mid-size companies, focusing our expertise on guiding unique, independent ventures to success."

I tilted my head. "Boutique? Like Lisa's clothing store?"

Derek didn't respond.

Josie said, "Boutique investment banks specialize in funding and investments under one billion dollars or so. Much smaller deals than the Wall Street mega firms."

"I see. Small investments," I said, letting slight skepticism creep into my voice. "Half of a billion dollars still seems rather large by most people's standards."

Derek waved off my remark, his earlier tension forgotten in his eagerness to impress me. "Yes, that's all relative, isn't it? To massive international conglomerates trading tens of billions a day, a billion may seem modest. But for a local mom and pop shop or creative startup, even ten thousand dollars can be a game changer."

"And you handle things that small?"

"Of course."

"Well, regardless of the scale, I'm sure Lisa must

have appreciated having your expertise available to help grow her boutique fashion business," I remarked, watching for his reaction.

"We always aim to foster the success of visionary local entrepreneurs and innovators. It's the backbone of the economy, after all." He flashed his polished teeth. "Unique independent ventures like Threads and Trends are the lifeblood of communities. That's where true innovation happens."

Innovation...

A clothing boutique?

Josie smiled. "How wonderful. Though I imagine not all such innovators and dreamers will have the business acumen to strategically invest the profits from their creativity." She tilted her head, meeting his gaze. "Some will need proper guidance to ensure their ventures remain stable and lucrative long-term, yes?"

"Precisely! You understand." Derek's eyes gleamed, sensing he had hooked his wealthy fish. "That ability to strike the perfect balance between creative freedom and shrewd business strategy is why so many companies seek our services. We allow the spirited dreamers to focus on what they do best while ensuring the financial side is handled with expert care."

He went on describing Boldman Bracket's unique services and approach, rattling off client success stories and statistics and percentages that blurred together into more boilerplate sales patter. I made occasional noises of polite interest, though my attention kept drifting to the windows overlooking the moonlit lake.

Somewhere out there, Lisa's luxury yacht sat upon the glimmering waters.

Or perhaps it lay beneath them.

The not knowing left a queasy feeling in my gut.

I must have drifted off too long, for Derek's voice sharpened. "Of course, managing such exponential success requires discipline," he was saying. "Bold vision demands bold action."

"Hm? Oh yes, naturally." I plastered on an invested look.

What secrets might Lisa have discovered that created such danger for her?

Had prosperity perhaps led her to overextend herself, requiring loans from less reputable sources? Or had she, in the creative spirit Derek touted, pushed back against investors aiming to control her vision?

My gut said Derek knew far more of Lisa's fate than he let on.

But without evidence, extracting the truth from him would prove impossible.

A shrill buzz jarred me from my contemplation. Derek fished his phone from his suit jacket and glanced at the screen. "You know what? It is getting rather late," he said. "Why don't I show you lovely ladies out so you can be on your way? We can pick this chat up after the two of your have discussed things."

Well.

That was abrupt.

We stood and Derek herded us politely but firmly down the hall. As we stepped out onto the front porch, he added, "I'll call you tomorrow so we can meet again soon to discuss Boldman Bracket's services. I'm certain we can tailor an investment strategy to help you maximize profits from the Blackwell inheritance."

"That sounds lovely," I told him as the two of us continued down the paved path toward Josie's car. Derek waited in the doorway until we had pulled out of the driveway and had driven out of sight.

It wasn't until the modernist lake house had disappeared from view in the rearview mirror that Josie steered the car to the side of the road and turned off the ignition. She turned to me, eyes gleaming.

"All right, let's see what secrets Lisa was hiding away." She pulled out the small leather-bound book from the hallway, waving it.

"You know stealing is against the law, right?"

"Oh please, I'm not stealing anything. I'm borrowing possible evidence without explicit permission in a totally ethical manner befitting an officer of the court investigating potentially illegal happenings," Josie replied. "We can mail it back to her with a friendly note once she resurfaces from her impromptu sabbatical. Whenever that may be."

Chapter Eight

BEFORE SHE COULD OPEN IT, HEADLIGHTS WASHED over us. I turned to see another car slowing on the dark road behind us. It came to a stop, the parking lights glowing red.

My breath caught. "Josie—"

She shoved the book at me. "Here, take this and hide it."

My mind raced, pondering where on earth I could stash the leather-bound book in Josie's pristine Mercedes without it being spotted.

The glove box?

No, too obvious.

Under the floor mats?

Equally conspicuous, and probably crawling with crumbs.

Beneath the seat?

A valiant attempt, but likely futile given the cramped dimensions barely large enough to accommodate my ample rear end—

That's it.

My rear end.

I jammed the book under my legs as Josie reached beneath her seat.

A muffled click echoed through the dark footwell. With steady fingers and a calm inhale, she removed the deadly object from its cradle. The checkered grip fit into her palm like car keys.

My eyes went wide. "Is that a gun?"

"Of course it's a gun. What does it look like?" Josie replied, checking the chamber. "We don't know who that is, and we just came from a missing woman's house. Just in case."

"What are you doing with a loaded gun in your car?"

"I have a concealed carry permit. This is the world's fastest in-car gun deploying safe with an elevator style holster rack system," she explained as if discussing the weather and not a deadly weapon. "It presents the firearm into my hand as the lid opens."

I stared at her. "Why do you need the world's fastest gun drawer in your Mercedes?"

Josie gave me an incredulous look. "Um, hello? I'm a lawyer. You think I don't receive death threats on the regular from the ticked off plaintiffs when I win cases?"

"No, I didn't think so."

"Well, I've gotten one or two in my time. You gotta be prepared out here as a woman alone, Ellie."

"This is a tiny Texas town, not the streets of Gotham City."

"Why don't you ask murder victim Fiona Blackwell how safe this tiny Texas town is?" Josie asked me. "Hey, you never know what might go down out here. I don't take chances." She kept the gun low but ready.

I shifted atop the book, cringing at the thought of what this might look like to whoever had pulled up behind us–two middle-aged women parked on the road-side late at night, one of them brandishing a handgun.

Hardly a scene to inspire trust.

I looked back and squinted against the glare of a flashlight bobbing toward us. The beam swept over the interior of Josie's car, momentarily blinding me.

"What are you ladies doing parked out here so late?" a gruff voice called out loud enough to be heard through the closed windows.

Josie bristled, offense creeping into her tone. "I could ask you the same question. What right have you to inter-rogate citizens parked along this public byway? I didn't see any blue and red lights."

The flashlight beam dipped away from our faces.

Blinking to clear the blotches from my vision, I stared through the gloom at the shadowed figure.

That gravelly voice... I knew that cranky tone.

"Mr. Henderson?" I asked. "Is that you?"

The flashlight slipped from Henderson's grasp, its harsh beam spinning wildly in the trees before flickering out. Cursing under his breath, he bent his stiffened knees, fingers scooping up the flashlight before rising with a painful groan. With a smack of his palm, the light flared again across our faces.

"Ms. Rockwell?" His bushy brows shot up in surprise.

"Yes?"

"What in tarnation are you doing out here?"

To Josie, I said, "This is Lisa Hartman's neighbor, Ethan Henderson. He's a widower that lives next to her —you know, the one who's been feuding with her over developing the land."

Josie slid the gun off her lap but kept it at the ready as she eyed our older visitor. "Charmed," she said.

"Pleasure, ma'am," he muttered to Josie. His eyes darted between us, still suspicious. "Now mind telling me what the two of you are up to at this hour? Sittin' in a parked car with the lights off right by Lisa's drive?"

"You still haven't mentioned what authority granted you the right to run around asking questions of people in public," Josie responded.

Henderson's flinty gaze remained guarded.

"Oh, fine. We just had a meeting at Lisa's house with her boyfriend about a potential investment opportunity." She rested a proprietary hand atop her leather briefcase. "We realized we might have left an important document behind, so we pulled over to look for it before we got too far along."

Once again, the casual mistruth flowed effortlessly from Josie's lips, leaving me torn between admiration and unease at her selective flexibility with facts. It was rather like watching a contortionist bend themselves into alarming shapes—impressive flexibility on display, yes, but also visually disconcerting and vaguely disturbing in a way you couldn't pinpoint.

I shifted atop my lumpy seat cushion, the concealed book's spine digging into my thigh. It was a tactile reminder we were both mired in a bit of deception.

Henderson's frown deepened, etching new creases into his already-wrinkled face. "Investment document? At Lisa's place? With that shifty banker friend of hers?" His shoulders tensed. "What business does he have being there if Lisa's still missing?"

How much should we share with this prickly old man? He clearly harbored animosity toward his neighbor, but perhaps he also had insights that could prove useful. "Well, you see—"

Josie cut me off. "I'm sure you've seen Mr. Sutton there without Ms. Hartman in the past, haven't you?" She flashed a polite, close-lipped smile. "He asked us to meet him at her home, and so we did. It didn't seem that unusual to us, considering the two of them are together."

"Should it have seemed unusual to us?" I asked.

Henderson's dark eyes bored into me as if searching

for any hint of reasoning or motivation behind my questions, and I tried not to squirm under his scrutiny.

Finally, he gave a grumbling sigh, shoulders shrugging.

"I suppose. Lord knows that jerk got involved in the fights that woman and I are having and between you and me? I think he made them worse." He scratched his scraggly beard. "Just find it mighty odd, is all. Ain't seen that Hartman woman in near a week. That ain't normal."

"Has it been that long?" I asked (as if I didn't know.)

Henderson spit over the guardrail into the roadside weeds. "Yep. Not that I'm complainin'. Fewer of her damn boat engines piercing my eardrums at all hours." His laugh sounded more like a hacking cough. "Still, woman up and vanishes without a word? Folks start to wonder."

Josie kept her tone light. "Yes, well, we should get on our way, Mr. Henderson. Lovely chatting with you."

Henderson looked disappointed to have his nosy neighborhood sleuthing cut short. "Well, suppose I'll head on home and leave you ladies to it. But you call me if that shifty banker gives you any trouble, ya hear? I'll come running with my twelve-gauge." He pantomimed aiming a shotgun.

"Thank you for the offer," I said. "You have a good night now."

With a tip of his tattered trucker hat, Henderson trudged back to his mud-spattered pickup. The engine rumbled to life, and he pulled a sloppy three-point turn before rattling off down the road toward his home.

Josie expelled an exasperated breath that sent a wayward strand of hair fluttering as she watched Henderson's taillights vanish into the night. "That nosy old coot. We're fortunate his powers of scrutiny extend no further than a flashlight bulb can illuminate," she remarked as she returned her handgun to the gun safe bolted to her car. "Heaven help us if he comes nosing about again. That man finds more intrigue lurking in his bushes than six seasons of *Murder, She Wrote*."

With a resolute jab, she fired the ignition.

"I can't picture him wishing harm on Lisa," I said once we had put some distance between us and the encounter. "He seems to harbor a lot of bitterness toward her for a bunch of reasons, but murder?"

"He volunteered to shoot Derek for us."

"Yes, but that's just something people say, right?"

Josie mulled it over. "Hard to say for sure. He strikes me more as a petty annoyance than a violent threat." She steered the vehicle around a curve, picking up speed as the road straightened. "But his uneasiness over Lisa's absence did seem rather eager, didn't it? The police haven't started looking for her, but he's noticed something's off—did he notice, or did he do something?"

"It seems to me he notices everything happening

over there. If anyone has clues about the days and night before she disappeared, it's likely him."

"If that's true, we need to tap into that repository of neighborhood observation. Disgruntled as Henderson may be, he could prove a useful source of intel." Josie slanted a sly look my way. "Perhaps you could pay him a friendly visit tomorrow and see what else you can get him talking about. Play nice and charm his story out of him."

I grimaced, already dreading another round of sly insinuations from the odd recluse. "Do you think he'd even tell me anything?"

"Can't hurt to try," Josie said. "Go over there and bring a pie. Apologize for scaring him tonight. Bring Landon, get him reminiscing about the good old days before the fancy house was built. Ask about Derek. Play into his contempt for Lisa. Men like Henderson love having a receptive audience for their ramblings. Get him monologuing about what a thorn in his side that woman was. If you do that, who knows what may slip out?"

She had a point. Curmudgeons did love an excuse to vent their grievances to an attentive ear. "Worth a shot, I suppose."

We fell quiet as the dark ribbon of road unspooled beneath Josie's headlights. Pecan trees towered like shadowy sentinels along the hill country roads, trailing beards of wispy moss. The only other cars were an occasional set of approaching headlights that swept by in a whirl of wind and vanished once more into the night behind us.

"Why don't you pull out that leather book now?"

I flipped open the blank leather cover and angled it to catch the faint glow of the courtesy lighting. Creamy vellum pages filled with an elegant script flowed past beneath my thumb. The first pages held only names and dates, some repeated across entries a year or two apart.

Further in, full paragraphs and inscrutable notes appeared. My eyes snagged on cryptic phrases as I skimmed—investment portfolio, development plans, liquidity event. The business jargon may as well have been ancient Sanskrit for all I could comprehend.

I clapped the book shut with a huff of frustration. "It's all finance mumbo-jumbo. I can't make heads or tails of it." I waved the journal. "For all we know, this could be Derek's, not Lisa's."

Josie held out an expectant hand. "Read it to me."

"Okay, this section mentions large dollar amounts for something called 'BB Retreat'," I told her. "Boldman Bracket? It says funds allocated for 'marina phase one' and 'golf course land prep'."

Josie's brow furrowed. "So, some big luxury development that Derek's company is financing?"

I flipped ahead through dense columns of figures. "Looks that way. Wait—here's a ten million dollar transfer to something called 'Wilde Luxury Homes LLC'."

Josie steered the car around a tight curve, whistling

under her breath. "So, if 'Wilde' means to Wildebridge, that's our county. And ten million? That's not a boutique clothing business money. Lisa's involved in some major development deals."

"If this is even hers," I said, scanning for more clues. "Oh wow. Here's another transfer for twenty-five million to 'LW Marina Properties'." I glanced up at Josie's profile glowing in the dashboard lights. "It's much less than a billion dollars, but that all seems like a lot of money."

"Anything else?"

I tapped a paragraph. "This mentions Ronnie Earle. So this has to do with Boldman Bracket."

"But does it have to do with Lisa?" Josie's brow furrowed in concentration beneath the passing street-lights. "It sounds like funding allocations and transfers for some type of large development project. All very vague language, but the dollar values are clear enough."

"Tens of millions of dollars. For what, though?"

"Excellent question." Josie squinted at the cramped scrawl in my hand. "One I don't have the answer to."

We were all gathered back in my office. Evie sat in a chair on the side of my desk, laptop open in front of her, while Landon and Charlie occupied the two chairs across from me. Josie leaned against the bookcase, arms crossed as she listened to Evie explain what she had uncovered.

"So I dug into those two companies you guys mentioned—LW Marina Properties and Wide Luxury Homes LLC," Evie began. "And I found some pretty interesting stuff connecting them to Ronnie Earle and Derek Sutton."

"Derek already told us Ronnie Earle owns Boldman Bracket," I said. "What did you find out?"

"Well, that's one of the weird things. I searched all the business records I could access, and there's zero evidence Ronnie Earle has any ownership stake in Boldman Bracket. He's not listed as a shareholder, officer, nothing. But both of the real estate entities are tied to him in the corporate paperwork."

Josie's eyebrows shot up. "Then who does own Boldman Bracket?"

"Still trying to unravel that," Evie admitted. "The ownership structure is complex, with shares divided between lots of anonymous LLCs. I need to dig deeper to connect the dots."

"What did you find out about those companies connected to Ronnie Earle?"

"Shady stuff, that's for sure." Evie enlarged a map on her screen. "See all these plots of land around Lisa Hartman's place? In the last two years, nearly all were purchased by Derek Sutton himself. But then, within days or weeks of the purchase closing, he sold them off for two or three times what he paid."

Fluffy, Flip Flops, and Foul Play

"I wonder how I get in on that deal," Charlie chuckled.

I narrowed my eyes, scanning the map. "Sold to who?"

"Wide Luxury Homes LLC," Evie told me. "Every single one. They're snatching up all the land surrounding Lisa's property, almost like they're using Derek as a proxy. And get this—" she enlarged a document, "when I pulled Lisa's credit history and financials, there's nothing showing she ever earned the money needed to afford that massive modernist house she lives in. Or the yacht and speedboat Mr. Henderson mentioned."

"What are you saying?" Landon asked, leaning forward with interest. "She doesn't own that place?"

Evie shook her head, eyebrows raised. "Nope. The owner of record is none other than Wide Luxury Homes LLC. Same with the boats and a hangar at the municipal airport. All registered to that company Ronnie Earle controls."

"Whoa." Charlie let out a low whistle. "So Lisa's place is just one of this guy's luxury properties? He lets her live there?"

"Seems that way," Evie said. "The boutique she runs with Samantha appears legit and successful, but not enough to finance the extravagant lifestyle on display. She's living large on someone else's dime somehow."

"Huh." I rubbed my chin. "So what's her link to

107

Boldman Bracket? Where does Derek's investment bank come into this?"

"That I'm still trying to piece together," Evie admitted. "But Derek has to have close ties to Ronnie Earle to be brokering all these lucrative land deals on his behalf. I just can't prove yet that Boldman Bracket itself is connected."

Landon leaned back in his chair and raked a hand through his hair. "So if I'm following you right, seems we've got a tycoon who likes to keep his name off things, an unstable banker making shady deals for him, a missing woman living large in the tycoon's house, and a lot of secret LLCs tying them all together."

"Something like that," Evie agreed. She closed her laptop with a definitive click. "I'm telling you, there's something funky happening under all this glitz."

Josie tapped her chin. "Here's what I don't get—if Lisa's lifestyle was bankrolled by this Ronnie Earle through his web of companies, why would Derek want to harm her? Wouldn't he need to stay in Earle's good graces since he profits from brokering the land deals?"

"Not if he's skimming or scheming in some other way," Charlie pointed out. "He wouldn't be the first crooked banker helping himself to more than his fair share. I've seen that movie before."

I thought back to the tense phone call that had pulled Derek away during our meeting at Lisa's home. "So, is Derek working on behalf of Ronnie Earle or not?"

"And if not, what if Lisa found out about his shady

dealings?" Landon suggested. "Maybe she learned things that could expose him, and he had to silence her."

"Okay, but what could she have learned?" Josie asked. "She runs a clothing store, for goodness' sake. She knows she can't afford her house. I doubt she stumbled into a complex investment scheme complete with shell corporations in her spare time. She's got to be part of this, doesn't she?"

"Not necessarily. You never know these days, with the internet and all," Charlie said. "Folks stumble across all kinds of things online. Maybe she spotted irregularities in her financial records that traced back to Derek and started digging."

Josie conceded the point with a nod. "It's possible. Her business partner did say it was strange for Lisa to just disappear without notice. Perhaps she did uncover inconvenient truths that made her a liability."

I thought for a moment. "Derek got called away when we were talking to him at Lisa's house. He seemed upset by whatever alert came through on his computer. Is there any way for us to know what was sent?"

"Maybe," Evie said, perking up. She tapped away at her keyboard again. "His back was to those gigantic windows. I might be able to see something in the reflection."

Landon cleared his throat. "Let's not get ahead of ourselves just yet. I agree that Derek's suspicious in more ways than one, but you're focusing on him to the exclusion of everyone else. Like Ethan Henderson. I

Leanne Leeds

think we should unravel the financial web, but visiting
Mr. Henderson tomorrow? That was a good idea. Maybe
there's a reason he's been burying Lisa in lawsuits and
complaints, and it isn't the normal nasty neighbor
reason."

We had enough disjointed clues to suspect Derek
and Ronnie Earle of shady dealings—perhaps even
harming Lisa to conceal their activities. But without
concrete proof, we were theorizing in a void.

110

Chapter Nine

THE BEDROOM WAS ILLUMINATED BY THE WARM glow from the bedside lamps, casting a cozy ambiance over the plush carpet and oak furniture. Before I pulled my nightshirt down over my head, I stole a glance at Landon. He sat on the edge of the bed, shirt already off, running a hand through his tousled waves of salt and pepper hair.

My mind drifted back to the conversation Josie and I had in the car earlier that evening—the one Landon likely overheard through my hidden lapel camera. A flush of embarrassment crept up my neck as I realized I couldn't put off discussing what he heard.

"So..." I began, padding across the room. "I'm guessing you heard everything Josie and I said in the car?"

Landon's head lifted, his deep brown eyes locking with mine, a kaleidoscope of understanding and concern swirling within their depths. He exhaled a heavy breath, his broad shoulders falling. "You're right, I did overhear everything back in Josie's car," he admitted, giving a solemn nod.

Reaching out, he took my hand in his callused grip, the rough pads of his fingers grazing my skin as he spoke in a low, earnest rumble. "I never meant to make you feel suffocated or like I don't trust your judgment, Ellie. That's the last thing I want." His brow furrowed, eyes holding mine in an intense, soulful gaze. "You have to know that."

I settled onto the bed beside him, drawing my knees up to my chest. "It probably didn't sound like it, but I know you mean well," I said, my voice softer than I intended. "It's just... after being on my own for so long, having someone worrying over me? It takes some adjustment."

Landon tilted my chin so our eyes met. "I'm not trying to control you or take away your independence," he said. "I have complete faith in your abilities and judgment. You're one of the strongest, most capable women I know."

A lump formed in my throat as his words washed over me.

And yet...

Did he truly see me that way—strong and capable?

Or was this just what he thought I wanted to hear?

Doubts nagged at the edges of my mind, memories of being dismissed and let down creeping in. Even as the recollections came flooding back, Landon's expression was earnest, and it made me pause. Maybe this time will be different. Perhaps I could allow myself to trust a little more and open doors that had been sealed shut for so long.

I blinked to hold back the unexpected tears that pricked at the corners of my eyes. "I want to believe you, Landon, but I have to ask—if that's the case, why do you question my decisions so often?"

He gave me a crooked smile, his thumb grazing my cheek. "Because I care about you, Ellie. More than you know. The thought of anything happening to you tears me up inside." His expression grew serious. "I'm not trying to be your protector or keeper because I think you need one. I just want to be there for you, to help shoulder whatever burdens I can. You're not obliged to carry the weight of it all."

My chest tightened as the weight of his words sank in.

Ever since my divorce, I had grown accustomed to shouldering every responsibility, every challenge, on my own. Having someone who wanted to share those burdens—not out of a desire to control but out of care and partnership—was something that would take a while to find my equilibrium within.

"Letting someone in..." I began, my voice catching in my throat. I swallowed hard. "It's still a work in progress for me. After Evie's father walked out, I made a vow to myself—I'd never leave myself vulnerable like that again.

Never put my trust in someone else only to have it shattered.

"From that day on, I was done relying on anyone but myself. I could shoulder any burden, face any challenge, with my own strength." A rueful chuckle slipped past my lips as I met Landon's eyes once more. "Though maybe I took that 'self-reliance' thing a little too far over the years."

Landon's arms enveloped me, and I rested my head against his broad chest, drawing comfort from the steady thump of his heartbeat. "You don't have to push me away to prove you're strong, Ellie," he murmured, pressing a kiss to the top of my head. "Accepting help from those who love you doesn't make you weak. It makes you human."

A tear slipped down my cheek as the carpenter whittled away at the walls I'd constructed.

Maybe he was right.

Maybe I had equated vulnerability with weakness, shutting others out in my need to showcase my self-reliance. Landon's words reminded me that true strength came from the courage to open oneself up, too—to trust and lean on others when needed called for some serious bravery sometimes.

"I'm trying," I whispered, leaning into him. "I really am. It's just... old habits die hard."

Landon pulled back slightly, his broad palms cradling my face with a tenderness that belied their rough surfaces. His eyes shone with a fierce determination as he held my gaze captive. "We'll get there together, you and me," he said, the rumbling timbre of his voice reverberating through me. "Methodically, one measured pace succeeding the last, one day at a time. However long it takes."

He leaned in, the faint scent of sawdust and sage mingling with his warm breath as it danced across my skin. "I'm not going anywhere, Ellie." His thumb grazed my cheekbone. "That's a promise you can take to the bank."

Our foreheads touched, his closeness enveloping me like a warm embrace.

In that moment, the world seemed to still, anchoring me to this man who had so effortlessly crumbled the walls I'd built up over the years. I could feel the truth of his words in the unwavering conviction of his stare, the steady strength of his touch.

Landon's embrace was like a cozy blanket fort—safe, warm, and a delightful place to get lost in for the night.

The scent of freshly brewed coffee mingled with the warm, earthy aroma of kibble as I stood behind the counter at the Silver Circle Cat Café the following morning. Sunlight streamed through the tall windows, casting a golden glow over the rustic wood tones and plush pillows strewn about for lounging customers.

Evie sat perched on one of the barstools, sipping her

latte while Landon leaned against the counter beside her, looking over some plans on his tablet. I smiled to myself watching them—my brilliant daughter and the steadfast, caring man who had become such an integral part of our lives over these past months.

The jingle of the bell above the mantrap announced a new arrival. I glanced up to see Laurie breezing through the entrance, her white lab coat fluttering behind her as she strode toward the counter.

"Morning, everyone," she greeted us with a warm smile. "You'll have to forgive me for dropping in and demanding tea. I haven't had a chance to catch my breath in what feels like days."

"No need to apologize, Laurie," I assured her. "We're always happy to see you. You want a hot tea?"

"Not in a cup. I want the gossip I've missed with an extra large coffee," she said, sliding onto the vacant barstool beside Evie. "Make it black as sin with a couple of those cinnamon buns Augusta Walton makes, if you don't mind."

Landon chuckled, shaking his head.

"You got it, Laurie. Coming right up."

As I set about preparing her order, Laurie leaned her elbows on the polished wood counter, head propped in her hands as she regarded the three of us. "So, what have you all been up to? I feel like I haven't seen any of you crazy kids in ages."

Evie snickered at Laurie's teasing term for us.

"You've been pretty swamped at the clinic by the sound of it."

"Ugh, don't get me started," Laurie groaned, rolling her eyes in exasperation. "Ever since that new subdivision broke ground on the south side of town, it's been a never-ending parade of frantic new pet owners bringing in their furry babies with every ailment under the sun."

She took the steaming mug I slid across the counter, inhaling the rich aroma with clear relish before taking a long sip. "I swear, first time owners act like their pup having the sniffles is a medical emergency demanding my immediate attention." She shook her head, exasperated. "I had an owner call at three in the morning last night because their six-week-old golden retriever puppy wouldn't stop licking itself."

"Oh no," I said with a laugh. "How did you handle that one?"

"Politely informed them that was normal puppy behavior they'd have to get used to, but to bring him by in the morning," she said, arching one eyebrow. "Then I hung up and went back to sleep."

I set a plate of Augusta's famous cinnamon rolls in front of her, and she immediately sank her teeth into the gooey confection with evident delight. Through a mouthful of sweet dough, she mumbled, "Can't take it personally, though. They're just nervous new pet parents." She swallowed and washed it down with more coffee. "Don't you remember when Evie was just a baby?

I bet someone fielded a dozen calls from you in her first year alone about every little thing."

"Dr. Cohen," I said, nodding. "And he was wonderful—as I'm sure you are."

"Naturally." Laurie studied us over the glazed rim of her coffee cup, green eyes narrowing in scrutiny. "No tea has been spilled, by the way."

I raised my eyebrow.

"You're being cagey with me this morning. What kind of trouble have you gotten yourselves tangled up in this time?" She glanced between our faces, catching the guilty looks we shared. "Aha! I knew it. You've been conspicuously absent from the café the past few days, and now you're all exchanging those looks." She jabbed an accusatory finger at each of us in turn. "Spill it. What drama have you stumbled into?"

With a sigh, I launched into the details, telling Laurie the full story of Lisa Hartman's abrupt disappearance and the abandoned kitten that had set our investigation into motion. I outlined the various clues we had uncovered — the shadowy ties between her boyfriend Derek and his alleged boss Ronnie Earle, the cryptic notes in the journal, her lavish lifestyle she couldn't have paid for, the feuding neighbor Mr. Henderson who may know more than he lets on.

As I narrated the developing mystery, Laurie's face cycled through a kaleidoscope of expressions—shock, outrage, confusion, suspicion—her eyes growing rounder with each new revelation.

"So you see," I concluded, "we still don't know what became of Lisa herself, but we have plenty of suspicious circumstances and motives surrounding her disappearance."

Landon nodded, expression grim. "More questions than answers at this point."

Laurie stared at us for a long beat, fingers drumming on the countertop. "You know, I was just thinking how I hoped another veterinarian would open up shop in town soon to help ease my workload." Her gaze swept over the three of us, eyes sparkling with fond exasperation. "But it seems no matter how much Tablerock grows from a small town into a suburb, this place will ensure I never lack for drama and excitement in my life."

"It does rather seem that way, doesn't it?" I chuckled, unable to deny the truth of her words. Whenever I thought things in Tablerock were settling into a peaceful routine, some new mystery or conundrum arose to thwart my hopes for tranquility.

Laurie gestured with her mug. "So go on then, fill me in. What's your grand plan for getting to the bottom of all this? I assume you're not just twiddling your thumbs waiting for the missing lady to show up safe and sound."

Landon spread his hands. "Well, as a matter of fact—"

"Don't tell me," Laurie interjected, holding up one hand. "You're headed over to chat with the curmudgeonly lion in his lakeside den and see if he drops any crumbs you can follow?"

I arched one eyebrow. "That's right, actually. We're going to pay Mr. Henderson a visit and see what insights he might offer from all the past year feuding with Lisa."

"I hope he gives you some concrete facts—it doesn't sound like you have many."

Landon spoke, his deep voice subdued. "You're right, we don't have all the concrete facts lined up just yet." He met Laurie's gaze. "Maybe we're not as close as we'd like to think, but we're getting there one step at a time."

Laurie traced the rim of her mug with one finger. Eventually, the skeptical line between her eyebrows softened, and she treated us to a lopsided smile. "Well, I suppose that's one way to look at it," she said. "Lord knows this wouldn't be the first time we bumbled around chasing wild geese, only to somehow stumble upon the answers we were seeking all along."

"We don't bumble," I told her. "We explore. We zero in."

She drained the last of her coffee with a decisive slurp. "Just don't go getting yourselves into too much trouble out there," she added, fixing each of us with a mock-stern look. "Let me know if you need my help. I'll try to pencil you in."

As I watched Laurie stand with a nod, I felt a profound sense of gratitude for these people who had become my chosen family over the years. No matter what curve balls life sent hurtling my way, I knew I wouldn't have to face them alone—not anymore.

And somehow, I had a feeling we would stumble our way to the truth.

Wild geese be damned.

I gripped the door handle as the truck jostled down the winding dirt road, peering out the window at the thickets of oak and cedar whipping past. We were heading deep into the hills surrounding Lake Wildebridge—a scenic drive under normal circumstances—but I found myself too preoccupied to appreciate the abundant natural beauty.

My mind kept drifting back to poor little Fluffy, the key eyewitness whose youthful exuberance made discerning concrete details from her account an exercise in futility. The scraps of information she could provide felt maddening in their scarcity—like a handful of torn puzzle pieces hinting at some larger picture we couldn't assemble.

"I wish Fluffy could tell us more about what happened with Lisa," I said, voicing my frustration aloud. "All we know is that they went to the beach, Lisa lost her flip-flop, and then somehow Fluffy got left behind. I could ask more, but..."

Landon glanced over, brow furrowed. "You think that kitten knows more than she let on?"

"No, I don't think so—she's just a child. She might know something, but she's too young to know what she

knows. I don't want to traumatize her by pushing, but..."
I sighed, resting my elbow on the door frame as we
continued our bouncing journey. "I'm just letting my
mind wander, I suppose. Wondering when Lisa got
Fluffy in the first place, how long she had her, and what
she saw."

Landon nodded, keeping his eyes on the road as it
curved deeper into the secluded lakeside enclave of
sprawling homes and cabins nestled amid the oak groves.
"The longer she's here, though, the more comfortable
she is. I don't think it would hurt to ask a few more questions. Especially about the beach."

"Maybe," I said. "What I can't figure out is why
Fluffy was outside in the first place. Why on earth
would Lisa take her to the lake? You don't just let a
kitten wander around outdoors unattended like that."

Landon shrugged one broad shoulder, the
muscles shifting beneath his faded blue shirt. "Some
folks do. My cousin Junior had this tomcat growing
up that was always out raising Cain, hunting whatever critters it could wrangle. He was a mean old
fleabag."

"This is a Scottish Fold kitten." I wrinkled my nose,
trying to picture the pampered, fluffy Fold kitten we had
at the shelter turning feral out here. "I doubt Lisa
intended for Fluffy to be an outdoor cat."

"You're probably right," Landon said.

We lapsed into thoughtful quiet as the truck
rumbled along. I gazed out at the lake glimpsed between

towering tree trunks, its glassy surface glittering like a mirror in the morning sunlight.

I couldn't imagine the cost of acquiring such a serene, secluded lakefront property so close to the city yet tucked away in splendid isolation. A tiny, exclusive community shielded from the noise and bustle, reserved only for those able to afford its high price of admission, or those that had been here for generations.

"You know, it is beautiful out here," Landon said, giving voice to my own thoughts as he navigated the curving roads. "Peaceful. I could get used to living somewhere like this one day when my business winds down."

I turned to study his profile, catching the wistful gleam in his eye.

Of course—Landon spent most of his days surrounded by the roar of power tools and the cacophony of hammers and heavy machinery, and when he came home, he had dozens of cats to look forward to. Retiring somewhere quiet must hold immense appeal for a man who builds things for a living.

"Is that a dream of yours?" I asked. "Buying a place out by a lake once you're done swinging that hammer?"

A crooked grin tugged at the corner of Landon's mouth. "Well, it's always been a little fantasy of mine. Nothing too fancy—just a cozy lakeside cabin where I can spend my days reading on the dock and piddling around with little projects in the workshop." He paused, eyes crinkling at the corners as his smile broadened. "Building myself a nice little wooden boat has always been at the top of my 'retirement bucket list,' if I'm being honest."

I couldn't help but return his grin, charmed by the simple pleasure such a quaint dream brought him. For all Landon's rugged exterior, the big carpenter harbored an unexpected sentimental streak that never failed to catch me by surprise—and tug at something deep in my chest.

"You want to build a boat from scratch? By hand?"

He bobbed his head, eyes sparkling with enthusiasm. "Sure do. Strip a few cedars, mill the planking myself, shape her hull nice and sleek. Maybe a classic little sloop with a bright white sail to skim across the water." He reached over and gave my knee an affectionate squeeze. "I'd take you out for sunset cruises every evening. We'd tie off at a secluded cove and watch the stars come out over the water."

"That does sound lovely," I told him. "Though it's hard for me to imagine not being surrounded by furballs at every turn these days."

Landon's brows arched in surprise. "Really? I'd have figured once Evie took over running the shelter someday, you'd be happy to finally relax and put your feet up."

I considered this, watching the scenery whip past in a blur of greens and browns. "The thought hadn't crossed my mind," I admitted. "When Evie was younger, I always assumed she'd be with me and need me to take care of her because of her illness, so I never thought about retirement. I guess some part of me wants her to keep the shelter in the family and take over for me once the time comes, but now that she's so involved with Matt and his PI work... well, I'm not sure her heart would be in running a cat rescue anymore. She seems to have found her calling elsewhere."

Landon chuckled. "She seems to have drug all of us into her calling."

"Don't forget the cat plate," I said. "It's a Gordian knot of a calling, really."

Landon was silent for a long moment, contemplating my words. When he spoke again, his voice was subdued, as if afraid to tread on uncertain territory. "You know... you don't have to make that decision today. Or any time soon, for that matter."

"What decision?"

"Whether Evie would take over, or who you'd leave the rescue to."

"Well, it's a non-profit. I don't own it."

With a gentle motion, he enveloped my hand in his, imparting a reassuring squeeze. "We've got plenty of years ahead of us before anyone needs to pass torches or hand over keys. Why don't you just enjoy running your cat circus for now—and let the future sort itself out when it gets here?"

He was right—no sense borrowing troubles before their time, as my grandmother would say.

The truck rumbled to a halt in front of a ramshackle cabin, distracting me from my swirling thoughts. Glancing out the windshield, I spied the mud-splattered pickup parked in the drive and realized we had arrived at our friend Mr. Henderson's humble abode.

Parked next to it?

A sleek black Escalade.

"Who's car is that?" Landon asked me under his breath as we climbed out.

Stepping toward that cabin, we strode into a viper's nest neither of us saw coming.

Chapter Ten

Before I could wonder who else might visit the reclusive Mr. Henderson, a sudden cacophony of shouting erupted from within the ramshackle dwelling, startling me. The muffled voices were indistinct, but the tone conveyed unmistakable anger and hostility.

I exchanged a puzzled look with Landon, his brow furrowing with concern as we hurried toward the cabin's front porch. What in the world was happening inside?

Landon reached the door first and rapped his knuckles against the weathered wood, the heavy thuds punctuating the din of raised voices within. "Mr. Henderson?" he called out, pitching his voice to be heard over the ruckus. "It's Landon Rogers and Ellie Rockwell. Everything all right in there?"

The shouting continued unabated, now accompanied by a series of dull thuds as if objects were being hurled about. My heart lurched with a surge of apprehension.

"I'm going to open the door," Landon told me, jaw set in grim determination as he gripped the tarnished brass handle and twisted.

It didn't budge; the lock held fast.

He tried again, grunting with the effort as his broad shoulders flexed, coiled bands of brawn tensed across his forearms. But the flimsy door refused to yield.

With a decisive nod, Landon took a step back and squared his stance.

"Wait, Landon—what are you doing?"

He slammed his shoulder into the door with a thunderous bang. The rickety structure shuddered, but the frame held firm.

"Landon, you'll hurt yourself!"

"You might be right. But I've got this," he told me. "Don't worry."

Don't worry, he says.

Easier said than done when the man you love is intent on channeling his inner action hero. I knew Landon was as sturdy as the oak he worked with, but that didn't stop my stomach from twisting into knots as I watched him square up for round two against the stubborn door.

"Maybe we should call the—"

In one fluid motion, Landon turned his back to the door, lifted his right leg, and delivered a powerful mule kick to the door, his boot connecting with the weathered wood just beneath the handle. The aged latch and hinges surrendered with an earsplitting crack as the door tore free of its moorings and crashed to the floor.

Landon and I found three figures stood frozen near the far wall of the cramped living area, their faces a mix of shock and trepidation. At their feet lay a scattering of figurines and collectibles that had been flung in their direction, judging by the shards of shattered ceramic littering the worn floorboards.

Near the center of the room stood Ethan Henderson wearing his signature faded overalls smeared with grime, his wild gray hair askew. In one gnarled hand, he clutched the battered stock of a hunting shotgun. The other fist remained clenched around what appeared to be a ceramic rabbit, poised to unleash it upon his cornered guests.

"You fellas best git out before I start shootin' what little lights y'all got left upstairs!" Henderson bellowed, his bushy beard quivering with rage. "I ain't sellin' a damn inch of my land over to you crooks for your stinkin' developments! Not one inch!"

His wild eyes darted toward Landon and me, widening as he took in our unexpected intrusion. "And you!" he shouted, jabbing the shotgun barrel in our direction. "Who in blazes gave you the right to bust down my front door like the dang'd cavalry? You better be ready to put that back together the way you found it!"

I raised my hands in a calming gesture, aware of the perilous situation we were finding ourselves in.

Henderson may be prickly, but something had sent him into a rage today. Before I could say anything to calm him down, one of the three men near the wall spoke up.

"Perhaps we've overstayed our welcome, sir," he said, adopting a mollifying tone as he held his palms out. "No need for anyone to get hurt."

The voice was familiar.

I squinted, trying to make out the man's face in the dark, when a sudden gust of breeze from the shattered doorway swung the overheard light toward the men. There, clear as day, stood the impeccably tailored form of one Bobby Daggett—a face I recognized from the Cinco de Mayo festival. Flanking him were his two smarmy colleagues from Town Prosperity Investments: William Woodfield and Daniel Patrick.

Oh, great.

More complications.

The sandy-haired one—Woodfield—stepped forward, shaking his head at Henderson. "Of course. We'll be happy to leave and let you cool down for now." He cast a pointed look at Landon and me, carefully avoiding any further escalation—I thought—until he said, "Though if these folks claim to have your power of attorney, we'd best let bygones be bygones for today and just talk to them."

"His what?" I blurted out before I could stop myself.

Woodfield turned to me, the coldness in his pale eyes undercutting the civility of his tone. "Well, I can only assume you're acting on Mr. Henderson's behalf here," he said with a thin smile that didn't reach his eyes. "Since he's not... well... let's just say Mr. Henderson seems to have become unmoored from the reality of his situation. Since you two broke down the door, I assume you're responsible for this old man?"

I opened my mouth to set these entitled developers straight, but before I could respond, Henderson erupted once more.

"Don't you patronize me, you vultures!" he roared, whirling back toward the trio of suited men standing against the wall. Another figurine whizzed through the air, shattering just shy of Woodfield's smug face. "I'm the only one responsible for me, and I know slippery jackals like you when I see 'em! Tryin' to trick an old man into signin' away his deed with your fancy words! You outta be ashamed!"

"We did nothing of the sort!" the paunchy one —Patrick—said, outrage creasing his features as he shrank back from another well-aimed projectile. "We were seeing if you might be interested in hearing about the generous offer the LLC has proposed for your property! Don't exaggerate, Mr. Henderson!"

"Aye, like the devil's 'generous' with eternal rooms for liars and thieves!" Henderson spit back, grip tightening on the shotgun. It wasn't pointed at anyone yet, but it seemed like that could change.

"Mr. Henderson," Landon said, once more trying to project a sense of calm authority over the escalating situation. "Let's all take a breath here."

Henderson's piercing gaze swung toward Landon. The old man regarded him with a blend of wariness and scrutiny for a long beat, analyzing my companion's neutral stance for any hint of malice or deception. Finally, he gave a nod, lowering the barrel of his shotgun a few degrees. "Fair enough," he said, a hint of reluctant respect creeping into his tone. "You ain't with them jackals—reckon I know who you are. At least you can fix my door."

With the immediate threat of violence momentarily defused, I seized the opportunity to address the smarmy Prosperity Investments partners still pressed against the far wall. "You gentlemen should leave," I said, striving to keep my voice even and firm. "Right now. Before this escalates any further."

"This is ridiculous," Woodfield scoffed, outrage flashing across his handsome features as he pushed away from the splintered wood paneling. "This is just a social call, and we have every right to be here discussing business opportunities with Mr. Henderson." His two cohorts exchanged uneasy glances, standing rooted in place even as Woodfield puffed out his chest, staring me down. "Mrs. Rockwell, isn't it? If you don't have power of attorney, you have no authority here. Maybe it's you who should leave."

My nails dug into my palms as I fought to keep my temper in check.

A protest formed in my throat, but I caught myself, swallowing it back before I unleashed the unrestrained intensity of my formidable tongue-lashing skills upon this arrogant suit. I took a breath and opened my mouth, but before I could utter a syllable, Henderson cut me off.

"Authority?" Henderson barked out a harsh laugh, lifting the shotgun and leveling it, gesturing toward the door. "They don't need no gall-danged authority in my home! They live in Tablerock. You don't! Now git!"

Daniel Patrick's gaze darted between the two barrels aimed in their direction as he swallowed hard. "It's enough, Bill," he muttered under his breath to Woodfield, placing a steadying hand on the taller man's arm. "The old coot's worked up enough without us antagonizing him more."

"He's the one antagonizing us!" Woodfield shot back in a heated whisper, his mask of composure fraying further. "This was supposed to be a routine—"

"You heard the man," Landon said, his words laced with steel as he cast the developers a withering look. "Get out. Before he shoots you or I decide to remove you myself."

For an extended moment, Woodfield looked as if he might dig in his heels and press his case. His jaw worked furiously, tendons straining in his neck as he battled an internal war between wounded pride and self-preservation.

In the end, self-preservation prevailed.

With a curt nod, he spun on his heel and stalked toward the doorway without a backward glance. Patrick shuffled out close behind him, his gaze still apprehensive as his line of sight shifted over his shoulder.

Bobby Daggett paused on the threshold, though, his practiced smile once more firmly affixed as he turned back to regard Landon and me with an unsettlingly amicable look.

"We'll be in touch, Eleanor," he said, inclining his head toward me as if we had been nothing more than courteous acquaintances enjoying afternoon tea rather than facing down shotgun barrels. "And Landon—a pleasure—"

"Stay away from us," Landon told him.

With that, he turned and followed his partners out to the Escalade, leaving Henderson, Landon, and me alone amid the shards of ceramic.

Ethan Henderson watched the sleek black SUV fishtail along the dirt path back toward the main road before turning his wizened gaze upon Landon and me once more. Slowly, he lowered the shotgun until the barrel pointed toward the floor, though his knuckles remained white from gripping it with such force.

"I guess I owe you some thanks," he grunted at last, his rheumy eyes boring into us. "Just because I owe you that thanks don't mean you don't owe me a new door."

<hr />

The din of hammering and sawing soon filled the cramped cabin as Landon set to work repairing the shattered front door he'd broken down. I swept up shards of broken ceramic knickknacks, gathering them into a dustpan while Mr. Henderson looked on.

"How's that door coming along?" he barked at Landon.

Landon paused mid-stroke of the hammer, glancing over his shoulder. "Be done in a jiffy, sir. Gotta reinforce the frame, but she'll be as good as new."

A wet snuffling sound drew my attention.

I turned to see a massive black Newfoundland dog sauntering through the gaping doorway, its shaggy fur dripping steadily onto the worn wooden floors. The dog paused, tongue lolling as it surveyed the interior with mild confusion, as if wondering why there was no door.

"Well, well, if it ain't old Rex deciding to show up," Henderson grumbled. He jabbed a crooked finger at the sodden canine. "Figured you'd sleep the whole day away by that spring-fed pond, you lazy mutt. Missed all the excitement on account of your nap."

Rex shook his head, sending a spray of water droplets flying in every direction. With a contented sigh, he ambled across the room and plopped down beside Henderson's recliner, brown eyes still roving between us.

"Some guard dog you are," Henderson muttered, reaching behind the worn cushions to produce a ratty towel. He held it out to me. "Here, girl, since you're already on maid duty. Mind drying him off for me?"

I accepted the threadbare cloth and began patting Rex's drenched fur.

As I worked, Henderson settled into his chair with a weary sigh, one hand absently stroking Rex's damp head. His eyes sharpened, narrowing at nothing in particular. "Those vulture jackals come sniffing around my property no less than once a week now," he growled, low and menacing. "Buzzing in that fancy black truck like flies swarming over rotten peaches."

I looked up from drying Rex's paws, sensing the resurgence of outrage simmering beneath the old man's grizzled exterior. "Who, exactly? The Prosperity Investments fellows?"

"Them. That girl's boyfriend. That girl. I could make a list." Henderson leaned forward, elbows braced on his knees. "They ain't the first slick developers to try bamboozling an old-timer out of his family land, but this bunch? They're the most persistent pack of mangy dogs I ever laid eyes on." He aimed a sharp, accusatory stare fixed upon Rex, who peered back with guileless eyes. "I shoulda got a dog that would bite their britches instead of a furry mermaid."

Rex's tail thumped against the wooden floor, the rhythmic thudding punctuated by a deep bark that reverberated through the small cabin.

"Sorry. Merman."

I rubbed the Newfie's head. "It sounds like you've been dealing with these aggressive land acquisition attempts for a while."

Henderson snorted, his gaze hardening into steel. He leaned back in his chair, tilting his head toward the shattered entryway where the Escalade had disappeared. "They been after every last inch of shoreline property around Lake Wildebridge for going on two years now. Relentless, they are. Soon as word got around that Fiona Blackwell planned to deed her estate to your shelter, these jackals started circling the area to scoop up whatever real estate was left."

Great.

So this was all my fault.

I recalled the details Evie had dug up about Derek Sutton's questionable land deals. Had Town Prosperity Investments been using him as a front to amass acreage around the lake? And if so, for what purpose?

Henderson scratched the wiry tufts of his beard, eyes narrowing with distaste. "Damn land pirates, if you ask me. They just keep comin' and comin', wavin' wads of cash at any property owner within ten miles of these shores." His gaze flicked toward the window, jaw tightening. "Seems like those three have even been sniffin' around Lisa Hartman's fancy lake house."

The breath stilled in my lungs. My eyes found Landon's, brows raised.

"Really?" I said, keeping my voice casual. "Did you notice anything... unusual over there while Lisa's been away?"

Henderson's eyes narrowed, his gaze locked on me with an intensity that made me shift uncomfortably. The crease across his wrinkled forehead deepened as he scrutinized my expression. Leaning back into the worn recliner, a flicker of resignation tempered the shrewd calculation behind his stare.

"I reckon I did, come to think of it." He jabbed a thumb toward the pristine waters shimmering through the window. "Last night I heard that big ol' yacht of hers rumbling out on the water. Pulled it in around midnight, sounded like."

I inhaled. "You're certain it was her yacht?"

"Only one thing on this part of the lake makes a racket like that. I oughta know—she takes that behemoth out more'n she don't." A muscle twitched in his weathered jaw. "Was idling out there for the better part of an hour before I heard it putt-putting away. Figured she was comin' back from one of her late night benders at the yacht club or some such."

So Lisa's yacht had been taken out in the dead of night, despite her disappearance.

But by whom?

It had to be Derek...

But Derek was at the house last night, and the yacht wasn't.

I was sure of that.

"Did you see who was on the boat, Mr. Henderson?"

The old man's eyes drifted toward the door, two deep creases etched between his furrowed brows. "Now that you mention it..." He paused, eyes squinting as if rewinding his memory. "I did notice a couple of fellas climbing aboard. Couldn't make out their faces from my place, but based on the ugly bright yellow jacket one of 'em wore, I'da put money on that banker snake Derek Sutton bein' one."

Beside me, Landon straightened to his full height, movements stilled by a sudden tension. "Derek Sutton was taking Lisa's boat out for a midnight joyride?"

"I guess," Henderson said with a shrug, as if commenting on the weather. "Like I said, hard to tell from here at night. But the way those two forms were movin' around, looked an awful lot like ol' Derek had himself a buddy for the cruise."

Lisa's missing yacht, taken out after midnight by her shady boyfriend and an unidentified accomplice?

It didn't bode well.

Landon shifted his weight, brow creased with grave concern. "Did you see them return to shore?"

"Come back?" Henderson blinked, his tone laced with puzzlement. "I musta conked out by then. All's I know is by morning, that monster wasn't at Ms. Hartman's dock no more."

Landon nodded. "Mr. Henderson... was there any sign of Lisa herself? Any chance you saw her around her property that morning? Or that the other person could have been her?"

"No, son. That wasn't her." The old man shook his grizzled head in a slow, resolute denial. "I know what a woman's silhouette looks like, and that was a man with Sutton. I'd bet on it. I haven't seen hide nor hair of that foolish woman. Believe you me, that yacht's eerie hollerin' at all hours has been about the only ruckus comin' from her place as of late."

My mind raced, pieces shifting and rearranging like a haunting kaleidoscope of theories, each more confusing than the last. I drew in a breath to respond, but he cut me off with a brusque wave of his hand.

"Now, I know what you're fixin' to ask, and I ain't got many more answers, I'm afraid." He heaved a weary sigh, suddenly looking every one of his years. "All's I know for certain is that shifty snake Derek Sutton has been around all week at night. Don't know how, don't know why, but I know I ain't never liked nor trusted that one."

I figured Derek Sutton was up to no good, but what could he have been doing lurking around Lisa's property in the middle of the night? A knot of dread twisted in my stomach as my mind raced with grim possibilities, each more unsettling than the last.

Henderson must have caught a trace of the apprehension clouding my features, for his grizzled face softened by a fraction. "I'll tell you this much more, girl," he said, his gravelly tone almost... gentle. "Ain't nobody knows this little slice of paradise better'n me and Rex. Kids moved away, the wife's gone up to be with the Lord. I got nothing but time now. If anything more comes to light, you can bet your tail we'll be the ones findin' it."

I managed a faint smile, grateful for the old man's

reassurance even as it did little to allay the pit of dread yawning within me. With Derek's suspicious behavior and Lisa's unexplained absence, it seemed increasingly likely that foul play was afoot.

I could only pray Henderson was right—that whatever secrets still lingered would soon be brought to light.

Chapter Eleven

THE TRUCK JOSTLED ALONG THE WINDING ROAD
leading away from Ethan Henderson's cabin, creaking
and groaning as we navigated the twists and turns. I
gazed out the window at the rolling hills and dense
thickets of oak trees lining the path, trying to sort
through the knot of thoughts and emotions swirling in
my mind.

With a heavy sigh, I turned to Landon. "Well, that
was... eventful."

He shot me a wry look. "You could say that." His
eyes crinkled at the corners as he let out a low chuckle,
shaking his head. "Leave it to us to stumble into the
middle of whatever mess those swindlers from
Prosperity Investments have been cooking up. There are
too many developers in this mess."

I couldn't help but smile at his easy humor, though
the weight of Henderson's troubling words still lingered.

So much remained uncertain—Lisa's fate, the true nature of Derek's activities, the looming threat of developers eyeing the countryside for their next "luxury living" conquest.

Trying to make sense of the tangled web threatened to leave me with a pounding headache.

"That poor old man," I murmured, feeling a pang of sympathy for the cantankerous Henderson and his desperate bid to cling to his cherished patch of land. "He's like a lion guarding his den against the circling jackals."

"He was wound pretty tight back there, that's for sure. Can't say I blame him, though—those land sharks would get under anyone's skin with their persistence." He pursed his lips, considering. "Still... Henderson did seem a tad unhinged, didn't he? Almost like maybe there was more to his fervor than just protecting family land."

"The man just wants to live out the rest of his days in peace on the property where he's spent his whole adult life," I said, unable to keep the defensive edge from creeping into my tone. "His kids have all moved away, his wife passed on some years back... that little cabin and that big dog is all he has left. Who can fault him for fighting tooth and nail to keep it?"

Landon's expression knitted into a frown, but he didn't respond right away. I could see the wheels turning behind his pensive gaze as he mulled over my impassioned defense of the prickly old recluse.

"You don't want him to be guilty of anything."

"I don't want anyone to be guilty of anything."

"Okay, you got me there." He exhaled a measured breath, like he knew I was going to call him out for whatever he was about to say. "Look, Ellie, I get where you're coming from—truly, I do," he said, his deep voice low. "Henderson's in a tough spot, and nobody enjoys being pushed around and bamboozled by shifty land-grabbers like those Prosperity goons. Believe me, I can empathize."

"But?" I asked.

He paused, casting a sidelong glance my way before continuing. "But you gotta admit... the way he flew off the handle back there? Hurling ceramic figurines and waving that shotgun around?" Landon shook his head. "Can't ignore that, sweetheart. There's clearly more going on under the surface with him than just a stubborn old-timer digging in to preserve his homestead."

Landon raised a fair point—the violence we had witnessed went far beyond simple ornery cantankerousness. Except for one thing.

"You're right, it looks like he went overboard back there," I said. "But can you blame the guy, Landon? He's all alone out here except for his dog, and those parasites keep coming to bleed him dry of his legacy. I'd probably lose my mind, too, if someone threatened to take the shelter and everything I've built away from me."

Landon considered this for a few moments before giving a slow nod. "Fair point," he said at last.

"Second, he hurt no one. He didn't shoot anyone. He

threw dozens of things at those developers, and he never hit one. Not once. No one's got aim that bad at five feet, Landon. I think he's all bark and no bite."

"Maybe."

"No maybe. He didn't hurt anyone."

"Okay, you have a point, but I'd be lying if I said I wasn't concerned about how easily he could snap if pressed—possibly in more dangerous ways. He was holding a gun. He may be a sympathetic figure in this whole mess, but that doesn't make him any less of a wild card or any less suspicious."

As much as I wanted to see only the curmudgeonly charm beneath Henderson's gruff exterior, Landon's caution served as a necessary counterbalance. We couldn't discount the possibility—however unpleasant— that the cantankerous recluse's erratic behavior stemmed from darker impulses.

"You're right," I said. "For now, we'll just have to keep Henderson on our radar and hope that whatever's driving his temper doesn't boil over into real trouble."

Landon nodded, though his expression remained somber. "Smart thinking. And hey—" he reached over, giving my hand a reassuring squeeze "—just because we can't rule the old coot out doesn't mean we're assuming the worst yet. Remember, our goal is to clear his name and everyone else's by finding the real culprit behind Lisa's disappearance."

"Or to find Lisa," I said, leaning back against the worn leather seat and letting the gentle sway of the truck's motions lull away the tension knotting my shoulders. "The best way to prove Henderson's innocence is to identify whoever's responsible—if anyone is. That has to be our focus." I let my head fall back against the headrest. "And frankly, Landon, the more I turn this over, the less convinced I am that Lisa is dead."

He shot me a sidelong look, curiosity flickering beneath his furrowed brow. "What makes you say that?"

"Well, think about it," I began as I sifted through the threads of possibility unraveling in my mind's eye. "Based on Fluffy's account, I think Lisa was running from someone or something when she lost her flip-flop on the beach."

"You think she was being chased?"

"Yes. No one's found an unattended beach set up. Lisa's car was here, not at the beach. I think she was running from someone, grabbed the kitten, and ran— and if she was fleeing from a threat of some kind, doesn't that suggest her attacker was trying to apprehend her rather than kill her? Otherwise, couldn't they have just..." I trailed off with an uneasy grimace. "Well, you know. Ended things right there while hiding in the trees? No one would blink twice at a gun going off out here."

For a long moment, Landon remained quiet, his fingers flexing over the steering wheel as he chewed over my reasoning. After what seemed like an eternity, he sighed. "You make a fair point," he said, the crease between his brows deepening. "If their aim was just to get rid of Lisa, leaving her out on that beach would have been simpler than chasing her down."

Bolstered, I pressed on. "And if we assume Lisa eluded her pursuer that night—whoever they were—it would explain why her yacht went careening off into the night not long after."

"I don't follow."

I leaned forward in my seat, animated by the thread of logic I was tugging loose. "Think about it, Landon. If Lisa managed to evade whoever was after her at the beach, a boat would be a good place to hide."

Landon drummed his fingers against the steering wheel, his expression one of intense contemplation. At last, he let out a slow exhale, inclining his head toward me.

"Maybe," he said, his tone laced with a newfound consideration for my premise. "If Lisa is still alive—and was the one piloting her yacht away from the area so she could hide from someone that's after her—it would explain why we haven't heard from her since."

"And it would make sense why she hasn't tried to contact anyone, like the shelter, about Fluffy. She's in hiding, terrified whoever came after her will track her down again if she reaches out."

Landon's brow furrowed once more, the pragmatist in him unable to resist poking holes. "That's one possibility," he said. "The other possibility is that whoever was chasing her got here. She no doubt has a radio on that boat. Why not call the police for help?"

I didn't have any answer for that one. My shoulders sagged, and I let out a dejected sigh. There it was—the persistent kernel of doubt or a piece that didn't fit, a fact refusing to be snapped into place even as the rest of my theory wove itself into a plausible tapestry.

"You're right," I said, deflating. "That part that doesn't quite add up. If Lisa is alive and on her boat, she should have tried to contact someone for help."

Unless...

"Unless she can't," Landon finished my thought.

❧

The truck rumbled along the two-lane highway cutting through the rolling hills outside Tablerock, my gaze drifting between the blur of trees whipping past the window and the peaceful waters of Lake Wildebridge sparkling in the morning sun. Landon kept both hands on the wheel as while maneuvering through the gentle curves and dips of the winding road.

A sudden flicker of red and blue lights in the rearview mirror made my stomach drop.

"Oh no," I muttered, twisting in my seat to peer through the back window. Sure enough, a patrol car had materialized behind us, lights flashing an unmistakable command to pull over. "Landon, I think you're about to get a ticket."

He glanced up at the mirror, brow furrowing as he registered the lights. "Huh? I wasn't speeding. At least, I

148

don't think..." Trailing off, he guided the truck onto the narrow shoulder and killed the engine. Landon pursed his lips. "Stay here. I'll see what's going on."

Before I could respond, he opened his door and stepped out onto the gravel verge. I watched through the windshield as he greeted the approaching deputy, his body language open and friendly despite the unwarranted traffic stop.

What were the odds of us getting pulled over right after leaving our chat with Mr. Henderson? Granted, Landon had a bit of a lead foot, but I was certain he hadn't been driving recklessly or breaking any obvious traffic laws just now. My hackles rose as I considered the possibility this might not be a routine stop after all.

My unease dissipated as I spotted the deputy's rumpled light blue shirt and languid swagger—an unmistakable gait I recognized all too well.

It was Don Markham.

I let out a relieved exhale, cracking my door to listen as Landon said, "Good morning, Don. Did I do something wrong?"

Markham interrupted him with a chuckle and an amicable wave of his hand. "You think I pulled y'all over for a traffic violation? You're killing me."

Landon's brow crinkled in puzzlement as I climbed out to join them. "Then... why did you pull us over?"

"Is that even legal?" I asked. "Pulling citizens over under false pretenses?"

Don shrugged, feigning nonchalance even as a wry

glint flashed in his eyes. "You've been hanging around Josie too long if you're about to lecture me on proper police procedure." He jerked his chin at Landon. "Besides, I just wanted to save myself the trip of swinging by the shelter, is all. You know how I feel about cats."

Our furry residents had an uncanny knack for spotting authority figures from a mile away—or perhaps they sensed the brusque, no-nonsense aura radiating from the grizzled lawman like a force field designed to repel all things soft, cuddly, and manipulative. Their disdain for the deputy matched his own thinly veiled distaste for their kind, an amusing clash of opposing natures that never failed to entertain me whenever Don paid us a visit.

Before either of us could respond, the deputy plowed ahead. "Speaking of information, let's chat about those yahoos from Prosperity Investments that y'all stumbled across out at Ethan Henderson's place today."

Landon and I exchanged a look, simultaneously realizing the reason behind Don's impromptu roadside rendezvous.

"You heard about that already?" I asked, surprise lacing my tone.

Landon tilted his head. "We just left his place."

Markham fished a pack of gum from his shirt pocket, picking one out before offering the pack first to Landon, and then to me. "News travels faster than a jackrabbit with its tail on fire around these parts. Especially scandalous news involving unhinged old codgers brandishing shotguns. Those developers are whining at Pedro's Cantina while they down margaritas to calm themselves. You'd think they'd never seen a rifle before."

Chuckling, Landon waved off the proffered stick of gum.

"So," the deputy continued, "Why don't you tell me the whole tale about Prosperity Investments dropping by this morning? My guess is they're trying to weasel Henderson out of his homestead."

I glanced sidelong at Landon, silently asking if he wanted to take the lead on this one. He gave a small shake of his head, deferring to me.

I launched into a recount of the bizarre scene that had unfolded when we arrived at Henderson's cabin—the shouts from within, the shattering of the door, the developers cowering in terror from a barrage of ceramic projectiles, and the grizzled recluse's defiant refusal to surrender another inch of his lakefront property.

Don listened with rapt attention, nodding along and not interrupting as I relayed each strange twist and turn we had witnessed.

"Can't say I'm surprised they've got their eyes on Henderson's ramshackle kingdom," he drawled at last. "Town Prosperity has been hungrier than a starving coyote with respect to snatching up land all around these parts, bless their greedy little hearts." He looked down at me. "The old man must like the two of you. I didn't get a call on either of you for trespassing or property damage."

"I stayed to fix his door, so no property damage," Landon said, letting the ominous rumble of a passing semi-truck fade before continuing. "Henderson mentioned they won't take no for an answer. It sounds to me like the insistence has stepped up."

"Those swindlers make televangelists look like Boy Scouts when it comes to hard-selling folks," Don replied. "Still, maybe the old coot went a mite overboard with the shotgun theatrics if all they were doing was dropping by for another sales pitch."

"I don't think it was theatrics," I said. "And I doubt his anger stems from malicious intent."

Don held my gaze for a beat, jaw working slow and steady as he chewed the matter over. "Fair enough," he said. "Any luck figuring out what's what with the Hartman woman's disappearing act while I've been busy?"

I relayed the scant details we had uncovered concerning Lisa's increasingly mysterious absence and the worrisome clues pointing to potential foul play by the likes of Derek Sutton. Landon chimed in from time to time, though I covered the bulk of the unsettling revelations—ending with Henderson's account of Lisa's missing yacht disappearing into the night and Derek's suspicious nighttime activities around her deserted lake house.

"Well, now," he murmured after a lengthy silence. "You two did uncover quite a doozy of a mess, didn't you? Lots of questions, but not a lot of answers."

"No kidding," Landon agreed. "The deeper we dig, the muddier the waters get."

Don grunted, giving a grim nod of agreement. "You still ain't managed to dig up a single trace of where that woman's fancy yacht went wandering off to?"

"We weren't looking." I told him, unable to keep the concerned frown from my features. "I was hoping you might have some new intel to share on that front from your lake patrol sources?"

To my dismay, Don shook his head, lips pressed into a grim line.

"Now you know if I'd heard a peep about where Hartman's boat went missing to, that woulda been the first thing out of my mouth." A flicker of grim resignation clouded his features. "I told 'em, but they only have one boat and a lot of drunk boaters to deal with. Way it stands, that vanishing yacht is still staying hidden unless we stumble on to it."

So much for hoping the authorities had uncovered a new lead to explain Lisa's peculiar absence while we had been occupied with our amateur sleuthing.

Landon studied the lawman for a lingering moment before clearing his throat.

"Actually, Don, there is one more thing we were hoping you could clarify for us," he began, his voice measured. "It has to do with a certain shady character."

Markham's brow arched, a flicker of piqued interest glinting in his eyes. "Oh yeah? Do tell."

Landon relayed the disturbing possible connection

we had stumbled across between Ronnie Earle's shadowy business empire and Lisa's opulent lakefront lifestyle—not to mention the tidy little land acquisition scheme Derek might have been orchestrating on Earle's behalf all around the lake.

The corner of Don's lip tugged upward in a grim smirk as Landon brought him up to speed, entertained intrigue mingling with the customary wry amusement that so often danced in his perceptive eyes.

"I'll be damned," he muttered as I wrapped up my summary. "Old Ronnie Earle's got his grubby mitts all up in this mess, does he?" Markham chuckled, a low rasp of sardonic bemusement. "Should've figured that snake charmer was slithering around somewhere nearby."

"Why do you say that?" I asked.

He glanced up, flicking his gaze between Landon and me. "I know everyone thinks he's a Texas real estate mogul, but if you follow the tangled trail that twisted son of a gun walks, you'll know all of his money comes from deals of the century—and he seems to make a deal of the century every six months. He's either the luckiest man in the world, or the crookedest."

Chapter Twelve

LANDON PULLED THE TRUCK AROUND BACK, AND WE hopped out, ready to head inside the shelter and grab a quick bite for lunch. As we approached the back door, it swung open, revealing Josie and Charlie striding out to meet us.

"Well, well, look who it is," Josie said, arching an eyebrow as she eyed us up and down with a smirk playing on her lips. "We were just about to send out a search party of cats to sniff you out."

Landon blinked, his brow furrowing in confusion as he glanced between Josie and Charlie. "Since break-fast?" He let out a half-chuckle, shaking his head. "What, did you two take a wrong turn on your way to court and end up here by mistake? Don't you have actual paying clients to torment?"

"Believe it or not," Charlie said, "this is about a case.

One that we just realized you two might have a vested interest in, as a matter of fact."

My curiosity piqued as they ushered us inside, and we all made our way through the café toward my office.

"You remember when I was arguing with Bobby Daggett on the phone a few days ago?" she asked over her shoulder.

I nodded, recalling the heated back and forth we had overheard at her office amid the tussle over environmental protections. "The golden-cheeked warblers at Rosa's place, right?"

"Exactly." Josie settled into one of the chairs facing my desk as Charlie closed the door behind us. "We've been going round and round with those TPI scoundrels over their plans to bulldoze everything on Rosa's lot— restaurant and all—despite my injunctions to preserve the land and trees where the endangered warblers nest."

A grimace twisted my features as memories of Rosa's warm, welcoming eatery at the center of Tablerock resurfaced with a pang. The thought of the establishment becoming just another casualty in Town Prosperity Investments' relentless pursuit of "progress" left an acrid taste in my mouth.

"They can do it since Rosa sold the property to them outright," Josie continued, "but they needed to submit a revised proposal outlining protections for the nesting areas before getting permits. I made them hit pause, but I didn't stop anything for long." She reached into her briefcase and withdrew a thick manila folder, slapping it onto my desk with a resigned thud. "Anyway, this is their newest attempt at placating the environmental review board so they can proceed."

"Okay." I glanced at the innocuous folder. "I'm guessing you don't find their revised proposal satisfactory?"

"Oh, I'm sure their plan is woefully inadequate—which is why they'll be tied up in court for the foreseeable future if they try ramming it through." A sly smile teased at the corner of Josie's lips. "But that's not the interesting part. When I was reviewing their proposal earlier, I noticed something intriguing buried in the appendixes."

She leaned forward, leveling me with a pointed look.

"One of the listed property owners for Rosa's land is Boris Stemple."

"Boris who?"

Charlie picked up the folder and cleared his throat, drawing my gaze to the folder in his hands. "Boris Stemple is the infamous valet and personal attendant to none other than Prince Baron Dragomirov." He opened the file and tapped a paper with his finger, eyebrows raised.

I squinted at the unfamiliar name printed there, feeling a crease form between my brows as I shook my head.

"Oh, come on. Prince Dragomirov?" Josie asked me.

My eyes flicked back up to Josie, then to Charlie, palms spreading in a helpless shrug. "I have no idea who that is." I leaned forward, peering closer at the typed words as if they might suddenly make sense. "Who is he?"

"Do you read anything other than cat books?"

"Wait..." Landon began. "Prince Baron Dragomirov... Isn't he that—"

"The notorious heir to the Herzoslovakian throne?" Josie finished with a curt nod. "The same. Known for his reckless playboy ways and the corrupt company he keeps." She glared at me. "I'm glad someone keeps up with current events."

"And Boris Stemple, who is part owner along with TPI," Landon said, "is his valet."

"Precisely." Josie tapped the folder, leaning back in her chair with a grim smile. "Despite his seeming role as a lowly servant, Boris Stemple is one of Prince Baron's closest confidants—a key player in funneling the Dragomirov family's ill-gotten wealth into their shady business dealings abroad."

I felt as though I had stumbled into a scene straight out of a soap opera miniseries, or perhaps an overheated airport paperback thriller penned by someone who had indulged in a few too many tiny bottles of airplane wine. Talk of reckless princes and shady valets, of illegal money laundering schemes spanning international borders?

It all sounded too lurid and far-fetched to be real, like a plot concocted by a bored author desperate to inject some excitement into the otherwise mundane lives of Tablerock's residents. I half-expected Josie to pause, push up the sleeves of her silk blouse, and declare, "But little did they know, the prince's valet was also... his long-lost twin brother!"

And yet...

"Didn't you watch that TV movie about the Stempka Lake Affair?" Josie pressed, no doubt reading the skepticism writ large across my features. "Baron Dragomirov was neck-deep in that entire environmental catastrophe back in Herzoslovakia. He let his family's factories dump toxic runoff into Lake Stempka for years." Her lips twisted in distaste. "With Stemple acting as his bagman, no doubt."

I had vague memories of something like that—lurid headlines and grainy photos splashed across the news detailing the Balkan nation's man-made ecological disaster. A grim-faced documentarian narrating shocking footage of dead fish bobbing in a mirrored slick of industrial effluent...

"Lovely bunch, these royals," Landon muttered, shaking his head in disgust.

"Wait, I'm still confused," I said, holding up a hand. My mind whirled, struggling to process how this convoluted tale of international corruption and aristocratic scandal could intersect with our humble mystery back home in Tablerock. "What does any of this have to do with—"

Then I remembered.

Lisa's boutique.

The designer dresses hanging in Threads & Trends, their placid elegance concealing an insidious global web of greed and exploitation stretching back to the Old World nobility of Herzoslovakia. All those intricate garments, each bearing that same tiny woven label —Made in Herzoslovakia.

A label sewn into the very fabric linking Lisa's quaint business to the shadowy dealings of a criminal empire headquartered half a world away in the halls of Baron Dragomirov's castle.

I mean, I assumed he had a castle.

I stared at the manila folder.

"This has to have something to do with Herzoslovakia, then, right?" I asked, voicing my thoughts aloud. "There's no way some international playboy prince would be interested in buying up property around here just for the heck of it. And if he was only after real estate investments, why go through so much trouble to hide his identity?"

"Maybe." Landon leaned back in his chair, brow furrowed in thought. "Derek and this Town Prosperity bunch must be connected to each other somehow."

"That would be my guess if I had to make a guess." Charlie tilted his head. "Boldman Bracket is an investment firm, while TPI is a development company. It wouldn't be that unlikely for there to be some kind of financial connection between the two corporations."

"Maybe Boldman invests in TPI's real estate portfolio?" Josie mused. "Funnel the prince's funds through Earle's bank to Town Prosperity to gain property for whatever shady scheme they're concocting."

"How can we find out for sure they're tied together?" I asked, feeling the first stirrings of urgency. As ridiculous as all this seemed, if an international criminal conspiracy was unfolding in our backyard, we needed answers—and fast.

"I could dig deeper through all the corporate paperwork filed with the Secretary of State," she said after a moment. "Search for any shell companies or LLCs that seem to link back to Earle, Derek Sutton, Boris Stemple —everyone involved. There are always breadcrumbs left behind for the discerning eye to follow."

"I could try tracing any financial ties with the money trail," Charlie chimed in. "Unusual transfers between accounts, that sort of thing."

"I think we should loop Evie in on this, too," Josie added. "She's a whiz with scouring social media sites and blogs. Maybe she can uncover connections we'd never think to look for."

I nodded, though the potential conspiracy we were sniffing out left me feeling uneasy. What had begun with a simple abandoned kitten now spiraled outward, each new revelation painting a darker, more complex picture than I could have ever imagined. "It all just seems like a lot to uncover from paperwork, doesn't it?"

"Paperwork trails are where the real clues always hide," Josie assured me. "That's why these snakes go through such convoluted lengths with shell companies and complex structures—to bury their misdeeds under layers of legalese. The key is penetrating that obfuscation, which—I don't mind bragging—my husband and I are quite skilled at." A confident smirk pulled at the edge of her lips.

"What about what you and Landon uncovered at Ethan Henderson's place today?" Charlie asked, leaning forward. "Any new insights about his connection to our wayward Lisa that could shed light on this Herzoslovakian entanglement?"

Landon and I took turns recounting the bizarre series of events at the cantankerous old man's cabin—the explosive confrontation with the developers from Town Prosperity Investments, Henderson's eruption of violence, the gun brandishing and figurine throwing... and of course, his clues about Derek's late night shenanigans on Lisa's property after her disappearance.

As we narrated the tale, Josie's brow creased deeper and deeper, a pensive frown stealing across her features. When we reached the detail about Henderson witnessing people bringing in and then taking out Lisa's missing yacht under cover of darkness, she sat back with a heavy sigh.

"Well, that's damning for Mr. Sutton," Josie said.

"Between that and the evidence of his involvement with this nefarious Herzoslovakian development scheme, that slimy banker had plenty of motive to make Lisa disappear if she was a liability to his and Earle's plans."

That was a stretch.

"What plans, though? I don't feel any closer to knowing what happened to Lisa, or why it might have happened to her," I said. "Even with all these new bread crumbs to follow, the trail keeps branching outward into more tangled threads of possibility rather than guiding us to the truth. Everything we've uncovered are just things happening around her. Why would any of this put her in danger?"

"Do you know what they call it when something insidious surrounds and envelops you?" Josie arched an eyebrow, letting the weighted question hang in the air. "A snare, Ellie. They call that a snare."

That still wasn't an answer.

"You want to get closer to Lisa?" she asked me, voice lilting with deliberate nonchalance.

"What do you mean?"

Josie's smile blossomed into a full-fledged grin, intent written in every crease around her shining eyes. "Why, if you want to find Lisa, it seems to me the simplest solution would be to go rent a boat and go looking where she was last spotted—out there on the lake. The police can't find a huge yacht on that small lake? Really? That seems ridiculous to me. Every ramp has cameras. Every dock is visible from their neighbor's terrace. Someone saw something if that boat is no longer on that lake, and if it's still on that lake, the sheriff's department isn't looking very hard for it."

Huh.

She had a point.

"You want us to go boating?" Landon said.

"Why on earth not?" Josie countered, leaning back with her hands folded atop her knee as she regarded him with a mask of serene self-assurance. "We have the resources at our disposal, don't we? There are boat rental places all along the lake. A little waterborne exploration could prove illuminating while we compile the paperwork to untangle this financial snarl."

Charlie cleared his throat, looking dubious about the prospect of a boating expedition. "Don't get me wrong, I love a bit of adventure as much as the next person," he said, casting Josie an uncertain glance. "But darling, are you suggesting we scour the entire sprawl of Lake Wildebridge? It's over sixty miles long, not to mention the open expanses on the water itself—"

"That anyone can see across. It's only four miles wide at its widest point," Josie interrupted, waving a dismissive hand through the air. "And I don't think we should do that. I'm suggesting the two of them do it." She waved in our direction. "They can read a map. They can start by scouring the areas surrounding Lisa's property, since that's where Henderson claims to have witnessed her yacht's last known whereabouts. With any luck, we may stumble across some clues that can steer us toward the truth."

I glanced sidelong at Landon, gauging his reaction to Josie's proposal—and found no trace of dismissive over-protectiveness in his expression, only thoughtful consideration.

"It could be our best chance of finding Lisa before anyone else does," I said, turning back to meet Josie's expectant gaze. "She's still out there somewhere, and we may be the only ones searching." A determined smile tugged at the corners of my lips. "So let's do it. I'm all in if you are."

Landon nodded, the crease in his brow smoothing out as the idea took hold. "If Lisa's yacht is our best lead, we'd be foolish not to chase it." He stood up. "I'll find a marina with the type of boat we need."

"Wonderful." With a decisive sweep of her arm, she snatched the folder and rose from her chair, ready to plunge headlong into the next phase of our crusade. "Just in case, though—you both can swim, right?"

Landon and I set off for one of the local marinas to rent a suitable boat for our amateur maritime investigation. The prospect of taking to the open water—well, okay, it was a lake, but still—filled me with nervous energy. It was part trepidation at venturing out of my element, part determination to pursue any lead that might crack open Lisa Hartman's murky disappearance.

As we pulled into the gravel parking lot of Wildebridge Marina & Boat Rental, my eyes landed on a promising candidate—a sleek white motorboat bobbing along the wooden dock. Its slender hull and open-air design seemed perfect for effortless cruising across the sparkling lake waters.

"Hey, what about that one over there?" I called to Landon as I unbuckled my seatbelt. "Looks speedy but stable."

Landon emerged from the truck, squinting against the glare as he followed my gaze. "Hm. Not bad, but it's got limited space for gear if we end up having to stay out overnight."

My eyes widened. "Overnight?"

"Mr. Henderson mentioned Lisa's yacht was spotted around midnight, right?" He scanned the flotilla of crafts along the dock, his experienced eye assessing each one. "If we're going to be out there for an extended search, we'll need something with more space and amenities."

I frowned. "I don't have any overnight supplies packed."

Landon's expression softened with a reassuring smile. "Don't worry, I came prepared." He jerked his chin toward the parking lot. "I tossed a go-bag in the truck bed with essentials for both of us—clothes, toiletries, snacks. Figured we might need to rough it a bit on this little nautical stakeout. I'll grab it once we're settled."

We made our way toward the tiny marina office, a squat wooden structure that looked like an outgrown toolshed with faded red paint peeling from its clapboard sides. As we neared, a shirtless teenager in raggedy cutoff jeans emerged from inside, tousling his shaggy mop of brown hair.

Hearing our approaching footsteps, he looked up and greeted us with a lopsided grin that spoke more of indolent rural cool than professional courtesy.

"Howdy, folks," he drawled around the toothpick clenched between his teeth. "Y'all here for a boat?"

"We'd like to rent something suitable for exploring some of the lake for a couple of days, if you have anything available," Landon told him.

The kid shrugged one bony shoulder with feigned nonchalance as he considered our request. "Well, shoot, you came to the right place. Mama keeps pretty much every watercraft you could ask for in these parts." He flashed another toothy grin, jerking his head toward the docks.

The price ended up being higher than I had expected—though Landon assured me it was par for the course given the length of our planned rental and the size of the boat we required. Soon, we were situated aboard a cozy but well-appointed 28-foot cabin cruiser, its creamy fiberglass hull able to cut a graceful line through the rippling lake waters.

While modest, the interior opened up to reveal a surprisingly spacious layout, with a small but efficient galley kitchen, a snug sitting area, and even a tiny bedroom with an adjoining head bathroom tucked away below deck. Twin outboard motors propelled us along with a satisfying rumble, promising ample power for our lakeside investigation.

"I can show you how to work the throttle and GPS if you like," the marina kid said as we settled into the cushioned chairs, Landon's grip tight on the polished wooden steering wheel. "Safety equipment's all stowed in the binnacles there, lifejackets beneath the benches, usual stuff. Sheets are clean. Plates, too. Map's got grocery and restaurant stops with docks." His drawl turned slightly more businesslike, though his slouching posture and casual demeanor remained in place. "Got you a full tank of fuel and your paperwork's all squared away. Just remember your boating laws—no drinkin' or carryin' on while puttin' around out there."

Landon gave him an appreciative nod. "Much obliged. Where I parked my truck is good?" He pointed.

"Yes, sir." With that, the scruffy teen untied our mooring lines and tossed them up onto the deck. His bare feet found the dock once more, his gangly frame crouching down as he cast off the last line, securing the bow. "Take 'er easy now," he called out with a cheeky grin as Landon fired up the engines, their throaty rumble thrumming beneath my feet. "Have fun out there, Mr. and Mrs. Rogers!"

With the twin motors thrumming at an idle, Landon eased us out of the marina's no-wake zone, our cabin cruiser gliding forward and leaving a gentle trail of ripples in its wake. Once clear, he opened up the throttle a bit more, and we surged ahead, the shoreline slipping past as I settled into the bench beside him.

Landon's hands moved with easy confidence over the steering wheel and controls, making minute adjustments as we carved through the lake. Trees and hills swept by on either side, the landscape slowly shrinking as he pointed our blunt prow toward the vast mirror-like expanse at the center of the lake.

With a deft twist of the throttle, he opened up the outboards to full power, and our boat responded with an invigorating burst of speed.

I grinned.

"You okay?" he asked.

"Wow," I breathed, unable to stifle the childlike sense of wonder blossoming in my chest. "Yeah, I'm just perfect!"

"It is a lot of fun," Landon agreed, his deep voice pitched to carry over the rumble of the motors. "I love being on the water." His eyes crinkled at the corners, lips quirked in an easygoing smile. "Glad to know you don't hate my dream of cruising around the lake in my own little watercraft."

For all the truths and lies yet to uncover about Lisa's fate, being out here—no buildings or billboards or signs of modern life within view, surrounded by the soothing splendor of shimmering waters and silent limestone bluffs—I couldn't help but feel a profound sense of peace settling over me.

At least until I remembered we were out here searching for any sign of where Lisa's missing yacht might be drifting.

And that was when the knot of anxious tension returned to my belly.

"So, I guess we should start looking around Lisa's area first," I said, glancing over at Landon for confirmation. "Based on what Mr. Henderson told us."

He gave a sober nod. "Makes sense to me. With any luck, maybe we'll spot something—or someone—out here that can point us in the right direction."

Landon turned back to the glittering horizon and gunned the throttle, sending our sturdy little craft surging onward, cutting a clean V-shaped wake—and carving a path toward answers to questions I hoped would recover Lisa safe and sound.

Chapter Thirteen

THE SLEEK WHITE CABIN CRUISER BOBBED ON THE glassy surface of Lake Wildebridge, its fiberglass hull gleaming in the sun. I let my gaze wander over the polished wood trim and brushed metal accents, admiring the spacious little boat that would serve as our temporary home during the maritime investigation into Lisa Hartman's disappearance.

We'd certainly staked out worse locations.

My gaze shifted to Landon, who stood at the helm, a rugged vision of capability in his faded jeans and worn chambray shirt. The sun's warm rays gilded the salt and pepper waves of his tousled hair, bathing him in a golden glow that highlighted the crinkles around his eyes and the faint laugh lines at the outer edges of his mouth. One of his large hands rested on the glossy wooden steering wheel, the other on the throttle, as he surveyed the vast, shimmering expanse before us.

A tranquil smile spread across his features, the kind
that can only come from a deep sense of ease and
contentment. In that moment, he exuded a serene confidence bordering on transcendence, as if the water were
an extension of himself rather than a space to navigate.

I couldn't help the rush of affection I felt seeing
Landon so clearly in his element out here on the lake.
His dream of owning a modest boat and cruising these
very waters in his retirement made sense to me.

Perhaps sensing my attention, Landon turned
toward me with an inquisitive arch of his brow. Warmth
crinkled the corners of his eyes as he regarded me.
"What are you looking at?" he asked, his voice a low
rumble just audible over the gentle thrum of the
outboard motors.

"Just admiring how at home you look out here on the
water," I told him, unable to suppress the swell of fond-
ness swelling in my chest. "You have a real sailor's poise
behind that wheel."

Landon ducked his head with a self-effacing
chuckle, a hint of color tingeing his tanned cheeks.
"Thank you very much, ma'am." He winked. "I don't
have as much experience as I would have liked to have,
but I can hold my own."

"I believe it," I said with a playful shake of my head.
"I do understand the feeling, too. There's something
transcendent about being on a boat, isn't there? So
peaceful and calming."

"It is, though I wish I'd taken you out here for better

reasons." Landon's fingers tapped an idle rhythm against the wheel's polished rim, his expression growing pensive as he gazed out over the placid blue waters stretching to the horizon. "But it's true. I've always loved this—being out on a boat with nothing but the breeze and the ripples and my lady for company."

Memories of our earlier conversation flickered unbidden into my mind.

The wistful fantasy he had painted of us cruising the sunset together in the warm contentment of our twilight years cradled in the gentle sway of our own hand-built wooden sloop—in that moment, the notion didn't seem like such a far-off dream.

"I wish that was all we were doing here. I can think of many things more pleasurable than chasing down mysterious missing faux millionairesses while potentially dodging bullets from crooked developers. Or whatever it is we're doing out here."

Landon's rich chuckle rumbled out of his broad chest. "Just your typical laid-back lake day is all."

"Uh huh."

"Maybe." His warm brown eyes danced with mirth as he met my gaze. "You didn't seem to be bothered by that scruffy marina kid calling us 'Mr. and Mrs. Rogers.'" He studied my reaction with a new wariness entering his expression.

Was he really that nervous to mention marriage to me?

I felt my features soften, an unbidden pang of

tenderness reverberating through my chest as I regarded this gentle giant of a man. Without conscious thought, I reached out, letting my hand come to rest atop his shoulder.

"It didn't bother me, Landon," I told him, and found that the words rang with complete sincerity. "Not in the slightest."

A trace of skepticism lingered in the furrow creasing his brow, chased by fleeting apprehension as he searched my eyes. "Even the 'missus' part?" he asked, the quaver of self-doubt in his tone so faint it could have been my imagination.

I pursed my lips, mulling over how to respond.

Sure, the idea of committing myself to another union still triggered that primal recoil—a knee-jerk self-preservation instinct that made me want to shy away and erect barriers against the vulnerability that came with that kind of intertwined intimacy.

And yet...

When I looked at Landon—this unwaveringly loyal, nurturing, steadfast man who strived every day to chip away at the walls I had erected around my heart—I knew he wasn't asking for some ironclad decree of matrimonial intent. He just wanted to know I was open to the possibility of him in my life.

Permanently.

Irrevocably.

"The idea of being anyone's 'missus' again after everything... it makes me feel a little queasy. A little scared. A little self-protective. But here's the thing—I meant what I said back there about it not bothering me. With you." I searched his gaze, silently imploring him to see the sincerity shining in my eyes. "I'm not appalled at the prospect. Just... not quite ready to take that plunge yet."

A wry smile pulled at the corners of his lips, softening the intensity of his attention. "Not quite ready. That means you're heading toward ready."

"Let's not go putting the cart before the horse."

Landon threw back his head with a hearty laugh, the sound rich and reassuring. When he faced me once more, his apprehension had melted away.

"Fair enough," he conceded, using his free hand to snag the brim of his cap and tug it down a touch lower over his brow. "I suppose there are a few more milestones we ought to reach before I start knocking together a picket fence, eh?"

"I haven't even met your kids yet. You hardly ever talk about them."

He grinned at that. "No need to rush into that fresh hell."

"Landon!"

"What?" He affected an exaggerated tone of innocence. "I'm just being honest." After a beat, his grin softened into a fond smile. "They don't make their way back to this backwater burg too often these days, truth be told. Remember, Hayley's an up-and-coming marketing executive out in LA, while Davis moved to

New York City and keeps threatening to write the Great American Novel if he ever finds time between shifts at the bar." He gave a rueful shake of his head. "My big city big shot children are too busy conquering the coasts to visit their old man back in Small Town, Texas."

"I'm sure that's not true," I said, unable to resist returning his smile. "But I'll hold you to that introduction one of these days. I want to see if those charming personalities inherited all their Dad's swagger."

Landon opened his mouth to respond, but whatever retort he had prepared died on his lips. His brow furrowed as his gaze snagged on something off in the distance across the lake's shimmering surface.

"Hold on a second—you see that?" he asked, gesturing toward a narrow inlet cutting into the forested shoreline. "I think that might be..."

I followed his pointing finger, squinting against the glare of sunlight sparkling off the water as my searching gaze landed on what appeared to be the stern of a large boat poking into view from behind the jut of rocky lakefront, partially shielding it from sight.

My breath caught in my throat, heart stuttering into a momentary gallop.

A yacht.

Or at least, the very distinct profile of one. Sleek and bulbous, all gleaming white fiberglass and tinted glass.

Almost like...

"You think that could be Lisa's yacht?" I asked,

unable to tear my gaze from the shape half-obscured by the tree line. "Just idling out there?"

"Well, it's an enormous yacht. Big, expensive one. Only one way to find out," he murmured, adjusting the throttles and angling our prow toward the narrow cove where the mystery vessel bobbed at anchor. "Let's get a better look before we jump to any conclusions."

As Landon cut the throttle, our sturdy little cabin cruiser slowed to an idle, the twin outboard motors' low rumble fading to a gentle purr. We came to a halt, bobbing on the gentle swell, far enough away from the mysterious yacht to avoid drawing unwanted attention—but close enough to see its distinctive silhouette.

It rode low in the water, its sleek white hull and large beam indicating that it was built for opulence rather than efficiency. Made of fiberglass with gleaming chrome accents, it exuded decadent luxury.

"Well, I'll be," Landon murmured as he studied the anchored vessel. "You think that's it?"

"Lisa's not the only wealthy person with a boat on this lake, Landon," I said, squinting to make out any identifying markers that might confirm its origin. "How many luxury yachts like that could there be out here? My guess is quite a few."

While not quite the sprawling mega-yacht one might envision moored along the sun-dappled riviera, the craft's sleek lines and generous proportions marked it as a serious investment vessel—the kind of craft that would feel more at home berthed in a private Monaco marina rather than lurking half-concealed in an inlet off the placid waters of Lake Wildebridge.

I looked over every inch of the exposed deck and hull for any sign of human activity that could confirm the yacht's occupancy. I could see no movement through the tinted floor to ceiling windows, and the sweeping teak decks appeared eerily deserted, save for a few deck chairs scattered near the stern rail.

My gaze landed on the cluster of towels draped haphazardly across the stern. "Look there," I said, gesturing toward the fabric fluttering in the breeze. "That's an awful lot of fancy towels."

Landon gave a noncommittal grunt. "Not if they have kids and they all went swimming." He worked his jaw, the taut muscle flexing as he scrutinized the draped towels. "But I don't see any kids."

"Or adults. The towels seem out of place," I murmured. Leaning closer, I could make out the faint outline of numbers and lettering beneath the thinner fabrics, but I couldn't identify them. "Landon, they're covering up the hull markings—the registration. Someone doesn't want this boat identified."

"Maybe." His expression darkened. "If that's on purpose, it would seem like confirmation this is probably Lisa's yacht and whoever is aboard didn't want to risk the patrol spotting the name or registry details."

He turned to me. "What was her yacht's name, anyway?"

Quickly, I retrieved my phone, pulling up the relevant conversation thread. "Baron's Bounty," I read aloud, my breath catching. "That's what Josie said it was called." I raised my gaze to meet Landon's, apprehension gripping me. "Baron... as in Prince Baron Dragomirov?"

A shiver ran down my spine, and I shook my head to dislodge the morbid thoughts coalescing like storm clouds.

"We can move around and see if we can spot the name on the ba—" Landon began, then froze.

Movement on the sundeck caught my eye, and a surge of adrenaline flooded my senses. A figure had emerged, moving with languid grace.

The man was tall and slender, with a bearing of studied poise. He was dressed in an impeccably tailored cream-colored suit cut in the sort of lightweight summer linen favored by old world aristocracy. An expensive pair of dark sunglasses shielded his eyes from our scrutiny, but I could sense his gaze lingering on us through the tinted lenses. After a long pause, he raised one hand in greeting and called out to us in a rich baritone with the distinctive Eastern European lilt.

"Ahoy there, strangers! Were you perhaps searching for something out in this remote corner of your beautiful little lake?"

My mouth went dry and my mind blanked.

How to respond?

Did we admit to seeking Lisa's yacht? Or should we feign innocence...

Landon took the choice from me, his rumbling baritone projecting outward with practiced ease. "Ahoy yourself," he called back, raising his hand in a mirroring wave. "We weren't looking for anything in particular, truth be told. Just out for a lazy afternoon cruise enjoying this gorgeous weather."

Smooth.

I couldn't have come up with a better casual deflection if I tried.

The man inclined his head, seeming to accept Landon's words at face value. "A most noble pursuit on such a beautiful day. And where might the two of you call home, if I may inquire?"

"Tablerock," I responded with a friendly smile, hoping to match the stranger's casual demeanor. "We're from Tablerock."

"A lovely town, no?" he said, gracing us with an approving nod. "You live near this lake, beautiful artesian springs... lovely place. It reminds me of what my Lake Stempka used to look like. Just lovely."

"We think so. We don't mean to intrude, sir," he called out in that same easy, ingratiating tone. "Would you prefer we give you and your vessel a bit more privacy?"

The man's smile broadened by a degree, his eyes crinkling above his high cheekbones.

"By no means," he replied with a dismissive wave of

his hand. "You are welcome to linger in this place for as long as the day holds out. There is ample room for all to enjoy these waters at their leisure, no?" With that, he executed a polite half-bow and turned on his heel, disappearing back through the cabin door.

Who talks like that?

Landon met my gaze with a pointed look, his forehead creased in a troubled frown. "Well?" he asked in a low rumble, casting a sidelong glance toward the yacht. "What do we do now?"

The distinctive groan of an engine rumbling to life came from the mysterious vessel's stern transom. That, combined with Landon's disappointed expression, signaled to me we were about to lose our last chance to observe.

My hand slid beneath the dashboard for my phone. I lifted it into view, fingers tightening as I framed the yacht's sleek profile through the viewfinder. With a decisive tap of the shutter release, I captured an image of the mysterious craft, towels and all.

Seconds later, the yacht's engines roared to life, but the name and registration numbers remained concealed by strategically hung tarps, towels, and canvases. Whether the crew suspected our presence was a problem or simply resumed their unexplained voyage, our brief encounter had ended. We watched in silence as the yacht pulled away, leaving a widening wake, and said nothing as the gleaming white yacht disappeared behind the rocky promontory.

I lowered my phone into my lap, mind racing. "No idea what to think."

Landon exhaled. "You could say that again. Who the heck was that guy?"

"His accent..." I trailed off, replaying the man's rich, melodic cadence in my mind. "It sounded Eastern European to me. Balkans, maybe. Considering how many times Herza... Hirza—" I took a deep breath as I tried once more to twist out the country's name. "—Herzoslovakia keeps coming up. I'd bet dollars to donuts that guy has something to do with Lisa."

Landon's eyes narrowed as realization washed over him. "You don't think—"

"Maybe." I met his gaze, giving a somber nod. "Boris Stemple, Prince Baron's valet? Maybe even Baron Dragomirov himself. I mean, it could be. Lord knows Austin's becoming riddled with celebrities and rich people lately."

"You think we might have just had a close encounter with Herzoslovakia's royal family?"

"I don't know. Maybe."

If that man was Boris Stemple or Prince Baron, and he was aboard Lisa's missing yacht, it meant her disappearance was—without a doubt—inextricably tangled up in the shady dealings of the Dragomirov dynasty.

"I feel like I'm on one of those television shows that play jokes on people," I told Landon. My fingers danced across my phone's screen, pulling up Evie's contact. "I'm sending her that photo," I murmured, thumb tapping out a message. "It looks like Lisa's yacht to me, but without seeing the registration number or name, I don't want to rely on my assumption. She can cross-reference the photo against specific details about Lisa's yacht."

"Good idea."

The phone buzzed in my hand as her reply came through, but my attention had already shifted. With a few deft swipes, I launched a search engine, typing out a query about the mysterious Prince Baron Dragomirov.

Images flickered across the small screen, including regal portraits and blurry paparazzi photos of lavish parties. I studied one, the furrow in my brow deepening as I analyzed the subject's refined features, before glancing up at Landon and shaking my head.

Angling the phone toward him, I displayed the photo. "I don't think that was our man out there. The resemblance isn't quite right."

"I agree. What about the valet?"

My fingers swiped across the screen, typing "Boris Stemple" into the search bar. The results populated rapidly, but as I scanned the images, a frown tugged at the corners of my mouth.

Shadowy figures, faces obscured by tilted hats or turned away from the camera. Blurred backgrounds and indistinct settings. In some shots, only the barest hint of a well-dressed form was visible, the rest concealed by crowds or strategic cropping.

I enlarged one photo and squinted at the pixelated display. A single man stood with his back turned, broad shoulders squared beneath a perfectly tailored suit. His head was angled away, with only a prominent jawline and the curve of an aristocratic nose to distinguish his features.

Swiping to the next result only deepened my frown.

Again, mere hints of Boris Stemple's presence rather than precise depictions. Silhouettes and half-glimpses, like the man himself, were little more than specters floating around the edges.

"I can't find a single clear photo of the guy," I admitted.

"That tells me more than anything else that might have been our man, and he's up to no good," Landon said. He looked past the rocky outcropping. "Let's go see if that yacht headed toward Lisa's dock. This lake isn't big enough to hide a boat of that size for long."

Chapter Fourteen

LANDON PICKED UP THE PACE, LEAVING THE secluded cove where we had met the mysterious yacht in our wake, but the boat was nowhere to be found.

"Faster than I expected," Landon muttered.

"That had to be Lisa's boat, right?" I asked once more over the rumble of the twin outboard motors. "I mean, the chances of another luxury yacht like that being out here at the same time she goes missing seem low."

"It could be. But this isn't a budget lake to live on or visit." Landon's jaw tightened, eyes scanning. "Sure, I'd say the odds are pretty darn good that was the Baron's Bounty," he agreed in a grim tone. "Especially after hearing the accent on that fancy-suited fellow and seeing more towels hanging from the bow than the Brady Bunch would require after swimming. He carried himself like a European aristocrat. And that could mean..."

His words trailed off, but the implication hung in the air—if the man we had traded pleasantries with was connected to Prince Baron Dragomirov, it meant Lisa's ties to the corrupt Herzoslovakian dynasty might extend far beyond the fabric used in the designer frocks sold at her boutique.

It still seemed crazy to me.

The idea of an international criminal conspiracy lapping at the shores of our sleepy Texas town seemed almost too ridiculous to be true.

And yet...

The pieces continued to fit together, creating an undeniable mosaic of intrigue—one that appeared to originate half a world away in the crumbling Balkan halls of Baron's feudal ancestral seat.

Something about his relaxed demeanor and casual invitation for us to linger nearby struck me as odd, considering the circumstances. "Do you think he knew we were looking for him? That man seemed awfully at ease. He practically granted us permission to lurk nearby."

Landon weighed my theory, the cords of muscle in his sun-bronzed forearms flexing as he turned. "Could be," he said after a contemplative pause. "I agree. He didn't appear to be paranoid or concerned about our presence in his little cove. If that was the missing boat and he was involved in Lisa's disappearance, he seems confident that none of it will cause him any problems."

If he was mixed up in Lisa's vanishing act, wouldn't he be more on edge about potential witnesses catching sight of him? "Do you think he wanted eyes on him? That he wanted to be seen?"

"Could be a lot of things, Ellie," Landon shot back over the roar of churning wake. "He could be toying with us on purpose to muddy the waters around Lisa's whereabouts. Or he might be hoping a couple of randos like us would be useful later if he needed a witness to say he was on the lake and not committing some crime somewhere. Honestly, I just don't know."

His eyes narrowed beneath the brim of his battered ball cap as he craned his neck, peering toward the stern. No other vessels were visible, but Landon seemed like a man expecting trouble to materialize at any second, regardless.

The strange reality I found myself in made me nervous.

And I didn't just mean being on a rented boat out on the lake searching for a missing woman or international criminals, which was unusual enough.

I hadn't spent much time with the cats at the shelter recently. As the mysteries and murky conspiracies surrounding Lisa's disappearance consumed my time, I missed the familiar routine of caring for my feline companions. It left me feeling a little disoriented, as if I were in a strange new world far from the reassuring familiarity of the Silver Circle.

I even missed Belladonna's sass.

And, well... truth be told, a part of me wondered if I was in over my head this time, chasing shadowy threats and international intrigues that appeared more appropriate for the pulpy pages of a paperback thriller than the quiet reality of small town life.

Even if I was, I couldn't just turn a blind eye.

Right?

As Landon and I made our way over the waters of Lake Wildebridge, I didn't know what to think. But I was equal parts sure we were getting closer to understanding what was going on and frightened of what new dangers might lie around the next hidden cove.

⤜◈⤏

"Over there," Landon said, his words cutting through my thoughts. With a subtle bank of the wheel, he altered our heading, angling our bow toward a bluff in the near distance. "If we tuck in close to that promontory, we should have a clear view of Lisa's property without it being obvious we're spying."

I peered in the indicated direction, shielding my eyes against the dazzling sunlight. Though still a fair distance across the water, the distinctive architecture of Lisa's lavish lakehouse crested the hillside a half mile up from

the dock, its minimalist angles and glass expanses
flanked by the rugged tree line.

It gave us a good view of the area.

"I think you're right," I told him. "That appears to
put us right in line with the cove where her dock is." My
pulse kicked into a higher gear as I considered what this
strategic vantage point might afford us. "If you pull up
along that bluff, we should have a clear look at her property up the hill, too—the house, the dock, all of it. I think
we'll be able to see Ethan Henderson's place, too."

"With any luck, we might just spot our esteemed
friends aboard the Baron's Bounty gracing us with an
encore appearance," he drawled, his voice dripping with
understated sarcasm. "Perhaps they'll even be kind enough
to extend us an invitation to their next gala fundraiser for
the 'Make Shady Dealings Great Again' foundation."

He cut his eyes toward me, one brow arching in a
silent "can you believe this?" gesture as he shook his
head. "I hear the caviar is to die for—literally."

A part of me felt guilty for dragging him into yet
another potentially dangerous situation as a result of my
and Evie's insatiable curiosity and refusal to leave well
alone after hearing a tale of woe from a feline on a magic
plate, but that self-recrimination faded as I realized—
with some discomfort—that without Landon's presence,
I really did risk falling into danger.

Again.

While the idea of needing a man's protection jarred

with my independent self-assurance, I couldn't deny the practical value of having an able-bodied companion (male or female) by my side. Having a partner willing to mule kick his way through whatever obstacles fate flung our way was a relationship bonus I could appreciate.

"Remember not to stare too obviously at Lisa's. If that gentleman in the cream linen was who we suspect, these people are big fish—the kind that eat nosy minnows for breakfast if given the chance, I suspect."

"I promise not to leap into the lake and start splashing around."

"Good," Landon said with a nod. "Let's find a spot to anchor."

He steered the cruiser parallel to the tree line, drawing as near the rocky outcropping as safety permitted. With the boat holding position, we trained our gazes along the curve of the inlet toward Lisa's waterfront estate.

My breath caught in my throat.

"Well, that doesn't look right at all, now, does it," Landon murmured.

"You're staring."

"So are you."

He was right. I was staring, and it did not look right.

Three dark forms moved in hurried tandem along the lakeside paths jutting from Lisa Hartman's property, barely visible beneath the trees and silhouetted against the backdrop of her opulent modernist manor. Though the distance obscured precise details, the interlopers' frantic, purposeful motions were unmistakable—as was the hefty duffel dangling from the shoulder of the person taking charge.

I watched the three shadowy figures disappear into a small outbuilding that appeared to be a storage shed, only to reappear seconds later with more overstuffed bags. They hurried back up the hill and vanished inside Lisa's home.

"I can't tell who they are."

"Me, neither."

"What should we do?" I whispered. "Call Don? Try to get closer and see what they're up to?"

"No, ma'am. We're staying right here for now."

"What could they be doing?" I felt a pang of sympathy for the missing boutique owner beneath the dread churning in my stomach. If she was wrapped up in whatever this was, I suspected she never understood who she was dealing with. "What could be in those duffel bags?"

"Hard to say," Landon said. He reached beneath the console and retrieved a pair of compact binoculars, extending them with a sharp twist and peering through the lenses toward the distant shapes creeping in and out of Lisa's abandoned home. "I can't make out finer details from this distance, but their actions sure look furtive. Like they're trying to be quick and quiet about hauling off whatever they have in those bags."

"But Landon, they're not hauling things off. They're bringing things *into* her house from the shed."

My statement made my sympathy for Lisa waver. We still didn't know whether she was a willing accomplice to whatever these schemes and depravities were, or an exploited pawn that was sacrificed once her role was played.

"If we were on the coast, I would say it's a smuggling operation of some kind, but this isn't the coast. It's a recreational lake in Wildebridge with a bunch of warblers in the trees and springs along the lakefront." He lowered the binoculars, expelling a grim sigh. "I can't see who they are."

"There's no boat at the dock," I said. "What about a car? Can you see a car?"

"Let me look." Landon gave a somber nod, refocusing the binoculars on the front of the house. "This isn't as good a vantage point as we thought. With all the trees and shade, I can't see anything from here."

We watched in tense silence, squinting against the sun's dazzling glare as Lisa's vacant mansion was visited in broad daylight by three people we didn't know. All told, it took them less than twenty minutes to complete their suspicious errand.

At last, a dust-shrouded SUV roared back up Lisa's long drive, tires spitting gravel as it sped up away.

"Quick, Landon! Can you get the license plate now?"

He squinted, tilting the binoculars as he focused on the retreating SUV. His brow furrowed, lips moving almost imperceptibly as he mouthed the sequence of characters emblazoned across the rear plate.

Finally, he lowered the lenses and turned to me. "SPRNG1."

I nodded, my trusty phone gripped in my sweaty palms. "S-P-R, N-G-1," I recited as I texted the number and a brief description of the fleeing vehicle bearing that registration number. "Josie can run it and see what pops up."

"You think that was Sutton and his crew again?" Landon wondered. "Or maybe Prince Baron's brood, coming to sweep away the trail they've left behind?"

"Remember, they were bringing things into the house, not taking things out. Though since we couldn't see what they put in the SUV, you could be right. They could have been removing things from the shed and through Lisa's into the car, I suppose. But what it was? I have no idea."

And I didn't want to think too hard about my guesses.

Landon looked over at me. "We need to get a look in that shed."

"Agreed. We need to wait until dark, though." I sighed. "What on earth did that girl get herself into?"

"Something she shouldn't have. Ellie, we're going to dig deep and untangle this," he told me, steel resolve ringing in each syllable. "And we're going to find Lisa— one way or the other."

I shuddered. "I hope you're right."

"I am. You'll see."

Whatever shadows gathered around this mystery—whether thuggish bankers, international crime lords, or corrupt aristocrats drunk on their own privilege—they had to have made a mistake somewhere.

⊰✿⊱

"Are you ready for a sandwich? I'm getting a little hungry."

Before I could respond, a faint sound from the nearby shoreline caught my attention—a pitiful, high-pitched mewling, barely audible above the rhythmic murmur of the lake kissing the rocks and the breeze rustling through the scrubby lakeside vegetation.

Landon heard it too, his head whipping around.

"Now what in the world?" he muttered, grabbing the binoculars and sweeping his gaze across the rocky shoreline near Lisa's vacant estate. "That almost sounds like—"

"A cat," I said. "It sounds like a cat."

"Ellie," he said, voice pitched low and urgent as he extended the compact lenses toward me. "Look over there near those blackberry brambles. Tell me if you see what I'm seeing."

I lifted the binoculars to my eyes and scanned the distant brush-choked stretch of shore he indicated. At first, nothing seemed amiss. Just the scrubby undergrowth expected in any lakeside thicket, complete with gnarled tree trunks, jutting boulders, and a carpet of—

I gasped.

A tiny figure hunched in the matted grass and dandelion tufts near the waterline, facing away but unmistakable even at this distance.

It was a kitten.

And not just any kitten, but a miniature carbon copy of the fluffy Scottish Fold brought to us—right down to the folded ears and distinctive squashed face I would recognize anywhere.

"Landon, take a closer look at that Scottish Fold kitten. It's the spitting image of Fluffy, down to the last whisker. Same size, same coloring, sitting on Lisa's property." What were the odds of stumbling across another abandoned Fold in the same desolate vicinity where Lisa had so mysteriously vanished? "We have to get that baby off the shoreline," I said, the words tumbling forth in a breathless rush as I surged to my feet, nearly upending my tumbler of iced tea in my haste. "Who knows how long the poor thing has been out there alone? It must be starving."

"Easy now," Landon cautioned, rising to join me at the prow. With a few deft twists of the ignition, the powerful outboard engines roared to life, thrumming with latent power. "We don't want to come charging in like a convoy of battleships and scare it away. Let's take it slow and quiet."

I stared at him. "Are you giving me cat advice, Mr. Rogers?"

"Oh. No, not... Well, I, uh..." He rubbed the back of his neck, a sheepish grin spreading across his face. "Look, I might have watched a few episodes of *My Cat From Hell* on Animal Planet before I moved in. You know, just to prepare myself."

"I promise it takes more than a few episodes of a television show to learn how to work with animals that are starving, scared, and very frightened." I smiled at him. "But I appreciate that you did. And you're right. As slow and quiet as we can."

"Right. Sorry."

"Nothing to be sorry about. Now hush."

Landon eased the throttle forward, guiding our prow slowly toward the lakefront across the way, where the abandoned kitten huddled. As we got closer, I could see its delicate features scrunched in a mask of misery, and a constant high-pitched keen emerged from its minuscule maw.

"Oh, you poor baby," I murmured as Landon cut the engines, their throaty rumble fading to an expectant hush. Only the lulling cadence of waves against the cruiser's hull punctuated the silence as we drifted toward the tiny creature.

The tiny Scottish Fold started at the sound of the idling motors being cut, its massive eyes blown wide with panic as it swiveled to face our approaching craft. For an endless, breathless moment, the kitten froze like a statue carved from sun-kissed sandstone, limbs splayed and trembling.

Then, with a mournful wail piteous enough to crack even the most jaded heart, it scrambled backward, batting helplessly against the tangled blackberry brambles that reached out to trap it in the shoreline thicket.

"Oh, you poor, poor thing," I whispered.

"Easy, little one," Landon murmured in a low, soothing baritone as he steered the drifting craft alongside the rocky shoreline a dozen yards or so from the writhing ball of terrified fluff. "We're friends. No need to be afraid."

If the strange kitten registered his reassurances, it made no visible signs. In fact, its haunches tightened and its sides heaved with panicked gasps, and it appeared to be about to fling itself deeper into the lethal tangle of prickly vines and branches.

"It's okay, sweet pea," I crooned, fighting to keep the tremor of distress from my voice. "We're not going to hurt you. We just want to get you somewhere safe."

The kitten paused mid-thrash, wide eyes locking onto my face with the intensity of a cornered wolf surveying an unfamiliar predator. I could see the wheels spinning behind its youthful, guileless gaze, the desperate calculation as it weighed the relative dangers of remaining trapped amid the thorns versus whatever awaited it in the company of me and Landon on our boat.

"I bet you know Fluffy, don't you?" I continued,

keeping my tone soft and melodic to soothe the wary creature's frayed nerves. "I bet she's your friend. Maybe even your sister, yes? Well, we have a magic plate that lets kitties talk, just like Fluffy." And she never told us about you, but that's a topic for another time. "She's safe with us. How about you let us take you to her?"

Whether that struck a chord of familiarity or the little one had exhausted its already meager energy reserves, the stricken Fold collapsed in a listless heap of matted fur and small ears. Its flanks rose and fell in ragged pants as a stream of high-pitched mewls poured forth once more, this time tinged with the unmistakable keen of bone-deep, desperate pleading.

"I hear you, darling," I heard myself saying, my voice catching in my throat. "Just let us help you, little one. Don't run, okay?"

Before Landon could object, I swung my legs over the side and plunged feet-first into the chill waters of Lake Wildebridge. The shock of the water (which was still far from summer temperatures) enveloped my body and took my breath away for a heartbeat, but adrenaline and worry for the tiny life in danger spurred me onwards.

"Ellie!" Landon's voice boomed across the water, his features contorted in a mixture of exasperation and disbelief as I struck out toward the rocky outcropping where the kitten cowered. "Have you lost your mind? You can't just go diving in like a crazed mermaid!"

I paused mid-stroke, treading water as I craned my neck. "I didn't dive," I called up to him. "I jumped."

"Ellie!" Landon dragged a hand down his face, his expression torn between amusement and frustration. "This is serious! What if there are snapping turtles lurking beneath the surface, just waiting to make a snack out of your toes?"

"There are no snapping turtles in Texas!"

"Alligator snapping turtles. Sure are."

Well.

Oops.

Ignoring his admonitions, I turned and covered the distance with a half-dozen more strokes, emerging upon the lakeshore just a few feet from where the bedraggled Scottish Fold trembled amid the prickly tangle.

Landon's chuckle carried across the water, mingling with the gentle lapping of the waves against the boat's hull. "You're impossible, woman!" he called out. "But I suppose that's why I love you—even if you do give me more gray hairs than I can count."

I swept my arm through the air in a grandiose gesture in silent response, sending droplets of water arcing through the sunlight, but I focused my attention on the kitten. "Easy now," I whispered, shuffling forward with exaggerated slowness so as not to startle the skittish creature any further. "You're safe. I'm going to get you out of this mess."

Inching nearer, I extended my hand, palm up in a

gesture of entreaty—but the kitten recoiled, shrinking tighter against the thorny vines imprisoning it...

...but an unmistakable flicker of unfocused, infant hope wavered in its eyes.

"That's it," I crooned. "Just stay nice and still for me."

With infinite care, I maneuvered beneath the hissing bundle of damp, matted fur, extricating it from the clutches of the blackberry bramble without so much as a single thorn piercing either of us. I checked the sex as I extricated it—male—and then rose to my feet, cradling the tiny boy against my chest, his sassy, hissy warnings giving way to a piteous mewling as he burrowed against me in search of warmth and safety.

"I know. I've got you," I murmured, planting a gentle kiss atop the kitten's damp crown before turning back toward the cruiser. "Let's get you someplace dry. Now, I know my going toward the lake will seem counterintuitive to accomplishing that, but trust me. We've got you."

I looked up to find Landon's expression had morphed from one of amused frustration to something more indecipherable—a mixture of awe, exasperation, and soul-deep affection that stole the words from my lips for a moment.

"How can I help?" he asked.

"I need to get him on the boat without scaring him."

Landon was immediately in motion once more as he angled the back of the cruiser toward me with a push pole. He maneuvered the prow until the boat's swim platform kissed the lake's edge and then, when close enough, extended a hand toward me to take the kitten aboard.

"You," he said as he accepted the damp cat, "are one hell of a woman, Ells."

My cheeks burned again as I climbed aboard using the back ladder, settling back onto a vinyl bench and snuggling the purring kitten close once more. "You would have done the same in just a few more seconds, I'm sure," I responded without hesitation. "Let's head back to the marina. I want to get this little guy to the shelter."

Chapter Fifteen

LANDON AND I ENTERED THE BACK DOOR OF THE Silver Circle Cat Rescue, the bedraggled Scottish Fold boy kitten clutched against my chest. Despite his ordeal, the tiny creature had settled into an exhausted slumber on the boat ride back, his delicate form rising and falling with each steady breath.

As we entered the shelter's main area, I spotted Laurie waiting for us at the foot of the stairs leading up to the second floor, her brow creased with concern. "Is that the—" Laurie began, eyes widening as she looked at the damp bundle of fur in my arms. "It looks just like the other one!"

I nodded, already moving toward the staircase with purposeful strides. "Another Scottish Fold kitten, just like Fluffy. We found him stranded out by Lisa's property next to the lake." I kept my voice low so as not to disturb the sleeping baby. "Poor thing got tangled in some brambles, scared out of his wits."

Landon and Laurie fell into step behind me as we climbed upstairs. Laurie bombarded us with questions, her veterinarian's mind already racing with the potential issues and ailments our unexpected guest could bring.

"Where did you find him? Any visible injuries or signs of distress?"

Landon fielded her queries as I focused on keeping the kitten steady. "Along the shoreline near Lisa's dock," he told her. "Hard to say how long, but he was pretty shaken up. Matted, probably hungry, the whole nine yards."

I braced my feet and leaned into the isolation room door, easing it open with my shoulder as the tiny Scottish Fold kitten began stirring awake. Belladonna raised her sleek head, whiskers twitching as her penetrating golden gaze met mine. Ginger's striped tail flicked lazily on the window perch while Fluffy untangled herself from her blanket nest and looked up, her oversized ears swiveling with curiosity.

Three sets of attentive eyes tracked the yawning new arrival cradled against my chest.

I carried the kitten over to the expanse of laminated block-style counter that stretched against one wall of the room while Landon brought Laurie up to speed on the rest of the details of our lakeside rescue. She listened, her expression growing more troubled with each revelation.

"It can't be a coincidence," she murmured, shaking

her head as she snapped on a pair of latex gloves she'd pulled from her pocket. "Another Fold kitten showing up abandoned? There has to be a connection." She looked back at Fluffy. "But if that one had a brother, wouldn't she have said something?"

"My thoughts exactly," I said, setting the now wide-eyed boy down on the counter. He blinked owlishly as he took in the unfamiliar surroundings. "Shh, it's okay, little one. You're safe now."

Laurie set to work examining him, her skilled hands probing for any sign of injury or illness as she assessed his overall condition. The room fell quiet, save for the soft mewls of protest from our pint-sized patient.

Laurie straightened up, a relieved smile forming on her lips. "Looks like he's in good health, all things considered," she announced. "A bit underweight and dehydrated, but nothing some TLC and a meal won't fix."

I exhaled the breath I hadn't realized I'd been holding, the knot of worry in my chest loosening a fraction.

Laurie reached for the microchip scanner, waving the wand over the curious kitten's scruff. The device beeped, and she squinted at the display. "Yep, he's chipped all right. And get this—" She held up the scanner so Landon and I could see. "The number is just one digit off from Fluffy's. Has to be Lisa's cat."

"Is that so?" Landon asked.

"It is, indeed. He'll need a natural flea bath just in case, and some fattening up," Laurie continued, oblivious to the looks Landon and I were exchanging. "But if you want to try chatting with him on that magic platter contraption of yours, I'd say he's stable enough."

We needed answers, and if this tiny newcomer could provide any insight into the enigma surrounding Lisa Hartman's disappearance and apparent ties to the shady Dragomirov dynasty, I wasn't about to wait.

I was also very curious why Fluffy didn't bother to mention him.

I crossed the room while carrying the small cat in my arms. He protested, but was quickly mesmerized by the shimmering inlaid surface as I set him down on the magic platter, the crystal pulsing with an ethereal glow.

In a voice barely louder than a whisper, he spoke.

"H-hello?" the boy kitten said, his tone tentative and uncertain. Wide, guileless eyes blinked up at me, a mix of trepidation and wonder swirling in their golden depths. "Am I doing this right?"

Before I could respond, a blur of motion caught my eye.

Fluffy, who had been lounging on a nearby cat tree, leaped to her feet with a ferocious hiss. Fur bristling and tail lashing, she launched herself across the room, hurling her tiny body at her unsuspecting brother with unbridled fury.

"Floofy!" she screeched, her normally sweet voice dripping with venom as she collided with her startled sibling. "What are you doing here, you stupid Floofy head? Buttface! Doodoo breath!"

Laurie's brow arched as the newly christened Floofy's name became known. "Fluffy and Floofy? Really?"

Tiny bodies collided in a whirlwind of hisses and furious mewls. Flailing paws and tufts of airborne fur filled the air as the kittens tumbled from the cubby, locked in a ferocious tangle. Laurie and I reacted on instinct, hands shooting out to pluck the combatants apart before blood could be drawn.

I cradled the squirming, spitting ball of rage—Fluffy twisted with primal fury in my grasp as I struggled to subdue her. Her miniature jaws snapped, pink gums exposed in a furious snarl aimed at the trembling Floofy cowering against Laurie's chest. With a sharp intake of breath, I tightened my grip as claws raked my forearm.

"Fluffy!" The reprimand tore from my lips, firm as I gave the irate kitten a gentle squeeze. "Enough of this, young lady. Is this any way to greet your brother?"

Another feral yowl of fury ripped from Fluffy's miniature maw, her tiny face—all squashed features and folded ears—contorting into a mask of apoplectic kitten rage that would have been adorable if not for the glint of murder in her eyes. She glared pure poison at her cowering brother, her fluffy hindquarters wriggling with furious effort as her wee legs pumped like miniature pistons, desperate to break free and unleash her—admittedly adorable—brand of vengeance.

Poor Floofy, meanwhile, shrank back against Laurie's comforting warmth, his wide eyes working overtime as he struggled to process this onslaught of rage from his sibling.

With a gentle shushing sound, Laurie brought the quivering ball of fluff toward the cubby once more. Ensuring my grip on the pint-sized velociraptor hadn't faltered, she deposited poor Floofy onto the gleaming conversation coaster once more—no doubt figuring the magic plate was as good a spot as any for airing the siblings' familial grievances.

"Is your name Floofy?" Laurie asked.

"Well. Mommy always calls me Floofy. But Fluffy calls me dumb-floof. So I go by Floofy. Because it's nicer."

"And Fluffy is your sister?"

"I thought she was my sister." And then the kitten hung his head. "But she left me when I couldn't run after her. It's not my fault my legs are shorter. That's not sister stuff. That's mean."

"Of course it's not your fault," Landon said, looking down at the angry female kitten. "But I'm sure she didn't mean to leave you. Maybe she was just running for help."

"No, she left me." Floofy nodded. "She's mad because I tried to chase the man instead of going after Mommy and then everybody just went all over the beach and then no one was together and she said it was my fault." He looked at Fluffy. "It wasn't my fault. But she always thinks it's my fault. She thinks I'm dumb. But I'm not dumb. I'm not dumb, Fluff!"

Fluffy's entire body tensed like a twanged rubber band as a guttural rumble reverberated from somewhere deep within her tiny chest cavity.

"I'm not dumb! I'm not!"

The sound blossomed into a full-blown intimidating growl that sounded like something more befitting a fearsome jungle predator than a kitten who couldn't yet operate the kick-stand on her hind legs half the time.

"You be quiet! I'm not dumb!" The words tumbled out in a dejected rush, his voice scaling heights of outrage and hurt. "I'm not, I'm not, I'm not!"

My heart ached for the poor dear, sensing there was far more to this story than met the eye—and that we'd need to calm him down to get it out of him.

"Floofy, sweetie," Landon said, leaning over to bring himself to the kitten's eye level. "Can you take a deep breath and tell us what happened? Let's start with how you and Fluffy got separated from Lisa."

The kitten hesitated, casting a wary glance toward his glowering sister. "Well... Mommy brought us to the beach by the shimmery water. She said we could explore and play all day! But Fluffy..." He swallowed hard, seeming to steel himself. "Fluffy didn't want to share Mommy's attention. She said I was a dumb baby, and that Mommy liked her best. She always said that."

Belladonna regarded the spiraling kitten showdown with an air of practiced ennui, her imperious golden gaze sweeping between the squalling combatants as if she were watching a mildly entertaining bit of street theater. Ginger, on the other hand, watched the drama unfold with rapt attention.

The furious cyclone of fluff in my arms let out a tiny snort of derision. It was the kind of haughty nasal exhalation you might hear from an eccentric old lady when she sees a group of edgily dressed teens daring to sully her evening mall power walk.

Floofy's little chin quivered, but he pressed on.

"She can laugh, but Fluffy kept trying to push me off things. The couch, the bed, the dock, the boat. Always saying it was an accident, but I knew better. She wanted me gone so she could have Mommy all to herself."

Laurie made a soft noise of dismay, rubbing soothing circles on Floofy's back. "You know, people don't believe me when I tell them some animals just want to be the only pet and get all the attention. I wish I could tape-record this and play it for them." She shot Fluffy a reproachful look. "Not that what you did was okay. It was very naughty of you, missy. You could have injured your brother."

Fluffy remained unmoved, affecting an air of supreme indifference.

"Floofy, can you go back to the day on the beach? The day that you and your sister got lost?" I prompted, sensing we were getting closer to the heart of the matter.

Even if it was just the black heart of a jealous kitten.

"Oh. Yeah. Okay." Floofy's ears drooped. "One day,

Mommy brought us down to the beach to play. She took off her foot-things and laid down on a towel to snooze in the sun." His voice dropped to a haunted whisper. "When Mommy wasn't looking, Fluffy head-butted me into the lake. I started to float away. I cried and cried, but Mommy didn't hear me because she was talking. Fluffy said she was teaching me to swim. I didn't really believe her because she didn't help."

Fluffy's whiskers twitched with the tiniest bit of self-consciousness. She looked away for a split second and rubbed her little paws on my arm, but as quickly as that tiny crack in her armor showed up, it closed back up again, defiantly re-establishing its iron grip.

"I'm so sorry that happened to you, Floofy," I said.

"It's okay. Turns out I could swim a little." The boy kitten shook his head. "I heard Mommy calling for us, but I couldn't get back fast enough. Then I heard Mommy yell something, and then... then she was gone. I got back on the beach and then I tried to follow the man, but he was running up the hill so fast and he had long legs. I didn't have long legs. I went back to the beach waited and waited, but Mommy never came back for me. Fluffy didn't, either."

Fluffy had the grace to look slightly abashed at this point, her bravado faltering once again.

"So then I tried to go home, but I got stuck by the water in the scratchy plant. Until you found me today." Floofy's golden eyes shone with gratitude as he looked up at us. "Thank you for rescuing me."

Fluffy hissed once more.

I opened my mouth, ready to delve deeper into the mysterious "man" Floofy had mentioned. But the words vanished with the sudden bang of the door opening as Josie and Charlie burst into the space.

Josie held a sheet of paper in her fist.

"You will not believe this," she announced, her eyes sparkling with the thrill of a new lead. "We ran that license plate you texted—SPR NG1. Guess who it belongs to?"

Landon and I exchanged a glance. "Derek Sutton?" I ventured.

"No."

"Lisa?" Landon asked.

"No. Boy, you guys are bad at this." Josie shook her head, a smug smile tugging at her lips. "That SUV is registered to none other than Ronnie Earle himself."

"Ronnie Earle?" Laurie repeated, her brow furrowing. "The guy that owns Boldman Bracket?"

"The same," Charlie confirmed, leaning against the door frame with his arms crossed. "And get this— according to Josie's sources, nobody has seen hide nor hair of old Ronnie in over a week."

I felt a prickle of unease at this revelation. "That's around the same time Lisa vanished."

"It is, isn't it?" Josie nodded. "It seems our Mr. Earle

has pulled a disappearing act of his own. By choice or not, who's to say?"

Landon let out a low whistle. "Well, if that doesn't scream suspicious, I don't know what does."

Fluffy perked up at the mention of Ronnie's name. She struggled out of my arms and bounded over to the platter, nearly knocking Floofy off in her haste. "Uncle Ronnie?" she squeaked, her earlier sibling animosity forgotten in the face of this new development. "Uncle Ronnie is missing, too? Like Mommy?"

I did a double-take, my gaze snapping to the little Scottish Fold. "Did you call Ronnie Earle Uncle Ronnie?" I repeated, incredulous. "Fluffy, are you saying Ronnie Earle is your uncle?"

Fluffy rolled her eyes, as if I were being particularly dense. "Well, duh. He's not my real uncle, obviously. But he's Mommy's uncle. She calls him Uncle Ronnie when he comes over all the time and brings us fancy presents."

Floofy nodded. "Mommy always looks happy when Uncle Ronnie comes to visit. They drink bubbly water and talk about business stuff."

Laurie's lips pressed into a taut line, eyes narrowing as she processed the complex details. "Let me make sure I've got this. Lisa Hartman, our missing boutique owner, was not only mixed up with Herzoslovakian royalty and their shady valet but also had a 'special friend' in Ronnie Earle? The same Ronnie Earle who owns the investment bank that employs Derek Sutton?"

"And who is now apparently missing himself,"

Landon added, shaking his head in disbelief. "This web just keeps getting more tangled by the minute."

I couldn't help but agree.

Every new piece of the puzzle seemed to complicate the picture further, rather than bringing clarity. I turned back to the kittens, hoping they might be able to shed a bit more light. "Fluffy, Floofy—do you remember what your mommy said when she talked about her business with Uncle Ronnie? Did she mention anything strange or scary happening before she disappeared?"

The kittens exchanged an uncertain glance. "I don't know," Floofy mewed, his ears drooping. "Mommy always made us get off her papers. She said numbers didn't need our footprints."

"And revenge!" Fluffy piped up, her tone turning gleeful. "Don't forget about revenge, dummy! See, you are a dummy!"

"Fluffy, stop that. Be nice to your brother. And what do you mean, revenge?" I asked.

The kitten puffed out her chest, relishing being the center of attention. "One time, Mommy and Uncle Ronnie were talking all serious-like. Mommy said something about how they were going to make that no-good Derek pay for what he did. She said he wouldn't get away with it. And she was very hurt."

Floofy nodded. "And angry."

"At Derek?"

"Yes."

Had Lisa discovered something incriminating about

Derek Sutton's activities? Something that made her—and by extension, Ronnie Earle—want revenge?

And if so, what did that mean for her disappearance? Or his?

Josie leaned forward. "What had Derek done, exactly?"

Fluffy shrugged. "I don't know. They didn't say. But whatever it was, they were super mad."

A shadow passed over Landon's face, his eyes darkening as he massaged his temples. "So let me get this straight—we've got a missing Texas mogul, his missing niece, a missing yacht, and a banker with a target on his back from the people missing, and they're all wrapped up in some sordid business deal with ties to Eastern European royalty?"

Charlie let out a humorless chuckle. "Sounds like the plot of a bad spy movie."

"Or a really good cozy mystery," I countered, trying to inject a bit of levity into the situation.

Fluffy, bored with the turn the conversation had taken, yawned. "Who cares about all that stuff?" she grumbled. "I'm still mad at Floofy for getting found and ruining everything. Now we're two Scottish Fold kittens. He's dumb, but no one will know he's dumb when they try to adopt him. And what if they want both of us again? I almost got rid of him, finally!"

Floofy's ears drooped even further, and he shrank back.

I sighed, realizing that the sibling rivalry between

these two was going to be an ongoing issue. "Fluffy, sweetheart," I said, using my sternest mom voice. "We talked about this. It's not nice to treat your brother this way. You both lost your mommy that day; you should support each other, not fight."

Fluffy grumbled something under her breath but didn't argue further.

Laurie reached out and gave Floofy a comforting scratch behind the ears. "Don't you worry, buddy," she cooed. "We're going to get to the bottom of what happened to your mommy. And in the meantime, you've got all of us here."

Floofy leaned into her touch, his purr ramping up a notch.

Josie cleared her throat, drawing our attention back to the matter. "Well, as touching as this family reunion is, we've got work to do," she said, tapping the sheet of paper for emphasis. "If Ronnie Earle and Lisa Hartman were plotting some kind of revenge scheme against Derek Sutton, we need to find out why. And more importantly, we need to figure out if it has anything to do with their disappearances. Maybe Derek found out and double-crossed them first."

"Maybe." Landon nodded, his jaw set with grim resolve. "You two need to dig further—this seems like it has its roots in some kind of business issue. Maybe go see Lisa's partner?" He looked at me. "We need to get back out to the lake."

"Someone needs to monitor Derek, too," I added, my

mind already whirring with the possibilities. "He might be the key to unlocking this whole mess." I looked at Floofy. "We can bring him with us. I can clean him on the boat and maybe if he's away from his sister for a bit, he'll talk some more. He's been around Lisa's house for days. Maybe he's seen something."

Josie raised her eyebrow. "How are you going to talk to him?"

"How do you think?"

"You're going to bring the platter?"

"Yes." I scooped up Floofy, tucking him against my chest as I turned for the door. "We can't leave our best lead behind to go toddle around Lake Wildebridge," I explained. "I think Floofy will be more relaxed and more forthcoming away from his sister, and having the platter there will allow us to communicate."

Landon's expression remained neutral, though his eyes betrayed a hint of skepticism. "You realize you'll be taking a cat out on a boat? That could get... interesting."

Adjusting my hold, I looked down at Floofy, who blinked at me with those wide, guileless eyes. "We'll make it work. Can you grab the platter?"

"Don't fall off!" Fluffy called out.

Chapter Sixteen

L ANDON STARTED THE TWIN OUTBOARD MOTORS AS he eased our cruiser away from the marina dock once more. Lake Wildebridge shimmered in the afternoon sun, its calm waters beckoning us back to its hidden coves and inlets—and to the mystery of Lisa Hartman's disappearance.

Floofy snuggled against my chest as Landon steered. The poor little guy seemed like he hadn't stopped shivering since we plucked him from the bramble tangle along the shoreline—whether from cold or fear of his shockingly unsympathetic sister.

"You've had quite the adventure today, haven't you?"

Floofy's folded ears twitched as he blinked up at me with those saucer-wide eyes. A reflexive purr rumbled forth, his miniature frame vibrating against my sternum.

"Are you ready for your spa day?" I asked him.

With a gentle mew, Floofy snuggled more deeply

into the bend of my elbow, seeking comfort in my warmth.

I smiled, leaning down to plant a gentle kiss atop his fuzzy head. "Don't you worry, sweet pea. We're going to get you all cleaned up, and you'll feel like a whole new kitten."

I carried the tiny Scottish Fold kitten down the narrow steps into the cozy interior of the boat, determined to get him cleaned up. Landon had stocked the galley with all the supplies—soft towels, gentle shampoo, a fine-toothed comb for working out mats and tangles.

"All right, Floofy," I murmured, setting the kitten down on the small galley counter beside the sink. "Let's get you cleaned up and feeling better."

The kitten blinked up at me, his ears twitching as I turned on the tap and tested the temperature against my wrist until it reached a comfortable one. He flinched at first, tensing beneath my touch and straining away from the water, but eventually relaxed as I worked the grime and debris out with gentle strokes.

He was sweet and good natured—which made me wonder how Fluffy could have treated her own brother with such callous cruelty?

Sibling dynamics could be thorny, sure, but Fluffy's actions went beyond mere petty tiffs and squabbles. It spoke of a cruel streak that unsettled me—the type of callous indifference toward a family member that, left unchecked, could calcify into a lifelong hardness.

Of course, they were cats...

Maybe I was anthropomorphizing the situation. I still didn't know what private hurts or perceived slights might fuel Fluffy's animosity toward her brother, and I had to admit her behavior wasn't really that uncommon —even if the words she spoke about him seemed unduly harsh.

In my years of caring for rescued litters, I'd often seen one kitten singled out by its littermates, subjected to harsh treatment or outright ostracization because of some perceived flaw or quirk. It was sometimes as arbitrary as a runt's small size drawing ridicule from its larger siblings. Other times, a kitten's distinct markings or temperament appeared to elicit resentment.

In the worst cases, the rejection went beyond kitten play, devolving into legitimate psychological torment or starvation as the outcast baby struggled to assert its position for attention or food.

"You know your sister's anger isn't your fault, right?" Floofy's ears twitched, but he made no reply.

Not that I expected him to—without the silver platter's power, vocalizations were limited to the normal ones available to any cat.

"Sometimes people—and kittens—lash out when they're hurting inside. It doesn't make it okay, but it's not a reflection of you. It's not your fault."

Unexpectedly, memories of my own childhood popped into my head—the sharp words and icy silences in the aftermath of my mother's abandonment of our family. The way my father's pain had sometimes spilled

over onto me, an innocent bystander. I'd internalized
that rejection, let it burrow deep in my early adult years.
It took time to uproot those insidious beliefs, to assure
myself I deserved better.

I didn't want Floofy to carry that burden.

"What Fluffy said and did was wrong. Full stop.
Pushing you in the water, leaving you behind, calling
you names—that's not how a family behaves." I shook my
head. "You did nothing to deserve that. You are a handsome, sweet little boy."

His wide golden eyes held mine, searching, and for a
moment I wondered if my message was penetrating
whatever linguistic barrier separated us without the
magic plate. Slowly, he pushed his damp little head into
my palm and a purr thrummed to life in his chest—tentative at first, but gaining strength.

I smiled. "You're a good boy, Floofy. Never forget
that."

We passed the next bit of time in companionable
silence as I scrubbed the lake grime from his fur and he
played with the washcloth each time it moved in his
peripheral vision. By the time I was done, his coat was
soft, and he smelled of green sprouts and clover—a fresh-
ness that always reminded me of springtime and new
beginnings.

I reached for the soft towel, bundling him up and
cradling him against my chest once more. He nuzzled
into the warmth of the terrycloth, his purr a gentle rasp
of contentment. I settled with him onto the built-in

bench, the matt splitter in hand, and set to work teasing apart the tangles left in his drying fur.

"You are such a handsome boy, Floofy," I said, my voice soft and melodic. "We're going to figure this out. We're also going to make sure you're safe and cared for no matter what happens. I promise you that." I worked with painstaking precision, slowly teasing apart each individual strand until every offending knot gradually loosened its grip. He was so trusting, so at peace nestled against me despite his recent ordeal. "I think that's the last knot. Feeling better?"

His liquid gold eyes flicking up to meet my reassuring gaze.

"Good. Let's see where that whatchamacallit is." I looked around for the magic platter. "Landon?" I called up the ladder. "I think we're about ready for the kitty plate widget thingy. Is it up there with you? I don't see it down here."

Footsteps thudded on the cruiser deck above, then a steady clomp of descent. Landon appeared in the galley, bag in hand. He set it down on the dining table and looked at Floofy. "Well, now, don't you look good, young man," he declared with an approving nod. "You work miracles, Ells."

"Oh, hush," I said, ears warming.

Landon smiled and moved to the portholes to draw the shades.

When he was done, dusky light still filtered through, but the possibility of prying eyes noticing our unconventional communication method and partner had decreased considerably.

I placed Floofy in the center of the platter. The moment his paw pads made contact, the otherworldly glow I knew—but the kitten was not quite familiar with yet—suffused the cabin with shimmering motes of light. The young cat startled, fur puffing in alarm, but I stroked his back until he calmed.

"It's fine," I soothed. "This lets us chat, like we did back at the shelter. Remember?"

Floofy blinked, the memory dawning. "Oh! Yes. It tingles." His voice emerged, high and boyish. "It tickles my feets." He sat down. "And my butt."

I chuckled.

"Before we get too involved here, let me go back up and anchor us better," Landon said. He rose from the bench, ducking his head beneath the low clearance as he moved toward the stairs. "It'll take me a second."

"Sure, no problem. We can wait."

Floofy's eyelids drooped as we waited, and his tiny body swayed when he let out a jaw-cracking yawn. He blinked slowly, attempting to refocus his bleary eyes, but the weight of drowsiness proved too great. With a contented sigh, he dropped onto the platter, his undersized ears twitching as another jaw-dropping yawn spread his miniature maw wide.

"We can wait..." he mumbled, the words trailing off into a soft snuffle as he crawled off the platter, then the table, and then hurled himself onto my lap and curled into a tight ball. Floofy's sides rose and fell with the gentle rhythms of slumber, his tiny pink nose twitching with each drowsy exhalation.

"My word, you are just the cutest," I whispered.

Through the slimmest of slits between the shades, I caught a fleeting glimpse of the secluded cove bathed in the fading rays of dusk. The sheltered inlet Landon had found was carved into the rugged shoreline across from Lisa's, its waters a lovely emerald hue where the depths remained shallow. The tree line curved toward the water, framing our vantage point across from the lakeside estate.

I could see the winding paths snaking up the hillside toward Lisa's home, the sleek lines of its roof jutting against the sky. Tucked away beneath a canopy of oak limbs stood her shed, its weathered clapboard siding nearly obscured by the verdant tangle of undergrowth.

This location provided an ideal staging ground for clandestine observation with a clear line of sight to any potential comings and goings on Lisa's property.

And her dock.

"I think that ought to do it," Landon called down from the deck, the metallic clank of the anchor chain rattling against the hull. "Shouldn't drift an inch." He ducked through the narrow doorway, his broad shoulders filling the small space, and looked at the sleeping kitten in my lap. "I didn't think I took that long."

"I think it's just been a long day for him." I brought the chatty kitty drink tray closer to me on the small table and placed the drowsy kitten on the platter, watching as the crystal inlay pulsed with otherworldly light. "He seems much calmer now that he's clean and comfortable. More relaxed."

Floofy's ears perked up and his eyes opened. "That's tingly."

"I know. Sorry to wake you from your nap, sweetheart, but we want to find your mom, and you might know some things about how she disappeared that can help us," I said. "You're safe here. Landon and I just want to know what happened at the water's edge on that particular day. We want to help find your mommy."

The kitten nodded. "I remember. The day Mommy disappeared. It was sunny. Mommy brought a blanket and some food. Fluffy stole my Kicky Bird toy."

"Wonderful. What happened when you got to the beach? Did you see anyone else? Talk to anyone?"

"Mommy sat on the blanket and stared at papers. Her phone rang over and over but she kept pushing the red button until it stopped." His nose wrinkled. "Then the angry man came."

"Angry man?" Landon asked.

My gaze drifted over to Landon, hoping to one day be blessed with the infinite reserves of patience he always seemed able to tap into—even when my own ran dry. To his credit, he leaned in with rapt attention, nodding along as Fluffy reiterated the cryptic confrontation between Lisa and the mysterious men on the beach that fateful day.

Floofy's voice took on a hushed tone—the way a child might recount a solemn secret or chilling ghost story. "The man Mommy works with. He stomped over and they started shouting."

She dated Derek, but didn't work with him, so it couldn't be...

I frowned.

No, wait.

She had worked with Derek. He shared that Boldman Bracket funded her boutique—but that meant Ronnie Earle invested in it. Floofy would know "Uncle Ronnie," but the kitten didn't seem to know this man by name.

"Can you tell me what he looked like?" I leaned forward. "Do you know his name? What were they shouting about? Could you hear them?"

Landon's eyes met mine, their depths shining with an unspoken reminder that we'd been showing restraint for a reason. I took a deep breath, the hectic flow of my thoughts slowing in response to his silent request, and I tried to will the knot of impatience constricting my chest to loosen its grip.

He was right.

We didn't want to pepper the poor child with too many questions.

"I don't know." Floofy's eyes went distant. "Fluffy pushed me into the water and everything got quiet. But when I got back..." He shuddered. "Mommy was crying. Saying she was sorry. That she didn't mean to betray Uncle Ronnie."

Ronnie.

As in Ronnie Earle.

I caught Landon's eye, anxiety looping in my gut. He gave a grim nod.

"The man said it was Uncle Ronnie's fault," Floofy continued, oblivious to the gravity of his revelations. "That his messed up deals got them into trouble."

"Was it Derek, this man?" Landon asked. "Do you know Derek?"

"Nuh-uh," Floofy replied, shaking his tiny head. "Derek was not the person I chased. He took off running like a scared bunny as soon as the shadow man appeared." The kitten's ears twitched. "He likes bubble water. And money."

"Okay, sweetie," I said, struggling to keep my tone gentle despite the dread seeping into my veins. "Let's go over this one more time, so we're clear. You're saying Derek was there on the beach that day—"

"Uh huh."

"As was your mom, your sister Fluffy, and this... shadow man you mentioned. That's five different people total, right? Including you."

Floofy bobbed his head, ears perking up. "Four folks,

yep! Well, four folks and one super spooky shadow man."

"And after Derek and your mom ran off," Landon interjected, his rich baritone low and level, "you tried chasing after someone else? Not the shadow guy, but another stranger who was there?"

Floofy's brow furrowed as he pawed at the platter. "Oooh," he said with a solemn nod. "One, two, three, four, five, six! He moved quiet as a field mouse, all slinky. He was trying to not be seen while he watched Mommy and Derek yelling about the house and the money. But I saw him."

I was both grateful for the additional information, and far more confused than I had been before talking to the kitten.

"Who was the first person who showed up on the beach?" Landon asked, his voice low.

"The sneaky man."

"And he's not Derek?" I supplied, feeling a curl of dread in my gut.

Floofy's head bobbed in affirmation. "Yes. Not Derek. He came later. They yelled a lot. Mommy said he betrayed Uncle Ronnie. Derek insisted he was trying to help everybody, that Uncle Ronnie's stupid deals got them in trouble." The kitten's nose wrinkled. "They used a lot of mean words. The shadow man just laughed."

I glanced at Landon.

"What happened then?" I asked.

"They saw the other man. The sneaky one. He walked like a cat hunting a mouse. Very quiet." Floofy shivered. "Derek ran away. So did Mommy. That's when I tried to chase the shadow man because he was just walking, but he was too fast. And then... Mommy was gone." His voice quavered.

I exchanged a glance with Landon, his furrowed brow mirroring the knot of unease coiling tighter in my gut. "So there were six people. Lisa and her two kittens, the shadow man, the sneaky man, and Derek."

But before Floofy could agree or disagree, a muffled clunk echoed through the hull. Landon's head jerked around, his eyes narrowing.

"What was that?" I asked.

Landon jumped to his feet, and all traces of calm curiosity vanished. His hand moved to his waistband, as if reaching for a weapon he didn't have. "Stay here," he snapped, already moving toward the stairs. "Could be nothing, but in my experience, people trying to shoot you rarely announce themselves first."

And then he vanished, his footsteps eerily silent as he ascended to the deck.

Gathering Floofy against my chest, I moved away from the platter, stashing it out of sight beneath one of the bench seats. The kitten burrowed into my arms, his tiny body trembling. "Shh, it's okay," I whispered, stroking a hand down his back. "Landon will check it out. We're safe here."

But even as the words left my lips, I felt a flicker of doubt.

The unseen threat looming beyond the boat sent my imagination into a dark twist. I thought about my daughter, who was not present, and Landon, and how I would cope if something happened to him.

I pushed the thought away.

I had to focus.

I crept toward the porthole, raised myself on my toes, and looked out at the darkening sky. While I worked with Floofy, the sky became streaked with bands of amethyst and copper that reflected off the lake's calm surface. For a moment, I saw only the beauty of nature's kaleidoscope and felt only peace and the gentle rocking of the boat.

It would have been breathtaking if my nerves weren't so frayed.

Floofy, sensing my distress, let out a mournful mew.

"It's okay," I whispered, wanting to believe my own assurances. "Probably just the fish getting their dinner, that's all."

Against the backdrop of that sunset inferno, the shadowed forms of trees and rocky outcroppings appeared stark and ominous. My eyes strained against the gloom, scanning for any sign of movement, any hint of who—or what—might have caused that soft thud against the hull.

The shoreline remained still and silent, its imposing silhouette indistinguishable against the gloaming shadows forming over the cove. A hush had descended, the kind of unsettling silence that made every nerve in my body tingle with increasing trepidation.

Then, without warning, a splash.

The poor kitten let out a soft mewl of distress, likely sensing the increase in my anxiety.

"Shhh, it's okay," I murmured in what I hoped was a soothing tone, even though my own voice sounded reedy and feeble to my ears. I was supposed to be the strong, reassuring presence here. But at that moment, blind terror gripped me. "Landon?"

There was no answer.

"L-Landon?" I ventured, hating the way my voice quavered like a terrified child calling out in the dark.

Silence responded, heavy and devoid of the carpenter's familiar presence. The hairs prickled along the nape of my neck as every irrational nightmare scenario flashed through my mind's eye—Landon floating face down, or perhaps already hauled away by malicious forces, leaving his broken body—

No.

No, I can't think like that.

Soft but unmistakable footsteps on the deck above.

When the broad form filled the cabin doorway a heartbeat later, I jumped so violently that Floofy let out an indignant squawk of protest.

Chapter Seventeen

"It's okay," Landon said, seeing my stricken expression. "We're all clear." He looked around. "Aren't we? You look like you've seen a ghost."

My sigh of relief ruffled the fur atop Floofy's head. "What was it? Did you see anything?"

Landon's hand came up, a familiar shape dangling from his fingers.

A mangled flip-flop identical to the one Fluffy came to the shelter with.

I blinked. "You found that floating in the water?"

Landon turned the battered flip-flop over in his hands, studying it as if it held the key to unlocking the mystery that had brought us out here to this secluded cove. His brow furrowed, eyes narrowing as he traced a finger along the worn rubber sole. "It must have just drifted up and tapped against the boat." He looked from the flip-flop to Floofy, a crease appearing between his brows. "Matching kittens. Matching flip-flops."

Even as the rational part of my brain dismissed it as a mere coincidence, an insistent voice within whispered that coincidences were the breadcrumbs that would lead us to the larger truth...

But sometimes a flip-flop was simply a flip-flop.

"You think it's Lisa's?" I wondered. "It looks like the one Fluffy has."

Landon shrugged. "Could have washed in from anywhere." He lifted his gaze to meet mine, a ripple of discomfort passing through his eyes. "But given that it matches the one your Scottish Fold dragged in..." He exhaled, a heavy sound. "I don't want to jump to conclusions. But two orphaned kittens showing up with two lost flip-flops in the same remote stretch of shoreline Lisa Hartman just so happened to vanish from?" Landon shook his head. "Strikes me as a mite too coincidental for my taste."

I looked down at Floofy, half hoping he'd jump in the plate and say something clarifying to help us figure out the answers, but the exhausted kitten had succumbed once more to the pull of sleep, his tiny body rising and falling with each gentle breath.

"So what does it mean?" I asked, frustration bleeding into my tone. "Where do we even begin to—"

An engine's rumble broke through, slicing the silence with its clear echo across the water in the dimming twilight.

Landon and I watched as a familiar white behemoth glided into view around the rocky outcropping flanking the narrow inlet—the same sleek yacht we had encountered earlier, its hull throwing back the shore lights from expensive homes as it cut an inexorable path through the darkening water.

Straight toward Lisa's dock.

"Where the heck did that thing come from?" I asked. "Were they parked on the other side of that outcropping?"

Landon was already moving, his hand falling to the small of my back as he hurried us away from the porthole. "I need to kill the lights," he ordered, his voice pitched low and urgent. "Turn everything off except the combination lights so no one drives into us. We need to stay out of sight."

He plunged the cabin into darkness with a few deft flicks until only the dim glow of the red and green navigation lights colored our movements to the upper deck of the boat. Floofy let out a faint mew of protest at the sudden shift that woke him, but I shushed him.

We hunched so we could peek out just above the gunwale.

"Try not to move too much," he breathed, the heat of his whisper brushing my ear. "It's a quiet night on the water, and if we can hear them, they can hear us."

Would we be able to hear them?

It didn't take long for activity to stir along the winding path snaking up through the trees toward Lisa's house—a flurry of motion at odds with the sleepy hush that should blanket the property since its owner disappeared.

I strained my eyes through the gloom, squinting to make out the solitary figure hurrying down the gravel track toward the water with purposeful strides... and felt my mouth go dry as the distant porch lights reflected off an unmistakable coif of tousled chestnut hair.

Derek Sutton.

I knew it.

He moved with an air of manic purpose, the denim and chambray that normally lent the banker a casual elegance replaced by midnight black slacks and a buttoned-up shirt rolled up at the sleeves. I thought I saw a pair of wayfarers in the bright pathway light, but I couldn't see him completely. His face was turned, shrouding it in unreadable shadow.

I sharpened my hearing as Derek hopped across and boarded the yacht, but the distance between our two crafts was too great to make out any words. My ears picked up little more than a series of urgent voices, their muddled cadences punctuated by the occasional surge of heightened emotion—fury, irritation... perhaps even fear?

I glanced at Landon, raising my eyebrow, and whispered, "Do you hear two men?"

He just shook his head, his jaw set in a grim line as he held a finger to his lips and tightened his grip on my hip. The message couldn't be clearer: be still. Wait. Listen. We wouldn't gain any knowledge if we didn't snatch every word we could hear right out of the air.

My neck ached from the contortion of holding myself (and the kitten) still and silent on the bench, but I didn't move—I tried not to breathe too deeply for fear of giving away our position.

After what seemed like an eternity—but was likely only a scant handful of minutes—the voices on board the yacht reached a crescendo before breaking into a burst of scornful laughter that slithered across the water to reach our ears.

They laughed and talked more, as if unconcerned someone might hear them out on the lake, but, to be frank, they had a right to be cavalier.

I couldn't make out a word they said, their muddled cadences and heated tones carrying only so far across the cove.

Who was Derek Sutton meeting on Lisa's dock?

On Lisa's boat?

And why did it seem like that humongous yacht could disappear off the lake in the blink of an eye?

The questions whirled until a furious shout sliced through the night, the thickly accented words dripping with menace.

"You assured me discretion was paramount, and look at where we are now!" The voice was tinged with a harsh Slavic rasp that raised the hairs on my nape. "We linger in plain view like sideshow performers while you dawdle! Get me those deeds immediately, or I'll show you the consequences for testing Baron Dragomirov's patience!"

Without warning, the sound of furious footsteps on the dock broke me from my shock with all the subtly of a bullhorn. I watched Derek storm up the dock, and I noticed there was something different about the set of his shoulders. Something uneasy.

Something rattled.

He reached the top of the path and disappeared from view into Lisa's house.

Landon and I remained crouched behind the gunwale, our eyes glued to the sleek yacht moored at Lisa's dock. After a few tense moments of silence, the cabin door slid open and two figures emerged onto the deck, their movements fluid and self-assured.

Even from this distance, I could see they exuded an air of aristocratic entitlement—the shorter man's sharp, weaselly features contrasting with his companion's tall, broad-shouldered frame and chiseled jawline. The taller one moved with a languid grace that spoke of a lifetime of privilege, while the other vibrated with a nervous energy that bordered on obsequiousness.

As we watched, a third man—small and wiry, with

the hurried gait of a harried servant—scurried out from the cabin, a silver tray laden with champagne flutes balanced precariously atop his palm. He approached the pair with a deferential bow, offering the sparkling libations.

The tall man plucked a flute from the tray with a dismissive flick of his wrist, not sparing the servant so much as a glance. His companion followed suit, though his movements were jerkier, less refined.

"More," the taller one commanded, his accented voice echoing over the water. "And be quick about it."

The servant bobbed his head and scurried back into the cabin, leaving the two men alone on the deck.

"I don't like this," the shorter one said, his reedy voice pitched high with agitation. "Sutton's taking too long. We should have had those deeds days ago."

"You worry too much, Boris."

I looked at Landon, my eyes wide. He met my gaze, his jaw clenching.

If the weaselly man was Boris Stemple, then the taller one had to be...

"Yes, Baron."

"Patience," Baron Dragomirov chided, his tone dripping with condescension. "Derek will deliver. He has no choice." A cruel smile played at the corner of his lips. "Not if he wants to keep his precious investments afloat. We have to secure these properties. The water is too valuable."

"And if he doesn't?" Boris pressed. "What then? We

can't just sit on our hands, waiting for that fool to get his act together. Every day we linger here, the risk grows that we will be caught."

Baron took a long, slow sip of his champagne. "Then we turn to our friends at Town Prosperity Investments and we turn up the heat on them in the same way we did with Derek," he said, his voice smooth as silk. "I'm sure they'd be more than happy to help us gain the properties—for the right motivation, of course."

My breath caught in my throat.

Derek was working with Baron and Boris to gain control of real estate in Wildebridge County.

How did Ronnie Earle and Lisa fit into this scheme?

The two men fell silent for a long moment, gazing out at the moonlit lake.

Landon leaned close, his breath warm against my ear. "Derek must have something they want. Those deeds, the properties they keep mentioning. Baron's using him to gain a foothold here."

I nodded, my mind racing.

"What are we going to do about Earle?" Boris asked, his voice cutting through the night. "He's getting restless, and I don't think he believes you're going to let him go. He's asking too many questions."

Baron drained the last of his champagne with a swift tilt of his head. "Ronnie is not our concern," he said, his tone hardening. "He dug his own grave by meddling in Herzoslovakian affairs beyond his skills." His lips curled in a sneer. "Once we tie up all the loose ends, we'll make sure his restlessness is cured."

Landon's grip tightened on my hip, his fingers digging into my skin.

They had Ronnie Earle.

And if they had Ronnie...

"The girl, too, then," Boris pressed on, a flicker of unease in his nasal whine. "What about her?"

Baron whirled on his companion, his eyes flashing with icy menace. "Do I need to remind you who's in charge here?" he snarled. "She's of no importance at all, merely something else to be discarded when no longer needed." With a flippant wave, he turned back to the lake view. "She'll be dealt with when she's served her purpose. I just need to transfer what she has, and we'll be finished. She'll be finished."

Before I could process the implications of Baron's chilling words, a piercing trill shattered the night's careful silence.

My phone.

In my front pocket.

Landon and I froze, his wide eyes meeting mine for a split second before the kitten-shaped grenade nestled against my chest came to life with a terrified yowl, Floofy's miniature claws sinking into my flesh as he scrabbled to escape the startling noise.

I grappled with the squirming ball of fluff, desperate to keep him from wriggling free, even as Landon's frantic hands patted at my hip and thigh in search of the offending device that threatened to blow our cover. Our arms and legs tangled in a graceless struggle, and I nearly tumbled over with an undignified yelp.

"Turn it off!" Landon hissed through gritted teeth.

"I'm trying!" I whispered back, my voice strangled. "Hold Floofy so I can—"

We flailed in the darkness, a mad tangle of limbs and fur as I fought to dig my phone out and shut off the head-splitting ringtone with increasingly clammy and desperate fingers.

Finally, blessedly, silence descended once more.

Panting, I leaned back against Landon, Floofy still clutched tight against my hammering heart as we both held our breath.

On the yacht, Baron and Boris had stopped, their heads swiveling with terrifying intensity—looking for the source of the unmistakable human commotion that had just shattered the night.

Chapter Eighteen

THE UNEXPECTED SOUND OF MY PHONE RINGING
had cleaved the night's tranquil quiet like a hatchet. I
watched the two men stride along the yacht's polished
deck, their purposeful strides betraying an unmistakable
sense of menace.

"Where did that come from?" Boris hissed.

They'd heard us.

Of course they had—the frenzied scramble to stifle
that blasted ringtone, all flailing limbs and muffled
curses, echoed like a dinner bell to savages. The two men
searched along the yacht's deck with purposeful steps,
their gazes homing in on our position with alarming
speed.

"Landon, they're coming this way," I breathed.
"What do we do?"

Floofy seemed to sense the danger, his miniature
body tensing like a bowstring as the electric charge of

fear crackled through the air. The poor kitten let out an earsplitting yowl, his needle-like claws digging into the soft cotton of my shirt as he fought to free himself from my grasp. I tightened my hold, grimacing as those razors pricked my flesh.

"We get the hell out of here."

With a few deft flicks of his wrist, Landon coaxed the cruiser's engine to a rumbling purr, its vibrations resonating through the wooden deck. Steely determination etched itself into the taut lines of his rugged features as he angled the steering wheel, propelling us out of the sheltered inlet.

Part of me marveled at Landon's calm efficiency.

Another part, however—the more vocal, keening inner voice that piped up during moments of crisis with all the tact of a klaxon blaring at midnight—couldn't help but wonder if the Herzi... Herszo... um, the autocrat prince might simply ram us off the lake like an errant tugboat.

Maybe, I thought, they hadn't seen us.

We hadn't gone far before the throaty roar of the yacht's powerful engines shattered the stillness behind us. A glance over my shoulder revealed the sleek white silhouette of Baron's craft surging through the darkness, its throaty rumble resonating within the waters as it devoured the distance between our two vessels, its elegant lines and opulent proportions belying the predatory menace emanating from its bubbling wake.

A low-speed chase across the inky waters of Lake

Wildebridge had begun, and it sparked a defiant flicker of irritation in me. Sure, the man commanded wealth and influence enough to make Willy Nelson look like a welfare case, but that didn't give him carte blanche to bully his way across the waters like some feudal warlord.

My fingers trembled as I fished my phone from my pocket with my free hand, the screen blurring with the boat's motion as I tried to see who had called. I jabbed Josie's name and the speaker phone icon with my thumb.

"Ellie, thank goodness! I've been trying to reach—"

"Josie, I'm sorry, but we're a little busy at the moment," I cut her off, my words tumbling out in a frantic rush. "Baron and Boris, they spotted us. We're trying to lose them, but—"

"Wait, the Baron is there? As in Prince Baron Dragomirov and his valet?"

"The one and only, in extravagantly tailored flesh," I told her. "Along with his coat-carrier, Boris. They're hot on our tails as we speak. No, Floofy, stop! Wait!"

As if on cue, the kitten jumped out of my arms as soon as I became distracted, landing on the floor and scampering away in a flurry of fur and clawed feet, vanishing down the galley stairs. I shot Landon a helpless look as the furry fugitive disappeared into the cabin's shadowy recesses.

"Ellie, listen to me," Josie said, her voice rising with urgency. "Boris Stemple owns one of the huge properties right next to Lisa's house. It used to be some desolate old hunting lodge, but now it's this sprawling estate with a private boathouse jutting out over the lake. One of those artesian springs on Ethan Henderson's land butts right up against the thing, and Boris has been fined for pulling water from it at least four times."

My mind raced, fragments of information whirling together like a kaleidoscope as Josie's words unlocked a flurry of connections. The springs... It felt like people kept talking about the springs. Josie had spoken of Herzoslovakia's acclaimed textile trade, the prestige afforded to their weavers' exquisite creations spun from those artesian—

"Wait, what did you say? A spring here on Henderson's property?"

"Yes, I have aerial photos showing Baron and Ronnie Earle sipping champagne on the back deck of the house overlooking it. Why? Do you think the spring has something to do with it?" I heard papers move around. "There are large-flow exit points for it on Lisa's property and Henderson's property."

Things fell into place with dizzying speed—the repeated mentions of springs, the Dragomirov family's connections to the Herzoslovakian textile trade...

"It's the water," I breathed. "That's it, Josie. It's the springs. You said Herzoslovakian fabrics are prized because they're made using the pure spring waters of the region." I thought back to the Stempka Lake environmental scandal. "But that show Evie watched was about the waters the Dragomirovs polluted with their factories..."

"You're right." Landon glanced over, brows knitting together. "They ruined their famous water back home."

"And are for an alternative water source," I finished, my blood running cold. "Josie, I think this is all about controlling Wildebridge's springs. This race to buy up the land isn't about more homes. It's about the water."

The cruiser shuddered as we thumped against something under the water, dishes and glassware clattering in the galley below. Landon's knuckles turned white as he wrestled the wheel, his jaw clenched tight as our little craft bobbed and rolled in the turbulent wake.

"Landon! Are we okay?"

"We're not going to sink." A muffled curse slipped from his lips, the kind a sailor might say when an errant wave slaps them in the face. Not the salty depths of a true seafarer, but enough vinegar to express his displeasure with our unwelcome visitors cutting through the night.

The yacht loomed behind us.

We weaved our little cruiser between the narrow coves and rocky outcroppings that littered the lakeshore. My heart hammered against my ribs with each evasive maneuver, equal parts exhilaration and dread pulsing through my veins.

But even Landon's skilled seamanship could only carry us so far.

One by one, our potential escape routes dwindled until there was nowhere left to flee, and I watched as Baron's captain expertly maneuvered the vast luxury yacht to block our path, its hulking mass sealing off the inlet's mouth like an impenetrable barrier.

We were cornered.

❦

"Josie," I said, fighting to keep my voice steady. "Baron and Boris have us pinned in a cove. We can't get away."

Landon's hand gripped the wheel, knuckles white as bone. Before I could blink, his phone was in his ear. "Don, it's Landon. We need backup." His gravelly voice took on an edge of urgency. "Ellie and I are blocked in on Lake Wildebridge by a large yacht. Can you get someone over here? I'm dropping a pin to our location."

The craggy limestone bluffs of the cove rose on either side, hemming us in. With the yacht spanning the inlet's mouth, its hulking mass made it impossible to pass.

We were well and truly trapped.

"Lovely evening for a moonlit cruise," Baron called out, his accented urbane tone belying the predatory glint in his eyes. He cradled a champagne flute in one hand. "Mind telling us what you're doing skulking about? Spying on the comings and goings of lake residents is quite rude, you know, and it's twice now that we've run into the two of you."

"We weren't spying," I shot back, injecting a note of offended incredulity into my voice. "For goodness' sake, we're just trying to enjoy a romantic night out on the water."

Boris smirked. "Ah yes, what's more romantic than eavesdropping?"

Landon bristled beside me. "I don't take kindly to being blocked in and accused without cause." His gaze darted from side to side, searching for an escape route even though it was clear the yacht's looming presence cut off any chance of slipping away. "We were minding our own business, the same as anyone else on this lake. We anchored in a cove to eat dinner, and we left when we finished to explore where we wanted to hitch up for the night. Not that we owe you any explanation, but I thought I'd offer it to be neighborly."

Baron tutted, shaking his head in a patronizing manner. He swirled the champagne in his glass, the liquid shimmering in the moonlight. "You have to understand our suspicion. It's not every evening we find strangers idling about in such proximity to, shall we say, sensitive discussions." Baron's eyes narrowed as he regarded us over the rim of his glass, his stare penetrating and accusatory.

"If you wanted privacy, maybe don't conduct your business out in the open for any passing boater to overhear," I retorted.

"So you were listening."

"I didn't say that. You just said you were having sensitive discussions."

Landon placed his hand on my shoulder. "Look, we

don't want any trouble. Let us pass, and we'll be on our way. Simple as that."

Baron stared at us. "Simple as that, is it?"

"Yes," Landon responded.

A charged silence fell over the cove, the tension crackling like static electricity. Baron and Boris locked eyes for what seemed like an eternity. Though no words passed between them, a silent exchange played out—minute shifts in expression, the subtlest dip of a chin or twitch at the corner of an eye.

They were so close to us I could see it all.

At last, Baron heaved an aggrieved sigh. "Very well. I'm feeling generous this evening. You may go—but I advise you to put this incident out of your minds. Idle speculation about the affairs of your betters rarely ends well."

My betters?

Did that jerk just call himself my better?

My gut instinct was to scold the arrogant twit for his flagrant display of elitist pomposity, but I stifled the acidic retort that was bubbling up in my throat. As much as I wanted to deflate Baron's overblown sense of self-importance with a few sharp words, I also wanted to get out of here.

Going toe-to-toe in a battle of wits with a man who clearly perceived himself as the heavyweight champion of the Snooty Rich Baffoon division would likely only goad him into changing his mind about unblocking the exit—and probably an even more insufferable spiral of condescension.

I wasn't sure would be worse.

While I was thinking about what to do next, Baron's hand sliced through the air in a sharp, decisive motion. Though he said nothing, the command carried—a muffled clatter of activity stirred to life somewhere within the opulent recesses of the yacht's interior.

But just as Landon reached for the throttle—ready to gun the engines and get the heck out of there—a flickering glow caught my eye. It seeped out from the galley below, pulsing with an ethereal shimmer. "Oh, you've got to be kidding me," I whispered.

The platter.

Floofy must have found his way to it while we were distracted topside.

I felt a knot of dread in my gut, my mind racing as I considered the possible consequences. If that sweet, innocent ball of fluff had wandered onto the glowing crystal's surface, it was impossible to predict what revelations would emerge in his tiny, piping voice.

How did the magic work? Would his words stay down below or would we hear them up here? My pulse thundered in my ears, the roar of anxiety drowning out all else until I felt certain the thunderous cacophony would give me away.

"Just wait a few more minutes, Fluffy," I whispered. "Just a few more."

No such luck.

"Shadow man. Sneaky man. They were with Mommy!"

Not only could we hear the words up here, but Floofy's high-pitched voice carried across the water, his kitten babble slicing through the tense silence.

Boris became rigid, his eyes narrowing to slits as he scanned the craggy bluffs that surrounded us, and then sputtered, a vein pulsing at his temple. "Did you hear that?" His gaze snapped toward me, piercing and accusatory. "You heard that, right?"

"Heard what?" I asked.

"Who said that?" Baron asked.

My mind raced, searching for an explanation. "Oh, that's just the radio," I blurted, wincing at the flimsiness of the deception. A rueful smile tugged at my lips as I made a vague gesture toward the galley. "Darn thing has been haywire all evening. It's driving me crazy picking up stray signals."

Landon played along, shaking his head. "Picked up some crazy preacher ranting about coffee being a sin earlier." His mouth twisted in a wry smirk. "I was about to fling it overboard before it convinced us to switch to tea."

Baron's lip curled, but his hawkish scrutiny remained unwavering. If the kitten's words had touched a nerve, he wasn't showing it—though the way his knuckles tightened around that champagne flute suggested our bumbling deflections might not have gone unnoticed.

The seconds stretched into an uncomfortable void, with the only sounds being the gentle lapping of waves against the yacht's hull. I resisted the urge to squirm beneath his piercing gaze. Just as the tension became unbearable, Baron exhaled a soft huff—whether of amusement or disdain, I couldn't tell.

"You are a curious one, aren't you?" Though his tone was filled with the dulcet cadences of aristocratic charm, each syllable had an unmistakable edge. A veiled threat. "Tell me, how does a humble cat rescuer from a speck of a town come to be in so many places she shouldn't be?"

"I'm not sure what you mean."

I knew exactly what he meant.

He paused, pursing his lips as he weighed his next words. "I've heard of you, you know. You enjoy making bold assumptions about matters far beyond your stature."

I bristled at yet another backhanded insult. "Just lucky, I guess."

"You are not as inscrutable as you think," he responded. "Either of you."

Landon chuckled. "We're just small town boaters."

"Are you?"

Disdain curdled in my chest, a simmering brew of annoyance and exasperation threatening to boil over into a full-fledged tempest of what my grandmother would have called "uncivilized behavior." The flippant dismissals, condescending sneers, and veiled threats wrapped in civility's silk pulled my last threads of patience and caution.

They unraveled like a cheap cardigan pulled taut.

"Do you think just because we noticed you and Derek Sutton attempting to buy up all the land around here, we're somehow different from everyone else in this town?" I asked, leveling Baron with a steady gaze. Diplomacy and restraint wilted in the face of his relentless arrogance like a debutante at a punk rock revival. "This is a small town. We all notice things out of the ordinary when it affects our home—like the fact that our springs produce the pure water you need for your textile manufacturing, just like you used to use in Herzoslovakia. You know, before you and your family ruined it?"

Landon's expression changed, with that telltale tic twitching at the corner of his jaw—the one that always emerged whenever I raced straight past whatever line he expected me to stay safely behind. I could almost hear the air for a resigned sigh gathering in his broad chest.

Which, I supposed, was fair enough.

Baron's eyes flashed, equal parts impressed and irritated by my assessment. "Very astute, Eleanor," he said, voice cool. "What is it the Americans say? Ding ding ding, give the lady a prize." He took a sip of his champagne, considering me over the rim of the glass. "Yes, a steady supply of pristine spring water is essential to our production process. And yes, Derek has proved instrumental in helping us secure it."

"And Ronnie Earle?" I pressed. "Does he figure into this scheme as well?"

"Who's Ronnie Earle?" Boris asked, smirking. "Our dealings are with Derek Sutton, and how he procures the properties is none of the Baron's concern. Tawdry details are beneath a man of his station."

Baron nodded. "I provide the capital to keep everything moving. Whatever machinations occur beyond that, well..." He spread his hands in an elegant shrug. "Mere trivialities, I assure you. Nothing that could be traced back to us."

Their careless attitude elicited a burst of frustration. "Do you know Lisa Hartman?"

At that, Baron's gaze hardened, all traces of affected charm vanishing.

"You ask too many questions," he said, each word precise and heavy with warning. "I don't know how things work in your country. But where I come from? Those who pry into the affairs of their betters often wind up sleeping with the fishes."

A muscle ticked in Landon's jaw, but his voice remained a monotone of composure. "We're not in your country, sir. You'd do well to remember that."

Baron's lips peeled back in a mocking semblance of a smile, the bared tips of his teeth glinting like fangs in the moonlight. With a disdainful sniff, he straightened, squaring his broad shoulders as if shrugging off an ill-fitting jacket. "Is that so?"

"Yes, sir."

"And what, pray tell, grants anyone the authority to rein in a Dragomirov? Make no mistake—I am the living embodiment of sovereign rule. My influence transcends your paltry borders and insignificant local fiefdoms. I answer to no nation, only the ancient bloodline that courses through these veins. Wherever I stand is Herzoslovakian soil."

"So you have diplomatic immunity?" Landon asked him.

"I have sovereign immunity. It's better. More exclusive."

Landon chuckled, the rumbling baritone reverberating from deep within his broad chest. "I'd wager you didn't study the United States—or Texas—too closely before you planted your flag alongside this lake, did you, Your Highness?"

Baron's brows arched, but the imperious prince said nothing—merely inclined his head in a silent challenge for Landon to elaborate.

"You might be able to bully your way across borders back in your country using your family name and noble lineage." Landon's lips quirked in a half-grin edged with mild amusement. "But this is the United States. We don't much care about titles or ancestry. Around here, the law applies to everyone—prince or pauper."

I couldn't resist adding my own two cents, undeterred by the dagger-sharp glint in Baron's eye. "No one is above being held accountable, no matter how lofty their heritage or deep their purse."

Baron observed us from the opulent deck, his expression unreadable. For a stretching breath, he said nothing —just swirled the dregs of his champagne in a slow, contemplative spiral. Finally, he let out a chuckle, the sound more bark than laugh.

"Nonsense, though it is a most quaint philosophy," Baron observed, sounding more amused than concerned. He set his empty glass aside with a decisive clink.

All at once, the night shattered—the shriek of an approaching siren reverberating across the mirrored waters. Blue and red lights strobe-flickered through the cove as a sheriff's patrol boat rounded the rocky outcropping, its running lights blazing.

Though his aristocratic features remained an impenetrable mask of composure, the muscle jumping in his clenched jaw betrayed his inner annoyance at this unwarranted interruption to our conversation.

"I believe that's our cue to depart. As engrossing as this little chat has been, I'm afraid we must be going." The prince sketched a mocking half-bow. "Do give my regards to the local constabulary."

With that, he and Boris retreated into the yacht's opulent interior. The engines roared to life once more, and the vessel surged forward, quickly putting distance between us.

Chapter Nineteen

AFTER BARON DRAGOMIROV'S SLEEK YACHT SPED
into the night, leaving a frothy wake to avoid the
approaching sheriff's patrol boat, I felt a wave of relief
wash over me. Despite the flashing red and blue lights
that got closer by the second, I couldn't shake the unease
Baron's menacing words had instilled.

Landon exhaled at my side, releasing tension from his
broad shoulders. His gaze remained fixed on the
approaching patrol boat until it joined us, its powerful
searchlight sweeping the cove. I recognized Deputy Don
Markham at the front of the boat, his expression an
inscrutable mask as he looked at us through the strobe lights.

I turned to Landon, my eyes wide with surprise as a
sudden realization dawned. "Floofy," I hissed, my heart
racing up my throat. "He's still down in the cabin with
that platter."

Landon's eyes met mine.

We were both aware of the dangers of leaving a chatty kitten alone with a magical cat-speech-enabling device for any period of time, especially with the police moving to board us. Without another word, I spun on my heel and dashed for the stairs leading below deck, taking them two at a time.

As I entered the dimly lit galley, my gaze fell on Floofy, perched atop the silver platter, his tiny paws covering the intricate etchings that allowed him to express himself. The otherworldly glow from the crystal inlay illuminated his fuzzy features in an ethereal blue light.

"Did I help Eleanor?" He squeaked, his high-pitched kitten voice full of eager expectation. "Did the police catch the bad guys?"

I scooped him up off the platter and cradled him against my chest before quickly moving the mystical object beneath the bench seat. "You did great, sweetie," I murmured, pressing a quick kiss on his head. "But let's keep that special plate a secret for now, okay?"

Floofy looked up at me, his small head cocked to the side as he processed my words. After a moment, he meowed.

I hoped that meant yes.

With the platter tucked away and Floofy safe in my arms, I climbed back up to the main deck where Landon and Deputy Markham awaited. The patrol boat had come alongside and two other deputies I didn't recognize tied it up to our cruiser.

Markham hopped across to our deck with agility, his keen eyes scanning us as he approached. "Ellie, Landon," he greeted, tipping his hat brim. "Y'all want to tell me what happened out here tonight?"

Landon began recounting an abbreviated version of the night's events, including our encounter with Baron and Boris on the yacht, the veiled threats and ominous references to Lisa Hartman's disappearance, and my theory about our local artesian springs.

"Water?" Don looked shocked. "You think this is about water?"

"I do," I said. "The Dragomirovs poisoned their own water supply in Herzoslovakia with their textile factories. That water makes their economy money. I think they are attempting to gain control of Wildebridge's spring water as an alternative source for their manufacturing."

Markham furrowed his brow. "Even if you're right, what does any of this have to do with Lisa Hartman?"

"I'm not sure yet," I admitted, stroking Floofy's fur while I thought about it. "But I believe Derek Sutton may have some answers. He appears to be at the heart of all these shady land deals and business connections."

Landon frowned. "Isn't he in on it? Working with that prince to force people off their property?"

I shook my head. "The more I think about it, the

more I wonder if Derek is involved in something bigger than he bargained for. What if this began as one of Ronnie Earle's typical get-rich-quick land grabs everyone knows about, but it escalated when the Dragomirovs became involved?" I met Landon's gaze, seeing my own troubled expression reflected back at me. "No one has seen Ronnie or Lisa in days. And based on what we heard tonight, I think Derek might be just as ensnared by the prince and his lackey as Lisa and Ronnie."

Deputy Markham took this in, his jaw working as he gazed out at the moonlit lake, deep in thought. After a brief pause, he returned our gaze with a speculative glint. "Are you planning to pay Mr. Sutton a visit to sort this out? Ask about your theory, maybe?"

His pointed tone conveyed a strong subtext: he was hinting rather than asking.

Landon and I exchanged a glance.

"Yes," we answered in unison.

Markham gave a slow nod, as if confirming something for himself. His gaze held ours, loaded with unspoken meaning.

"I thought as much," he drawled. "We need to keep our eye out for any more trouble, then. You two be careful now, you hear? Them folks you're dealing with ain't the type to play nice."

He saluted by touching the brim of his hat and then hopped back aboard the patrol boat, murmuring instructions to his deputies. Landon and I watched as they untied and motored away into the night, leaving us alone in the sheltered cove.

He looked back once.

Don Markham's gaze was a locked vault, yet the slight, knowing smile that tugged at his lips hinted at concealed schemes.

Landon guided the cruiser into the slip at Lisa's dock, the engines' low rumble fading to a soft purr as we drifted in. With no sign of the prince's ostentatious yacht nearby, the cove had become quiet once more.

We disembarked in silence, Floofy nestled in the curve of my arm, and made our way up the moonlit path leading to the modernist lake house perched on the hill. The night air was heavy with the tang of pine and rich earth, and the rhythmic trill of crickets created a hushed symphony in the undergrowth flanking the trail.

As we approached the house, I noticed a flicker of movement in the enormous wall of windows. I grabbed Landon's arm and directed his attention to the lone figure pacing the length of the living room, his agitation visible even from a distance.

Derek Sutton.

His polished exterior had cracked, exposing a man unraveling at the seams. He raked a hand through his tousled chestnut hair, causing it to stand on end as he walked across the gleaming hardwood. Even the rigid set of his shoulders beneath the crisp lines of his tailored shirt suggested a coiled tension lurking beneath the surface.

We climbed the steps to the back door, and Landon rapped his knuckles against the glass, a startling sound in the quiet night.

Derek's head snapped up, his eyes widening in undisguised shock as he saw us. For a moment, he remained motionless, like a deer caught in headlights. Then, with visible effort, he trained his features into a semblance of calm and strode to the door, pulling it open with a forced smile.

"Ms. Rockwell, Mr. Rogers," he greeted, his smooth baritone sounding strained. "What an unexpected surprise. What brings you out here at this hour?"

"We need to talk, Derek," I said, holding his gaze.

He shifted on his feet, but stepped back to allow us in.

As we sat on the plush leather sofa, I could practically feel Derek's anxiety radiating in waves, despite his attempts to appear relaxed. He busied himself at the bar cart, pouring a generous amount of amber liquid into a cut crystal tumbler. He cast a quick glance over his shoulder and raised the decanter in a silent offer.

Landon and I both declined.

Derek shrugged and took a sip, the ice clinking against the glass edge as he turned to face us.

"So," he began, a forced levity in his tone. "What can I help you with?"

I leaned forward, elbows braced on my knees. "Derek, we know about your involvement with Baron Dragomirov and Boris Stemple. We know they're strong-arming you to help them gain control of the local water supply."

Maybe an assumptive opening would get him talking.

Derek blanched, his fingers tightening around his glass. "I don't know what you're talking about," he blustered, but the slight tremor in his voice betrayed him.

Landon fixed him with a level stare. "They're holding Lisa Hartman and Ronnie Earle somewhere, aren't they? Using them as leverage against you."

The mention of Lisa and Ronnie seemed to drain Derek's strength. He retreated to the bar cart for support, his head dipping as if bearing a heavy load.

"Please," I entreated, softening my tone. "If you're in trouble, if they're threatening you, we can help. But we need to know where Lisa and Ronnie are."

"You don't know who you're dealing with," Derek whispered. "Baron and Boris... they're ruthless. They'll stop at nothing to get what they want." He dragged a trembling hand down his face. "If I don't get those properties signed over, if I don't do as they say..." He trailed off, his throat working as he swallowed hard. "They'll kill them."

I knew it.

Well, today I knew it.

I should have known about it days ago.

Even if it was ironic that the key to all this was the very first person I stumbled into, the validation provided a little comfort.

"Not if we stop them first," I said, injecting my voice with more conviction than I felt. "We have friends in the sheriff's department. They can protect you, get Lisa and Ronnie back. But you have to trust us, Derek. Tell us everything you know."

Derek paused for a long, lingering moment, his gaze drawn to the papers strewn across the coffee table—deeds and contracts awaiting his signature. I could almost see the war raging behind his eyes, fear and self-preservation clashing with the last remnants of his conscience.

Derek appeared to collapse on himself just as I thought he would refuse. A choked sob escaped from his throat, and tears streamed down his ashen cheeks.

"I don't know how any of this happened," he confessed, his words tumbling out in a broken rush. "It was just supposed to be another of Ronnie's land deals. Buy low, sell high to the prince. But then Prince Baron wanted assurances, then Lisa and her business got involved, and then... everything spun out of control."

"How did Lisa get involved?" I asked.

"We were dating. Ronnie's known her since she was a kid. We thought we were helping her get all her dreams fulfilled, but the prince just wanted her in a place he could use her to threaten us. I tried to kill the deal to get her out of it all, but it was too late, and Lisa thought I was betraying her." He dragged a shaking hand through his hair, his anguish palpable. "Lisa... she started asking questions. Getting suspicious. She went to Ronnie. Neither of them knew how bad these men were, what they were doing. Boris got a call from Ronnie, and he..."

Derek trailed off, a shudder rippling through him.

"It's okay," I murmured. "Do you know where they're holding them?"

Before Derek could say anything else, the sound of the front door banging open broke through the stillness. We all turned to see Baron Dragomirov, flanked by a scowling Boris and two hulking goons with guns drawn, striding in.

The prince's eyes blazed with malice as he took in the scene, with his attention fixed on Derek's tear-stained face. "I knew you were too weak to keep your mouth shut," he spat, bared teeth flashing in a cruel facsimile of a smile. "Once a coward, always a coward. You were so easy to manipulate. I should have known others could do so, too."

And just like that, Landon and I were staring down the barrels of real, lethal guns.

Again.

I tightened my grip on Floofy, feeling his tiny body tremble against my chest as he sank deeper into the crook of my arm. The poor kitten seemed to sense the danger in the air, and his presence provided some comfort even as my heart hammered behind my ribs.

Baron leveled his gun at Derek, a sneer curling his aristocratic features.

"Did you really think you could double-cross me, Sutton?" he asked, his accented voice dripping with disdain. "That I wouldn't find out about your little heart-to-heart with these meddling nobodies?"

Oh, that man and his insults were rankling me.

Landon leaned forward, putting himself between me and the line of fire. Despite the indignant feminist roaring within me—a voice that had grown a bit strident in recent months about my status as a self-sufficient, independent woman who did not require a man to protect her—I felt an unexpected surge of gratitude for my broad-shouldered companion.

Perhaps it was the adrenaline coursing through my veins or the gun pointed at my face, but the comforting bulk of Landon's frame protecting me from harm elicited not outrage at perceived chauvinism, but a strange sense of reassurance.

"There's no need for violence," my carpenter knight said, his deep baritone steady despite the tension thrumming through his frame. "Why resort to threats and kidnapping when you could have gained the properties through legal means? Negotiate a fair deal, work within the law?"

Baron barked out a mirthless laugh.

"Did I say something funny, your highness?"

"You simple fool. Why bother with the tedious formalities and red tape when I can take what I want?" He waved his free hand in a dismissive gesture. "I'm royalty. I'm not bound by the pedestrian constraints of lesser men."

"It had to be this way," Boris interjected, his nasal whine grating on my nerves. "The money lent to Hartman helped to secure his fortune beyond the international community's reach. They can't demand we repatriate what they don't know exists to pay for pollution cleanup or whatever."

I felt a flare of anger at his words. "You used Lisa to launder your money, didn't you?"

Boris shrugged one bony shoulder. "She was an unwitting pawn, but a useful one. She had no idea she was an accomplice to such dealings."

"And now that your funds are tucked away, you thought you could just sweep Lisa and Ronnie under the rug? Make them disappear once they'd served their purpose and become a liability?"

Baron's obsidian eyes glittered with malice. "A small price to pay to keep my money," he said, devoid of remorse. "With the international community baying for my family's blood over those unfortunate pollution incidents back home, I had no choice but to take measures to secure my wealth through alternate channels. What's a couple of insignificant lives in the grand scheme of—"

His words were cut short by a strangled yelp as a

crimson light flashed across his chest. Boris, too, let out a startled cry, staring down in horror at the glowing red dot dancing above his heart. So did the thugs with him.

"Bloody hell!" Boris exclaimed, his voice rising an octave as he broke out in a cold sweat. "Your parents sent assassins!" His gaze shifted between Baron and us, like a trapped animal sensing its impending demise. While licking his dry lips, he raised one trembling hand in an instinctive surrender gesture. "They know what we did!"

Before Baron or his lackeys could process what had happened, the front door burst open again. Deputy Markham and his officers entered with weapons trained on the prince and his entourage.

"Drop your weapons and get on the ground!" Don barked, his languid drawl replaced with the steel of command. "You're under arrest."

Baron sputtered, his face flushing an alarming shade of purple as he snarled at the intruding lawmen. "How dare you! I have immunity, you backwater cretins. You have no authority to—"

Don cocked his head, his eyes hardening to flint. "That immunity won't stop a bullet, Your Highness," he said, each word sharp as a razor. "I suggest you comply, unless you want to test the lead-proof properties of that fancy suit."

For a tense heartbeat, Baron appeared on the verge of doing something reckless. His grip on his gun tightened, and a vein throbbed in his temple.

But when confronted with the unwavering aim of

multiple officers—and the genuine threat of bullets ripping through his privileged flesh—the fight seemed to drain out of him. With a muttered curse, he dropped his weapon to the floor, Boris and the goons quickly following suit.

"Where's Lisa and Ronnie?" I asked as the deputies converged, forcing the men to their knees as they snapped cuffs around their wrists.

Fluffy, still in the bend of my arm, meowed.

As his posse was led away, Baron Von Arrogant shot me a venomous glare over his shoulder.

"You'll never find them," he spat.

Chapter Twenty

DEPUTY MARKHAM STRODE BACK INTO THE ROOM, his boots thudding against the hardwood floors. His fingers worked the chrome latch on his holster like he was a concert pianist tackling a tricky passage from Beethoven's Moonlight Sonata. "Neither of 'em is talking. Baron and Boris both clammed up tighter than a miser's coin purse when I asked where Lisa and Ronnie are. Just stared at me with those beady little eyes, smirking like they knew something I didn't."

I looked around at the assembled group—Landon, Derek, and the handful of deputies still securing the scene. It occurred to me, then, that an idea had been percolating in the back of my mind like a fresh pot of premium roast—the fragrant tendrils of realization wafting through my thoughts as pieces of this convoluted puzzle slotted into place one by one.

"I think I might know where they are," I said.

All eyes snapped to me, a mix of surprise and skepticism.

"How's that?" Don asked, his brow furrowing.

I took a deep breath, organizing my thoughts. "Remember when we first met Ethan Henderson, Landon? He mentioned something that stuck with me—he said Lisa's house and the one next door were built simultaneously. He implied it was with the same workers, even."

Landon nodded. "Right. He said some company owned the place beside hers, even though she owned this one. And that they were built together."

"Exactly. At the time, I thought little of it. But as we dug deeper, uncovering those shell corporations and Boldman Bracket's shady involvement, the two properties have to be linked."

Don looked at me, his face expressionless. "Linked how?"

"Well, Josie confirmed it," I continued, the pieces falling into place as I spoke. "During that phone call, the one that almost got us killed? She traced the ownership of the property next door to the prince. Also, it has a private boathouse on the water. Lisa was trying to get one just like it on her dock, but Mr. Henderson was fighting her. Remember?"

Landon's eyes widened. "Lisa's yacht. That's how it kept disappearing on us. They'd just slip into the boathouse and pull the door shut. Like a magician's vanishing act."

Derek slumped against the wall, shock etched into his features. "You're saying they've been right next door this whole time? Staying in the house I helped them build out?"

I nodded. "I didn't know you did, but I think so."

He dragged a hand down his face. "I feel like such an idiot."

Don snorted. "Frankly, son, it sounds like you should. I wouldn't be surprised if you're going to be spending some time with me in a small cell before this is all over. But standing around feeling sorry for yourself ain't gonna get Lisa and Ronnie back, so let's move."

The sudden burst of activity propelled us out of Lisa's sleek home like a startled kaleidoscope of butterflies emerging from their cocoons. Deputies fanned out ahead, their tan uniforms standing out against the manicured landscaping as they forged a path toward the suspicious neighboring property, weapons gripped with a solemn resolve.

I trailed behind, the rhythmic crunch of gravel underfoot serving as a metronome to the frantic pounding of my heart—a pulse of equal parts trepidation and curiosity.

Was I right?

Surely, I was right.

Little Floofy dug deeper into my neck, trembling as he pressed against my skin. Kitten breaths ruffled my neck hair in rapid succession. As the poor thing tried to merge into my embrace to escape whatever threat lay beyond my arms, delicate claws pricked my flesh.

"You're okay," I whispered.

A muted mew came in response.

Deputy Don Markham paused at the front door, fingers splayed, signaling his men to position with a subtle flick of his wrist. They fanned out behind him, weapons drawn but angled toward the ground in a loose grip—ready, but waiting.

"Should we be here?" I whispered to Landon.

The deputy took a steadying breath, the muscle in his jaw twitching almost imperceptibly. Then he gave a curt nod and tried the handle. It held firm, the deadbolt's obstinate refusal echoing through the silence like a challenge.

"Landon," I whispered, tugging at his sleeve. "Shouldn't we, you know..." I jerked my head back toward the tree line, eyes widening.

A callused finger rose to his lips in an exaggerated "shushing" gesture. "If there's anyone in there, they know it's the police," he whispered. "They saw their fearless leader hauled off."

If my years of binge-watching police procedurals have taught me anything, it's that our potential felons weren't necessarily deterred from inappropriate behavior by the knowledge that the police had arrived on their doorstep.

But it was too late now.

Don turned around, shifted on his feet, his chest

expanding with a sharp inhalation. Bent knees coiled like tightly wound springs as he gathered himself—eyes narrowed, jaw set in a taut line, fingers curling into a fist at his side.

Then he struck.

His booted foot lashed out behind him in a viper-quick blur, colliding with the door just below the handle with enough force to rattle the frame. The barrier exploded inward, sending splintered wood, tortured hinges, shards, and splinters cartwheeling through the air.

"Nice mule kick," Landon's rich baritone rumbled with dry amusement.

Don flashed a tight grin, the coiled tension in his frame unwinding as the splintered debris settled. "Thank you." He jerked his chin toward the decimated entryway. "Follow us once things are clear."

"Yes, sir."

An armed man dressed in black appeared in the doorway.

"Sheriff's Department!" Don bellowed. "Drop the weapon or so help me, I'll blow a hole through you! Hands where I can see 'em!"

For a tense heartbeat, the guard hesitated.

In one more beat, the gun slipped from his grasp, clattering to the floor with a dull thunk, breaking the spell. His shoulders sagged, all resistance and bravado gone in an instant as cold reality hit him.

"Where are they?"

The man raised his hands with halting motions, as if moving through thick syrup—palms open, fingers splayed in the universal submission gesture. He said nothing, and there was no need for him to. The slump of his frame, the despair etched on the downturn of his mouth, and the sheen of perspiration beading on his brow all conveyed the message.

"Where are they?"

The man shrugged at Don. "Lawyer."

The deputies swarmed in like ants on a sugar spill, quick and efficient in securing the guards that surrendered one after another after another. I saw the tough men fall to their knees, some with a spasm of relief battling glimmers of panic in their eyes as cold steel clicked around their wrists.

"Where are they?"

It was a question that kept getting asked, but answered with the same word, over and over.

"Lawyer."

My eyes swept across the lavish foyer. Expensive artwork adorned the walls, including oil paintings framed in gilded rococo cornices and towering marble sculptures that probably cost more than my entire net worth—and that included Fiona's inheritance.

Did a person really need so much extravagance around them?

It all seemed excessive.

Gaudy, even.

With each step deeper into the home's opulent depths, my disgust grew like an insidious kudzu vine. How could anyone live like this, immersed in such extravagant grandeur? The antique furniture sparkled with meticulous polish, bespoke pieces handcrafted by long-dead artisans flickering in the warm glow of gilded mirrors and crystal chandeliers. It was beautiful, I guess, in an extravagant way.

But it also reeked of careless privilege, of ill-gotten wealth amassed with reckless disregard for consequence or morality.

Every glittering bauble, every sconce, and every drapery heavy with the weight of dynastic affluence seemed not just a monument to success but a grotesque celebration of how far one could stray from humility, from compassion, when greed took root and grew unchecked.

I thought of the quaint, rustic charm of the other lake homes nestled along Wildebridge's tree-lined shores —residences meant for families, for shared laughter and memories around kitchen tables rather than gilded formal dining rooms. These were places of warmth and simple comfort.

How many cogs in the Dragomirov machine— servants, valets, and the invisible underclass—had given their lives, sweat, and blood to fuel this almost comical state of opulence?

How many once-pristine lakes and verdant forests had been poisoned or destroyed to ensure the imperial fantasy's continued prosperity?

This...

This was a palace of excess, a hermetically sealed jewel box with the outside world frozen beyond its pristine boundary.

"This place is... something," Landon murmured.

Each new chamber seemed to eclipse the gaudy excesses of the last in an ever-escalating game of one-upmanship—soaring coffered ceilings dripped with crystal, priceless chandeliers raining shards of kaleidoscopic light onto polished marble floors and hand-knotted Persian carpets soft as moss beneath our boots.

"I hope we don't have to confiscate all this stuff," Don said as another deputy escorted a sullen guard out to the waiting cruisers. "We may need to build a warehouse just to hold it all."

Derek opened and closed another door, growing more agitated by the minute. "They have to be here," he muttered. "Where else could they—" He froze mid-step, his eyes going wide. "The panic room."

"What panic room?" I asked.

Don turned around. "There's a panic room?"

Derek pivoted on his heel and bolted away, his long strides devouring the stairs with urgency, not giving us a second thought. The deputy rushed up the curving marble staircase after him, and the rest of the team followed in a cacophony of heavy footsteps and muffled grunts.

Landon's eyes met mine. "I guess we go up."

Floofy meowed.

My arms tightened around the kitten as I clutched his warmth against my chest, grounding myself in his solid presence as Derek led us up the stairs and then down a lavishly appointed hallway into what appeared to be the master suite.

Though, frankly, I'm not sure they didn't all look like this.

Derek walked across the cavernous bedchamber like a man on a mission, cutting a straight path through an opulent litter of discarded finery. Silk robes lay strewn about like discarded snakeskins, carelessly abandoned in the chaos of... whatever.

I didn't want to think about it.

His fingers danced in a strange pattern against the heavy wooden paneling, intricately carved with twisting grotesques and leering gargoyle faces, tracing over innocuous whorls and knotholes with a tendril of urgency coursing through each gesture.

A seamless panel slid aside to reveal a hidden keypad interface illuminated by a pale LED light. Derek leaned in and tapped out a rapid succession of numbers.

With a low whine of protest from its motors, the wall pivoted inward, swinging slowly to reveal whatever secrets lay hidden behind.

"Praise the Lord," Lisa gasped, stumbling upright as tears streamed down her delicate cheeks. "I thought we'd never be rescued."

Ronnie released a ragged chuckle, every crease in his weathered face radiating gratitude as Derek helped him stand. "Well, I'll be..." His voice cracked with emotion as he turned toward the deputy. "Never thought the day would come when I'd thank heaven for the sight of Johnny Law."

"Never dreamed we'd have to rescue you, either, Mr. Earle," Don said, steadying Ronnie on the other side with a firm grip as the older man swayed on his feet. "What on earth happened to land y'all in this mess?"

Gone was the self-assured tycoon who so frequently graced the society pages.

He'd been replaced, at least temporarily, by a haggard, haunted shell of a man aged well beyond his years by whatever tribulations he'd endured.

I couldn't help but feel a pang of sympathy.

"Listen, I've spent years playing middleman for foreign investors lookin' to scoop up Texas real estate on the down-low—nothin' criminal, you understand, but it sure as shootin' didn't win me any loyalist awards at the country club." Ronnie let out a dry chuckle, though no mirth reached his eyes. "When Baron came callin', figured it'd just be another routine land grab. Fella wanted a lake house, no big whoop. Then he wanted two... then three..." He trailed off, shaking his head as a grim smirk twisted his weathered features. "Should've seen the red flags from a mile away, but I didn't. And I introduced him to Lisa, which is unforgiveable."

"Oh, Uncle Ronnie, you didn't know." Lisa glanced at Floofy in my arms and then looked away as if she didn't recognize him. "He was so charming when we met. Flattered me, saying I should be having fashion week runway shows, that I deserved a boutique in Paris. Claimed he could make it all happen."

"But?" I prompted.

"But," she continued, "because his parents were determined to keep the money in Herzoslovakia, and with the country under such scrutiny after the Stempka Lake fiasco, he'd have to funnel the funds through shell companies. A 'loan' to help me get started. It sounded logical. I mean, he was a prince, right?"

Ronnie bobbed his head in grim affirmation. "That man funneled millions of his country's money into one of them offshore shell companies, then into Lisa's business and personal accounts with a bottom dollar loan and an inflated salary. That weasel Boris had her sign paperwork that he would inherit her portion of the business if anything happen to her, and he was supposed to own her lake house and rent it to her dirt cheap, but it somehow got deeded solely to Lisa." His steely gaze bored into Derek. "I'm guessin' that little sleight-of-hand was your bright idea, boy."

Derek fidgeted, running a hand through his hair as

embarrassment colored his chiseled features. "I thought putting her name on the deed would protect Lisa if... things went sideways. By then I knew Baron's plans reeked of corruption. I just couldn't figure out what they were planning."

"So rather than loop me in, you freelanced and single-handedly steered this ship away from one iceberg only to drive it straight into an even bigger one." Ronnie fixed the younger man with a pointed stare edged with weary disappointment. "Admirable intentions, but son, all your meddling did was paint a bigger bullseye on our backs."

"Me? You're the one who roped us into this entire fiasco!" Derek's voice escalated, a flush of anger coloring his chiseled features. "I tried extracting Lisa from the minefield you stranded her in!"

"And yet you just got her in deeper." Suddenly, his anger dissipated, and Ronnie seemed to deflate before our eyes, shoulders sagging. "But you're right, son. Can't argue with the truth." Regret threaded through each word. "I was blinded by my own hubris, same as Lisa. Both of us were arrogant enough to think we could tango with snakes like Baron and slither away unscathed."

"We were mistaken," Lisa whispered.

"We were dead wrong. Baron snatched us up, put a gun to our heads. Told us he told Derek he'd paint the lake red with our blood if that boy didn't snap to it and get them everything they wanted—Lisa's properties, the deed to Henderson's land, all of it. Like checking off a shopping list."

Deputy Don Markham's brow furrowed. "But why here? Why go to all this trouble in Wildebridge County, of all places?"

"The springs," I explained. "Baron and his ilk poisoned their own artesian wells back in Herzoslovakia. Now they need an alternative source to keep their textile empire afloat—and I'd bet the pure artesian waters bubbling up around this lake hit the mark."

Landon gave a grim nod. "Makes sense. Baron was aimin' to move his whole sordid operation right here under our noses, unfettered access to a fresh water supply."

I bit my lip. "Maybe."

Landon raised an eyebrow.

"I'm not convinced it was that straightforward," I said. "The way Boris reacted when those laser sights appeared across their chests? He thought assassins from the royal family had caught them. Why would they be afraid of the Baron's own parents? My gut says our charming prince planned to sever all ties with Herzoslovakia—cut his parents and his homeland out of the equation to keep every ill-gotten penny of future profit for himself."

"Well, Mom and Dad can discuss whatever business plans they need to with Junior over a jail phone," Don drawled. "I'm sure the boys in holding will be thrilled to host royalty during visiting hours."

As we led Lisa and Ronnie out to a waiting ambulance to get checked over, it all seemed too fantastic to be real. Royalty, international embezzlement... It was like a Jason Bourne movie.

As I glanced at the weary faces around me—the victims, the bystanders, the police, the unlikely feline heroes—I knew that this was a story that would be etched into Wildebridge County lore for years to come.

Well.

Minus the feline heroes.

Chapter Twenty-One

"DID YOU HEAR WHAT HAPPENED?" EVIE BURST INTO the Silver Circle's office, her cheeks flushed with excitement. "They threw everything at Baron and Boris. Like, everything—kidnapping, embezzlement—the works!"

I glanced up from the paperwork strewn across my desk with a start. "Already?"

Evie plopped down on the overstuffed armchair. "Word travels fast in this town, I guess. Don called Matt because they needed some help to investigate the overseas stuff in the case. Matt, of course, called me and told me everything." She leaned forward. "There's some huge international investigation brewing over Baron siphoning money out of Herzoslovakia. His own parents won't lift a finger to help!"

A low whistle sounded from the doorway.

"Eavesdropping, are we?" I asked.

"You know the whole lobby can hear you when the

door's open." Landon stepped inside. "I have to admit, I didn't see that coming. Figured the whole 'sovereign immunity' spiel meant his family would go to the mattresses for him."

"Nope. Matt said they've practically disowned him. It sounds like Prince Baron overplayed his hand. Once the king and queen realized the extent of his money laundering and corruption, his parents washed their hands of him. Said he was a disgrace to the crown or something and then took his title from him."

For someone who'd strutted around like he owned the lake itself, it was a startling reversal of fortunes to see the arrogant prince abandoned by his own dynasty. "So much for aristocratic privilege," I said. "That's got to sting."

"Oh, man, it gets worse." Evie was unable to hide an unladylike hint of relish. "The feds froze all his offshore assets before he could liquidate them." She leveled me with a pointed look, her eyes sparkling with mischief. "He's not as loaded as he wanted us to believe. Well, not anymore, anyway."

Landon's rich laughter rang out, a deep baritone peal that filled the room. "Don't that just beat all? So much for sovereign immunity when Uncle Sam comes callin'."

I raised an eyebrow. "You seem pleased."

"Well, I'm not an arrogant man, Ellie. I don't like to see anyone suffer." He shrugged, but the crooked grin spoke volumes. "But I do take a certain amount of satis-faction in seeing bullies get their comeuppance."

"Speaking of comeuppance..." My brow furrowed as realization dawned. "What about Lisa's house? Where does that fall in all this now?"

"It's forfeited to the federal government! All of it—house, boats, everything." Evie tapped the toe of her sneaker against the hardwood floor, bobbing her head in emphasis. "From what Matt said, the feds are going through and seizing every asset connected to Baron, Boris, and their web of dummy corporations. That entire stretch of waterfront property Boris built beside Lisa's place? Uncle Sam's now."

Landon let out a low whistle. "Well, I'll be. I'd feel sorry for old man Henderson, but now he's got to be tickled pink watching his nemesis's gaudy lake house get claimed by the government."

A snort of derision echoed from the doorway behind us.

We all turned to find Old Carl lounging against the frame with the grizzled nonchalance of a vagrant crow perched on a fencepost.

"Tickled ain't quite the word for it. More like spittin' mad is what I reckon Ethan's feelin'. Him and that over-grown mermaid Rex done been howlin' up a storm ever since them fed'ral varmints rolled into town with their jackboots and started struttin' around takin' over anything that ain't nailed down."

Of course the two of them knew each other.

"He'll be fine when they all return to Washington, where they came from," he said, his eyes crinkling with a hint of genuine warmth that belied his perpetually cantankerous air.

"The feds probably came up from Austin, Carl," Landon told him. "They have an office over on Research, you know."

"Now, how would I know that?"

"You seem awfully calm about the whole thing," I teased. "I thought a herd of federal agents trampling all over the county would be the perfect fodder for one of your trademark conspiracy rants."

"Oh, it would be—if I was plannin' on spouting any blasted conspiracies." He took a long draft, throat working as the piping brew flowed down to settle in his belly. "But this isn't a conspiracy theory. It's a fact. I ain't gotta look hard to tell you the goverment's up to their standard mischief. All their sneakin' and land grabbin'? It was all an inside play to line their pockets, mark my words."

Landon arched a brow. "You figure the deputies and feds were in cahoots with Ronnie Earle and Baron all along? That they started this harebrained scheme to seize property for themselves?"

I had no idea why Landon asked the questions, but that was all it took.

"Don't get me started on that snake-oil huckster Earle," Carl growled, his faded eyes sharpening as he pinned Landon with a withering glare. "Victim my backside! He's been greasier than a Yankee truck stop's fryin' pan for decades longer than you been wearing long pants. Why d'you reckon he was happy to roll over and give those self-important bluebellies everything they wanted? He's up to his armpits, is why."

A series of stifled snorts and muffled chuckles escaped Evie as she fought to maintain her respectful composure as Old Carl barreled onward with the blustery vigor of an ill-tempered bull.

"I ain't talkin' about no official conspiracy with Earle. I'm sayin' the whole shebang is just the latest chapter of that old game—gov'ment gets wind of a big score, so they manufacture some 'emergency' to ride in and take it all while pretendin' they're the good guys cleanin' up after the bad guys."

Before I could ponder the implications of Carl's conspiracy further, Lisa slipped inside my office archway, her delicate features arranged in an expression of contrite gratitude. "Am I interrupting? Darla said I could come on back."

"Lisa," I called out, standing to greet her. "Oh, honey, it's so good to see you up and about. How are you feeling?"

Lisa offered me a brave smile. "I'm well, all things considered. Or I will be, at least." Her eyes sparkled with a resurgence of the vivacious spirit that must have fueled her business ambitions. "Thanks to you and Landon's actions, and your refusal to leave well enough alone, I survived."

"I'm glad to hear it," I told her. "We were worried sick about you."

"Well, you needn't worry anymore. I wanted to come thank each one of you who played a role in my rescue. I'm only sorry it ended up being so... chaotic."

"Chaotic is one word for it," Carl drawled from behind. I shot him a glare as he stood up next to us. "What? I reckon the little lady's entitled to know we was only tryin' to get her runaway hairballs back when y'all stumbled into the thick of Baron's falderal."

We?

I didn't remember Old Carl contributing anything to... well, anything.

And what on earth was a falderal?

"Thank you again." A faint blush stole across Lisa's cheeks. "I also wanted to come retrieve Fluffy and Floofy."

Evie sprang to her feet and hurried out of the office.

"Of course," I said. "Though I have to confess—I'm afraid I've become rather attached to Floofy." The thought of parting with the darling little Scottish Fold kitten brought a pang of dismay I couldn't quite suppress. "He's been such a little delight to have around."

"Really?" At this, Lisa's expression morphed into one of amazement. "I'm surprised to hear you say that." She paused, chewing her lip as if trying to decide how best to articulate her thoughts. "The two kittens don't... well, they don't get along. At all. Floofy's a bully."

I blinked.

She thought Floofy was the bully?

"Why do you think Floofy is a bully?"

"He's always fighting with the little girl kitten," Lisa replied. "Poor things seem convinced they're mortal enemies. They've been tussling nonstop every time they're in the same room together, to the point I have to keep them separated. With everything else going on, caring for them—and cleaning up after their spats—has become... trying."

Evie popped up from the back, toting a wire carrier frothing with an angry tide of writhing fur and plaintive objections. Floofy and Fluffy were a seething cyclone of fluffy combat, all slashing paws and furious glares despite the cramped confines of their enclosure.

"Some things never change, huh?" Evie said as she closed the office door behind her.

I cast a sympathetic glance at the feuding siblings. "Lisa, you wouldn't want to re-home one of them with another family, would you? I could arrange for that, if it would help. This level of aggression isn't good for either kitten."

Lisa opened her mouth to respond, but whatever words she'd intended to offer were drowned out by a ragged chorus of furious yowls as Evie undid the carrier's latch. A heartbeat later, the kittens came pouring forth—Fluffy leading the charge with murderous purpose while Floofy fled in blind panic, tail ramrod straight as his miniature paws scrambled for purchase on the slick floor.

The terrified little fellow scurried toward me, crying

out with comical desperation as he struggled to scale my pant leg. I bent down and scooped him to my chest, cradling his trembling form while casting Lisa an imploring look.

"Well," she said, gathering Fluffy into her arms and straightening. Her eyes shone with an emotion somewhere between relief and resignation as Fluffy glared daggers across the space at her brother. "He does look like he's attached to you. More to you than to me. And Fluffy and I get along so well."

A triumphant purr rumbled from my furred companion as he snuggled deeper into my embrace, peering up at me with wide, adoring eyes. My daughter —who knew better than to put the two kittens together in a single carrier like gladiators thrown into an arena— looked like the cat who not only got the cream but drank the entire dairy farm dry, eyes dancing with impish delight.

"We'll take good care of him."

❧

The sun was high in the brilliant azure sky, its radiant warmth enveloping the rocking deck of our modest rental boat as it bobbed on the shimmering expanse of Lake Wildebridge. I reclined in a plush deck chair, taking in the relaxing atmosphere—the gentle lapping of waves, the distant call of birds wheeling overhead, and the aroma of fresh-cut grass wafting from the shoreline.

With the chaos and tension of recent events dissipating, I let myself sag deeper into my seat, taking in a deep, cleansing breath. My gaze shifted from the cloudless cerulean panorama above to my companions lounging on the deck.

Charlie lay sprawled on an adjacent chaise, sleeves rolled up and hat tilted over his eyes, as gentle snores whistled from his gaping maw. Josie sat nearby, a long-stemmed glass of crisp white wine swaying between her fingers, exuding effortless aristocratic elegance despite her casual cotton shift dress and oversized shades.

Landon reclined with ease, his broad shoulders sinking into the plush deck chair while holding a frosty bottle of beer in one callused hand. Despite his sturdy build, every line of his body exuded a languid, tranquil repose—from the rolled up shirtsleeves exposing tanned forearms to the upturned bottle tilting back for a long draft.

His deep chuckle was a soothing rumble, his eyes crinkling at the corners as a lopsided grin spread across his handsome face. Landon exuded complete contentment, as if he had found his rightful place among the lake's lapping waves and soothing breezes.

When our gazes met, I returned his amiable smile with a subtle nod and tilt of my chin, a silent reassurance that everything was fine in our sun-dappled world, at least for this brief, blissful moment.

Everything was fine—even better than fine, to be honest.

With Baron and his shadowy consortium defeated, an ineffable sense of reassurance had settled over me, like a soft quilt of serenity draping across my shoulders, erasing any remaining uncertainty. Sure, the fallout from their scheme would last for months, with federal investigations, international indictments, and diplomatic snarls to unfurl.

But the existential threat had passed.

I watched as the feds began hoisting plastic-shrouded bundles to the open rear doors of an idling moving truck, conveying an unbroken conga line of mystery cargoes from the disgraced prince's palatial digs. The scene unfolded like an elaborate mating dance, each bundle passing from agent to agent to agent in a flurried sequence of ritualistic movements that deposited them into the van's belly.

"They ain't wastin' any time strippin' that place bare, are they?" Landon's wry observation floated toward me from across the deck.

"Nope," Josie chimed in, her usual breezy insouciance sanded to a sleepy rasp as she rode the same languid wavelength of relaxation as the rest of us. "They'll have that entire mausoleum of gilt and gaudiness divvied up and cataloged before supper. Mark my words. Probably auction it all off to the highest Monaco casino mogul or Russian oligarch bidder once the case is over." She paused, tilting her face toward the blinding sunlight with a catlike stretch.

A flicker of motion across the cove snagged my peripheral vision.

Squinting against the dazzle reflecting off the lake's mirrored surface, I made out the hunched silhouette of none other than Ethan Henderson himself, the wiry old coot trudging along the narrow deer trail snaking through the underbrush. Rex ambled ahead, his tail swishing with cheerful canine obliviousness as his tongue lolled out in a gleeful doggy grin.

Though they appeared small from this distance, Henderson exuded an infectious vigor that belied his advanced age. As if sensing my gaze, he turned and raised a hand in a cheerful wave across the glittering waters.

I waved back, grinning as the crusty former suspect waved once more before vanishing around a copse of towering oaks.

Despite the man's months-long vendetta of litigious harassment and erratic behavior, I couldn't help but feel a bit of affection toward the cantankerous old coot—his observations had played an invaluable role.

"Well, I'll be," Landon murmured. "Look at him, swaggerin' around his kingdom like a conquering sultan."

"He's been working for this day," I told him. "I imagine he hopes those eyesores will finally get stripped off the landscape he loves so dearly." I shot a sidelong glance at Josie, unable to resist needling her. "I don't think it's going to work out the way he wants, but I hope he has some time enjoying the quiet once the feds are gone."

A peaceful silence fell between us once more, broken only by ospreys making high-pitched whistles as they wheeled and dove over scraps along the shoreline.

All was right with the world.

Well, with our little corner of it, anyway.

"Anyone want another beer?" Landon asked, his voice a low, soothing rumble pitched not to disturb the fragile peace cloaking our little craft. "I've got a few more cold ones here in the cooler."

I cracked open one eye, my gaze trailing from his outstretched hand—callused and sturdy, yet cradling the frosty bottles with a tenderness that stirred something deep inside me—to the warm crinkles around his eyes and the impossibly fond expression playing across his tanned features.

In that moment, a wave of bone-deep contentment washed over me like the gentle lull of a rippling tide.

No, all wasn't well, I corrected myself with a smile as my fingers brushed Landon's with undisguised affection.

All was perfect.

Thank you for reading! I hope you enjoyed the seventh book in the Silver Circle Cat Rescue Mysteries!

As the last page turns, things continue to unravel in the

eighth installment, "Sunbeam, Sunflowers, and Sabotage."

Set against the picturesque backdrop of a sunflower farm in the Texas Hill Country, this tale of secrets, betrayal, and danger will keep you guessing until the very end!

KEEP UP WITH LEANNE LEEDS

Thanks so much for reading! I hope you liked it! Want to keep up with me?

Visit leanneleeds.com to:

Find all my books...

Sign up for my newsletter...

Like me on Facebook...

Follow me on Twitter...

Follow me on Instagram...

Thanks again for reading!

Leanne Leeds

Find a typo? Let us know!

Typos happen. It's sad, but true.

Though we go over the manuscript multiple times, have editors, have beta readers, and advance readers it's inevitable that determined typos and mistakes sometimes find their way into a published book.

Did you find one? If you did, think about reporting it on leanneleeds.com so we can get it corrected.

Artificial Intelligence Statement

Portions of this book were created with the assistance of AI tools used for editing, proofreading, and refining the text. However, the ideas, storyline, characters, and overall creative vision remain my own original work.

While some aspects of the cover image were generated using AI tools, it was done so under my creative direction and curation.

I want to acknowledge the use of these technologies as part of my creative process, while affirming that the essence of this work comes from my own imagination and effort.

Leanne Leeds